After Anatevka

Center Point
Large Print

Books are produced in the United States using U.S.-based materials

Books are printed using a revolutionary new process called THINKtech™ that lowers energy usage by 70% and increases overall quality

Books are durable and flexible because of smythe-sewing

Paper is sourced using environmentally responsible foresting methods and the paper is acid-free

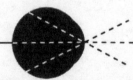

This Large Print Book carries the Seal of Approval of N.A.V.H.

ALEXANDRA SILBER

CENTER POINT LARGE PRINT
THORNDIKE, MAINE

This Center Point Large Print edition
is published in the year 2017 by arrangement with
Pegasus Books.

The text of this Large Print edition is unabridged.
In other aspects, this book may vary
from the original edition.
Printed in the United States of America
on permanent paper.
Set in 16-point Times New Roman type.

ISBN: 978-1-68324-584-1

Library of Congress Cataloging-in-Publication Data

Names: Silber, Alexandra, author.
Title: After Anatevka : a novel inspired by Fiddler on the roof /
    Alexandra Silber.
Description: Large print edition. | Thorndike, Maine :
    Center Point Large Print, 2017.
Identifiers: LCCN 2017039218 | ISBN 9781683245841
    (large print : hardcover : acid-free paper)
Subjects: LCSH: Jewish families—Russia—Fiction. | Large type books.
    Jewish fiction.
Classification: LCC PS3619.I5425 A69 2017 | DDC 813/.6—dc23
LC record available at https://lccn.loc.gov/2017039218

Foreword

In the theater, it's customary for a performer to create a "back story" for the character she (or he) is playing. This is a history of the character's activities up to the moment when she (or he) steps onto the stage.

With *After Anatevka*, Al Silber has done exactly the opposite. After performing the role of Tzeitel (Tevye's oldest daughter) in the most recent production of *Fiddler on the Roof* at the Broadway Theatre in New York and previously playing Hodel (Tevye's next-oldest daughter) in London's West End (a production through which I came to know her), Ms. Silber has written a book which begins after Hodel has *left* the stage.

The last time we see her in \ , Hodel is waiting with her father for the train that will take her to Siberia to join her fiancé, Perchik. After a brief prologue in which Hodel accepts Perchik's marriage proposal, Ms. Silber catapults us to Siberia, where we discover that Hodel—shortly after her arrival—has been imprisoned. We are plunged immediately into a highly dramatic situation where the scenes take on an almost cinematic reality. We meet a cast of arresting characters who have little in common with the engaging villagers in *Fiddler*. And Hodel

5

undergoes trials that test the limits of her strength and courage.

As the lyricist for *Fiddler on the Roof*, I was curious to see how Ms. Silber's novel related to the story we tell in our musical. I wondered whether one had to have seen *Fiddler* or read the Sholem Aleichem stories on which it's based to understand or appreciate *After Anatevka*. Once I read the book, I found that prior familiarity with the underlying stories is unnecessary. It's a beautiful coming-of-age story that will speak to all readers. But for those who *are* familiar with the original tale, Ms. Silber has provided a number of rewarding bonuses. Although the title *After Anatevka* suggests that the novel will concern itself solely with Hodel's adventures after leaving home, Ms. Silber manages to provide gratifying and entertaining glimpses of Hodel's life with her parents and her four sisters throughout the novel. Those vivid and detailed flashbacks serve to intensify the contrast with the desolation Hodel finds in Siberia.

Over half a century ago, Jerry Bock and I wrote songs based on the characters and dramatic situations in Sholem Aleichem's *Tevye's Daughters*. I can only marvel at the fact that, after all of these years, Alexandra Silber produced an entirely new work stemming from the same font. Inspired by a character she played in *Fiddler on the Roof*, Ms. Silber has employed her formidable intelligence, her lively imagination, her poetic sensibility and what must have been extensive research to create *After Anatevka*, a powerful and gripping tale of love, loyalty, bravery, and endurance. I hope you are as moved by it as I am.

Sheldon Harnick
New York City
April 2017

prologue

Get me out,
for indeed I was stolen away
out of the land of the Hebrews,
and I have done nothing that
I should be in this place.
—*Genesis*

When he asked her to be his wife, clumsily, and with agonizing effort, she was uncharacteristically silent. All went still. Perhaps in the deepest recesses of his psyche, he understood that she was already tethered to him. That, for her, their marriage was already complete, their spirits already one, so veritable was her feeling, so steadfast and unwavering her love. She gazed at him and smiled.

Perchik—there he was: all sternness and swagger. For all his education he could not overcome the anxiety of such a moment. He wanted her. She knew that. Though it did not need to be said, for she could see in his sorrowful eyes a new expression of unerring devotion. More than that—a shared covenant, and the longing she knew to be identical to her own. This

9

vision of him promised a future, and that future would be in Perchik's arms. The eyes of a man capable not only of seeing but also of creating more majesty in the smallest corners of existence than any other being she had known or ever would know. She simply nodded her acceptance.

He wept, embracing her completely as they had both longed to since the very first moments.

"You will follow me, Hodel?" he asked, clutching her hair and holding her close.

She pulled away to look into his eyes, then answered without smiling, "Forever."

BOOK ONE

Siberia, 1906

One

Dim light crept in, followed by her consciousness. Savage cold. Harrying voices.
The fierce grips of unfamiliar men. Endless
rooms and corridors. A door opened. She was
deposited into a dark room, placed in chains,
plied with questions in Russian, then pulled
upright.

They flung her in a solitary cell. She ricocheted
off the back wall, fell with a thud, screeching
herself hoarse and scratching at her body when
she discovered the floor was swamped in
excrement and crawling with vermin, the chains
about her preventing every attempt to destroy
them.

Here it comes, the guards thought as they
looked on. *The break.*

It took only a moment. Just a moment for the
stab of realization to snap the neck of her spirit.

There it is. . . .

She clutched her body and crumpled to the
ground, weeping.

After how long she did not know, Hodel
opened her eyes. The dark enclosing her was
thorough—so thorough, it instilled a type of calm
and moved her to stand, and when she did she
found the floor beneath her to be of vile frozen

stone. It reminded her at once of where she was.

How long have I been here? she thought. No answer came.

But something was off—a familiar odor of dusty earth wafted up as her body adjusted to standing, and she realized at once that her ankles were no longer constrained by shackles.

She took an unpracticed step. Her long-limbed stride wobbled but advanced her. Though toward where? Toward what?

Another step. Another. The *thud* of each foot rang out. She thought of her family, feeling closer to them with each step. She had been there what felt like only moments ago. . . .

Onward . . . onward, she thought.

Hodel was accustomed to fending for herself. Second-born and nearly three and a half years younger than her elder sister, Tzeitel, Hodel had been born in the middle of a scorching summer. "Perhaps that is what made her so fiery," her mother teased.

Hodel was the proud one, the one with the quick tongue, the one just like her mother. All of these epithets got her into trouble—trouble she gave right back to anyone who crossed her.

Hodel felt perpetually passed over. Tzeitel, as the eldest, commanded a great deal of attention as the natural homemaker and the first in their family to be wed. Their younger sister Chava, on the other hand, commanded attention because, as an incurable dreamer, she required looking after. The two youngest sisters—Shprintze and Bielke—had been regarded as babies nearly all their lives and constantly doted on. But Hodel was neither in command, nor a dreamer, nor doted upon. Instead, in a family of women with sturdy, strong, compact frames that bespoke humility, Hodel was tall. Her height made her feel conspicuous, isolated, as if she physically were not a part of her family. A *langer lucksh*, neighbors would call her—a long noodle.

With a height established well before the age of twelve, Hodel would almost have met her father's eye if it weren't for her defiant slouchiness. For a long while, she slumped over so much, no one could see the lovely developing shape of her breasts or the dainty curve from her waist to her hip. And her clothing certainly did not help. Tzeitel would get new clothes as she grew, and despite the vast difference in their heights and shapes, Hodel would get Tzeitel's hand-me-downs. She had to tug them over her long limbs. Even worse, after the wear and tear of two sisters, the hand-me-downs were too worn out, so Chava would also get new clothes. It was intolerable! Hodel understood frugality, but she so rarely had anything new, something that was *just* hers.

One day her mother, Golde, took her aside and gave her a basket of linens to hang in the yard.

"For you alone," she instructed. "Come find me when you are done."

Hodel sulked. Heavy lifting was always her task, and she despised it. She grudgingly walked out into the yard, heaving the basket along with her. But then she saw it: new laundry lines, hung from the higher branches of the trees, crisscrossed one another like the flight patterns of birds, their clean white lines heralding hope and ascension.

She looked down. At the bases of the trees stood little footstools employed earlier by her mother and sisters. But Hodel didn't need any help to reach these new laundry lines.

It was a reason to stand tall.

She set to work, and after clasping the last of the corners of the freshly washed linen upon the line with clothespins, Hodel stood back. She stretched her body as the wind lifted the sheet clear off the ground, cracking the fabric in the air with each gust. Her frame lengthened— her head erect, back taut, shoulders revealing her heart to the gusty, chalk-colored sky. Her eyes locked on the linen—a flag of newfound dignity.

"Done?" her mother inquired as Hodel brought the empty baskets back inside.

"Yes, Mama."

"Good," replied Golde, not looking up from her chopping board. "It will not do for us to have the bottoms of our linens soiled because the lines were not high enough. We must aim them a bit *higher,* yes?"

"Yes, Mama."

"Good. You should only live and be well. *Ver volt dos geglaibt?*" she muttered to an unknown and unseen audience. "Who would have believed it? Come help me with the stock."

Hodel stood tall evermore.

The thin line of light before her was no wider than a fingernail, and it was impossible to tell whether it was inches or miles away. Hodel moved toward it, the weight of her steps squishing in the ever-softening earth.

"You!" a faraway voice barked from the darkness. *"You!"*

She turned and stared hard into the endless black, pupils aching—nothing. But then, suddenly, a familiar voice.

"Hodel!" It was his voice.

Her eyes shot open as she clutched at the walls to steady herself.

"Perchik!" How close he was! "Where are you?"

"Hodel!" It was a desperate cry. "I am here!"

She jolted upward and flung herself to the bars.

"Perchik!" she wailed. *"Perchik!"*

She thrust the full weight of her body upon the bars.

The voice was gone. But his scent remained—

17

Hodel sensed it so strongly, she could taste it in her throat. But with each moment of crashing silence that followed, it grew further and further away.

All at once, she was seized by her shoulders and shaken vigorously.

"You! Wake up!"

She opened her eyes: the same unfamiliar cell.

Farkuckt, she thought.

two

Her keepers were concerned she was dead, for she had slept well over a day without stirring. When she woke, she was seized and escorted to the showers by the forbidding arms of a truculent woman—her hair fixed tight, with gherkins for fingers. Hodel's chains were still fixed as the woman scrubbed her red, then redeposited her into the cell and exited with the deftness of a general.

Hodel got to her feet and trudged in chains from one side of her cell to the other and back again. Her hands traced the stones as her fingers discovered names carved with struggle into the walls. She shuddered; these walls seemed to whisper things.

She examined her surroundings. The cell was painfully small and flanked with gray stones on three sides. Iron rods made up the fourth. The solitary window at the top of the back wall was barred and nearly useless, and she listened to the scream of wind insisting itself from beyond the bars. A filthy mattress lay upon the floor. A chair. An earthen stove.

If only the window were lower, she thought. *If only I might see out.*

Somewhere from the world beyond her cell

came a surge of wretched wails, and at this, she began once more to weep.

Sat low, the daughters of the dairyman crouched beneath the cows and pulled the milk from their udders, as they had every day since the age when they were first able. It was more regimen than routine. They secured the cows by tying them to sturdy stanchions with a halter, cleaned the teats with soapy water to help bring down the milk, then patted them dry. They placed buckets beneath the udders and squatted down upon milk stools low enough to afford comfortable access to the underside of even a cranky or uncooperative cow. They applied animal fat to lubricate their hands, wrapped them around two of the four teats, squeezed the base down to push out the milk (maintaining their gentle but firm grips on the base of the teat so the milk didn't flow back up into the udder), and continued until the udder became deflated.

The sisters rarely spoke throughout the morning, and they each had their own way of going about the work.

Shprintze was hostile toward the early hour and would often silently weep at the work, as if enslaved. Chava and Bielke shared the method of fooling themselves that they were somehow still asleep by leaning their heads forward so they were face-to-udder with the cow, eyes still closed, hands working habitually, without apparent consciousness. Tzeitel preferred to seize the milk from the cow just as she had seized herself from slumber—a zealous act of victory before daybreak!

"Done!" declared Tzeitel in triumph, as if winning a competition no one else had entered, lifting her two pails of raw milk and making her way to the back of the barn with brisk and lively steps. She would join their mother in the kitchen and be the first to prepare the house for the day—which was her inclination anyway.

Hodel smirked and called after her sister, "Mazel tov, Tzeitel!" If the others had not had their half-sleeping heads buried in the body of a cow, she was certain they would have laughed. Tzeitel turned back and simply lifted her pails a little higher, indicating that, petty or not, she was off to the warmth of the kitchen while Hodel was still freezing beneath a cow.

The mechanical sound of each rhythmic tug and the subsequent tinny splash accompanied by the incessant groans from the beasts themselves was the music of home—its dull cadences almost soothing. But the sound was accompanied by a stillness—a feeling of unbearable emptiness that had been growing there for as long as she could recall. It was a longing as insidious as the odor from the stables: oftentimes unnoticeable, but a particular turn of the breeze, a sweltering afternoon, or in returning from inhaling the clean air of the river, and the feeling would grab ahold of her consciousness before she was permitted to continue on. People would call upon their family from the village and she would not know what to say. She did not want to be social in the old ways, do the same old things. But if she didn't belong here, then where did she belong? She wasn't entirely sure who she was anymore. She didn't even look the same to herself. She wore an expression she did not recognize. *Who is this?* she would ask the person in the glass. The image would shrug her shoulders. It didn't know either.

Her eyes were intent on the milk rising in the pail when the repetitive music of the work came crashing to a halt. She suddenly felt void of more than just her energy; it was a collapsing of life purpose, as if the oil had run out, extinguishing her flame.

"What is it, Hodelleh?" Hodel did not even notice that Chava's concerned hand was upon her shoulder.

"Nothing . . ." Hodel dismissed the feeling, brushing it away. "Nothing at all."

But of course it was something—and she wanted it gone. She ached to feel once more, even for the briefest of moments, the fellowship of her community, her faith, and, above all, her affinity with Chava and the rest of her family. She longed to grow—inward, outward, taller still. She longed to burst through the barn doors and run toward any kind of rescue, across vast distances, through the mists of the morning, until the collapse of her body matched that of her spirit. All of a sudden she was quite nauseated with it. Hodel shook herself, threw back her head, and smiled with reassurance at her sister before returning to the udders with a forced resolve.

That was the summer she turned sixteen—the summer before she met Perchik.

He had come into their home as a Sabbath guest of her father, Tevye, one early autumn day.

"He has no beard!" Shprintze exclaimed, spying from the kitchen. "Nor prayer shawl!"

"I think it's exciting," said Bielke. "A stranger from the city!"

But Hodel had hated him at the start. She didn't like his flouting of tradition and of the old ways. Perhaps she was overly defensive—of her way of life, of her family, of all she had ever known. Hodel's irritation was only exacerbated by the stranger's pride when he told the family he was not only a teacher but also a "very good one" at that.

Pah! she thought, rolling her eyes. *Vanity.*

As Golde set a place for the stranger at their Sabbath table, Perchik smiled, glancing Hodel over and chuckling to himself. He'd been dealt worse. This only riled Hodel further, and she spun on her heel and went into the kitchen.

"He certainly does not appear to have trouble joining us unannounced," Hodel whispered to her sisters from the domestic refuge. "Of course," she added quickly, catching her mother's stern glance her way, "I would never be uncharitable to strangers. Or judge people at first sight. Of course."

"Oh, of course," said Chava, rolling her eyes before making her way back to the table, arms full of plates and serving dishes.

Once seated at the table, Hodel virtually steamed as she kept an eye on the stranger. She could barely eat. Who was this person who came to their table? He claimed to be a teacher, but from all she could see, he was an itinerant—an overeducated man doing the job of a beggar. For the first time in all her life, Hodel was glad to be Tevye the milkman's daughter, for though her family was far from wealthy, she was glad at least of her father's popular social position in their community. And Tevye had invited Perchik in, which meant that Perchik was indebted to her father, and thus—quite spectacularly—to her. The delight of that thought sustained her through the meal and in the cleanup that followed. She was making a final trip back to the dining room to grab the last of the dishes when she turned the corner and ran face-first into the stranger himself.

"Good Sabbath," said Perchik.

Hodel, caught like a startled animal, jerked herself away.

"Good Sabbath," she replied, almost inaudibly, as she retreated from him in both her shame and her disquiet. She smoothed the length of her hair with her trembling hands and breathed deeply. *At least vagrants come and go quickly,* she thought as she straightened her spine and followed Chava into the kitchen. *That, after all, is the nature of vagrancy.*

But he returned again a few days later, as the agreement had been that Tevye's family would welcome him for the Sabbath if he would provide the two youngest daughters with lessons.

Hodel watched from a safe distance as Perchik sat outside with Shprintze and Bielke, bent over a heavy book that sat between them. She examined the threadbare tunic stretched across the muscular length of his shoulders, the planes of his beardless face. She inched back. She did not want to come too close; something about it felt sinful, so she observed from afar, protected by the distance. Hodel admired how the broadness of his shoulders curved above the volume as if he were cradling the very thoughts upon the pages with his entire body. She could have remained there, eyes intent on him forever, but for the gust of wind that whipped her rippling blanket of hair across her body, forcing her to quickly gather it up and tuck it in a woven knot beneath her headscarf. When she looked up once again, she saw that Perchik was no longer gazing into his book: he was gazing at her.

Hodel bolted upright and returned his gaze. She was self-consciously aware of her neck exposed from the openness of her work shirt. He tilted his head and made a little bow. She wasn't sure what it meant, but it rocked her.

Despite every attempt to stay away, Hodel returned a few days later, just as the lessons were concluding. As the little ones scampered off to play, Hodel looked over Perchik's stack of travel-worn books with their lofty titles.

"You don't belong in the shtetl, do you?" she finally said. "You don't talk like a teacher, or a Jew, or any other proper man I've ever come across. What did you do before you came here?"

"I worked all my youth for my uncle. At university, I was a newspaper editor. Then a barman. I've been a joiner, a carpenter, a common laborer."

"So," she asked, "does a scholar such as yourself find it very tedious to teach children?"

"Sometimes," he replied with a wry smile. "Depends on the student."

Perchik's expression made Hodel uneasy, and she bristled in his gaze, pinned and squirming beneath the heat of his appraisal.

"Well, then how does such an advanced thinker stomach such a task?"

Perchik paused a moment, gripping his notebook. "When I fall asleep at night, in the moment between sleep and wakefulness, I can feel a kind of crushing panic. I have been experiencing this every night since I was a young boy. It is a dread that this is all life might be made of—that beauty and truth and the simplistic gifts of a righteous life might not be enough." He looked over her house, off into the distance. "Yet I drift off in peace and sleep quite soundly most nights. For I trust that tomorrow might be the day. It might be the day that may have that new idea or spark. Tomorrow might be the day some kind of glory, peace, or freedom arrives. It gives me courage to continue with my life." He swept his gaze back to her face, where it rested.

Hodel closed her eyes. He was speaking of the thing that she had felt. She knew his weariness, shared it, felt it creep heavily within her—denser than any Sabbath wine.

"Hodel!" she heard Mama cry, rattling her back to reality. But she ignored the call.

She looked at Perchik sharply. "Why are you here?" she demanded.

"Where?"

"In Anatevka!"

"I am here for the shelter and food your father is paying me in, Hodel." Perchik smiled. His study of her felt assured, uncompromising. "Why? Should I remain here for any other reason?"

Hodel squirmed in the glare of his scrutiny. But as he took a step toward her, she saw that his eyes were filled with both a blazing intellect and a terrible sadness.

"*Hodel!* Where are you?" she heard Mama call again. "It is time to wash!"

"Coming, Mama!" Hodel shouted back, then turned away and hurried back into the house.

three

The bread was rotten and the broth nothing more than dirty water, but it was there. Though eating in the iron cuffs was no easy feat.

How she longed for her mother's bread; the effort of half a day was always worth it. The girls had learned the secrets of bread-making from Golde, who in turn had learned from her mother, and so forth—down six generations. Grandmother Tzeitel was said to have always prepared the very best challah loaves for her family of nine. And, for Golde's unit, baking bread had become a tradition of family pride, filling their home with the golden aroma of tufts of soft-baked dough and warm crusts glazed with egg.

Suddenly, Hodel was struck by an idea. If hunger was a torture used upon the prisoners, then she would try to protect herself by accumulating what provisions she could. She grabbed the remaining bread and, looking about, hid it in the open pipe behind the stove.

"Oi!"

She heard a cry from the darkness and returned to her corner, praying no one had seen her stash away the loaf.

From the corner, she stared into the dark. Down

the bleak dimness of the corridor, Hodel caught a pair of eyes—sunken, like two tiny pieces of nearly snuffed-out coal, burning at her. There sat an ashen-looking man whose vacant expression called to question the triple mark of *VOR* (for the Russian meaning "thief") branded upon both cheeks.

It was a jailer.

This, then, was the overseer of the convicts? A felon himself—oh God! Hodel returned the jailer's gaze, which must have conveyed all the indignation of her spirit, for he rose and moved to stand before her.

His eyes dropped, and he spoke with a complacent posture in heavily accented Russian. "Well, what can I do? They order me to watch you, and I must execute my orders."

A thief for a jailer? she thought. *What has become of me?*

She went breathless, sucking in frozen air as a cold sweat burst over her skin still aching from disinfection. She desired nothing more than to open up her chest like great window shutters and rush out. She pressed her head between her hands in a viselike grip until at last she breathed again.

The jailer addressed her. "What is the name of your intended?"

Hodel edged herself upright with renewed hope. "Perchik Tselenovich."

"Ah. And his prisoner number, do you know it?"

"Nine hundred thirty-seven—it was in the letters he sent to me weeks ago."

"Mmm . . . " he muttered, scratching a few lines upon the papers before him.

"He wrote that he was being held at this location. He *is* here, yes?"

But the jailer gave no reply.

"I do wonder, sir," she said, "why I am being held here at such length."

"Have you committed a crime?"

"No, sir! None. I only wish to join Perchik. To work beside him." She mustered as sweet a smile as she was able, entreating the jailer to pity her, but he merely stared with the same vacancy as always.

"Food will be sent," he said, "though it's hardly that. Cook's no good, no—what do you Jews call it? No *baleboosteh*, that's certain." He moved to take his leave of her. "The other prisoners are whispering of your loyalty to your intended," he added, almost smiling. "Like a little tiger—that is what they are calling you—*Tygrysek*. It's Polish." He shrugged. "So . . ." Hodel watched him as he examined her.

"Now, get up," he said. "You must be cleaned."

"Cleaned?"

"Yes."

It could not be. "I have just been washed."

"You must be cleaned again."

"But I am red."

"Never mind. You will. Until they are satisfied. You stink of Pole."

The truculent woman returned, hair pulled somehow tighter than before, bucket and scouring cloths secure in her hulking arms.

"Pole? But—"

"Jew, then. Scrubbed."

"Sir—!"

"Again."

He unlocked the cell and nodded to the woman. "Every nook and cavity."

four

Tzeitel always had been a little woman. Tzeitel—the boss, the serious one. The wife-in-training.

Their mother, Golde, called her *kallehniu*—the little bride.

"Baleboosteh!" Golde would exclaim, the utmost compliment to a great homemaker, and she'd grin incessantly at her good fortune. Tzeitel was her protégé; she need only teach her daughter a recipe once, and off she went! Even finding ways to alter and improve it.

Tzeitel's slim, efficient body took after their mother's—a muscular, upright posture with full breasts and long limbs both strong and lean. She moved like an eldest daughter, with a sharp, exacting precision. Her hands were small but sturdy, crafted perfectly for both work and tenderness. Her gestures reflected that her mind regarded her work as that of celebrated rigor; a lifelong calling unique to women who felt they had been chosen for this life of delicious, harsh exactitude.

But Tzeitel also possessed an incredible softness, a deep kind of femininity different from that of her sisters and mother. This was evident in her dark and lustrous hair, in skin smooth and clean as morning upon her heart-shaped face (and, to Hodel's great irritation, the button nose she shared with Chava)—a face ignited with a fierce, determined gaze. Slight she may have been, but also beautiful and mighty.

All this filled Hodel with the distant worship reserved exclusively for gods and older sisters, and from that admiration, of course, sprang jealousy. Hodel watched Golde watch Tzeitel—*a protégé! A disciple!* Hodel seethed, marinating in a wash of envy and inadequacy.

Tzeitel seemed to relish household chores. She attacked the laundry with visible signs of pleasure, extracting every last particle of grime from aprons, tucking a bed linen in a perfectly angular manner. The deep degree of contentment that spread over her after a day of baking, mopping floors, washing, ironing, and giving baths to the little ones left her thoroughly at peace. She was just where she ought to be within her God-given role. *Home,* Tzeitel would muse. *The holy realm.*

Tzeitel had always been the one her less-than-domestically-blessed sisters would come to for practical advice. How to dice. How to remove a stain. Holiday traditions. Which food blessing would be expected. How to fold a bed linen versus a tablecloth.

Chava, however, was no homemaker, but she tried her best to hide it. She had a spectacular routine developed to obscure the fact that she couldn't cook, hoping no one would notice. Tzeitel did. Chava's sneaky tricks and stealthy dodges might have fooled their preoccupied mother, but not Tzeitel. The only reason Chava could manage even minor kitchen tasks was because of Tzeitel's watchful eye, her patience, her guidance, and, most important of all, her insistence.

"After all, these skills are to become our life's work," Tzeitel said when she asked them to plait the challah, clean the windows, hang the bed linens, and beat the carpets, *again*.

As young children of seven and six, Hodel and Chava had loved to climb trees and get their knees bruised playing outside. Persuading them to comb their hair or style it neatly was hopeless, for they considered such ladylike things to be bland. Tzeitel was undeterred—it was her role as eldest to set an example, and set an example she did.

One day, when the sisters were finally in the early buds of womanhood, Tzeitel felt it was time for real action. It was now her duty to impress upon her sisters what she considered to be the subtle arts of being a lady (for Tzeitel was, above all else, a natural lady, and as far as she was concerned, that had nothing whatsoever to do with being bland).

She sat them down upon overturned milk

buckets in the barn and stood before them with the kind of upright authority she envisioned a yeshiva teacher might possess. She paced back and forth, treading a path in front of their muddy boots and soiled skirts, calmly reciting the pleasures and virtues of womanhood.

"Observant women such as we must make certain to always look pleasant," Tzeitel instructed. "Not to do so would reflect negatively on the God whose imprint we bear."

Hodel rubbed her eyes and shifted on her bucket. The movement made a hollow clang, and Tzeitel turned her head sharply and fixed Hodel with her signature stare, which her sisters simply referred to as "the black look."

"Sorry," Hodel murmured.

Tzeitel inhaled and continued. "Surround yourself with what prettiness you can find—a lovely tablecloth with a handsome centerpiece on the table goes such a long way."

Chava yawned.

Tzeitel caught this and winced. She had nothing against her sisters, but she did not doubt that God had given Adam a partner and not a slave. Adam *needed* Eve.

"Watch your step and posture, and walk gracefully—and don't walk too quickly if there is no need for it! Also, watch your voice—is it soft and gentle? Is it unnecessarily loud?"

Hodel snickered and buried her face in Chava's

shoulder; Chava responded in kind. They were of course thinking of their mother. Hodel put her lips to Chava's ear.

"It doesn't matter how often Tzeitel's future husband changes his job," she whispered to her sister. "He is always going to end up with the same boss." They fell off the buckets in fits of hysterical laughter.

Well. Tzeitel never attempted that tactic again.

Sharing the larger bed with Chava was one of the purest delights of their upbringing. Hodel and Chava would often talk deep into the night, hands folded beneath their heads, face to face, foot to foot for warmth, eyes alight.

"She is in love with him!" Chava cooed, remarking on Tzeitel and her lifelong love of her childhood playmate, Motel Kamzoil.

"Oh yes."

"Just like you with the rabbi's son!"

"No!" Hodel protested. "He is merely the best available there is! In truth, Mendel is really a bit stuffy—

"—and humorless—"

"Certainly. No. This is different. Haven't you seen the way they look at each other? Like in all the books you read to me. Like in the poems."

"You're right," said Chava, smothering a giggle. "But she is so serious!"

Hodel looked away, thoughtful. She had always

felt Tzeitel was particularly hard on her, and their lives in Anatevka were dotted with foolish disputes between the two eldest daughters.

"She hates me."

"No!" Chava insisted, clearing Hodel's hair away from her eyes.

Three and a half years did not appear to be so great a difference now, but it certainly was when they were children. By the time Hodel was born, Tzeitel had been speaking in sentences and was fiercely independent. Hodel's arrival was unwelcome at best.

"Oh, Hodelleh, Tzeitel is hard on all of us," Chava continued. "But perhaps because you were the very first to come along? Like Jacob and Esau, or Cain and Abel!"

"But those are all brothers," Hodel said with dismay.

"Yes, but it's the same thing."

"No, it isn't—boys are completely different."

At this, Chava buried her face in a pillow.

When they were very young children, Tzeitel perhaps not much older than seven or eight, they shared a room with two tiny beds—Tzeitel in one, Hodel and Chava in the other, slightly larger one. Tzeitel was adamant that Hodel specifically not cross a self-proclaimed line onto her "side," nor touch anything she kept around her bed. Of course Hodel did—frequently. Tzeitel never let Hodel borrow anything, not even a hairbrush or a ribbon, unless specifically instructed to do so and only then begrudgingly, out of a sense of obedience.

These days, all the girls shared a larger room divided into sleeping camps: Tzeitel behind a partition in her own small cot, Shprintze and Bielke at one end of the room in small stacked beds, Hodel and Chava at the other on a larger mattress. It allowed these late-night talks to persist without *too* much bother to the others.

"Well, I think it is perfectly unfair," Hodel said. "One can't help being born! I have only ever wished to please Tzeitel." *To love her,* she added to herself.

"Perhaps it's how your dark wit developed?" offered Chava.

"Please, Bird, that's from Mama."

"No!" Chava thought a moment. "Well, yes, but listen—"

"It is not my imagination, then!" Hodel interrupted, hands clasped around her face. It broke Hodel's stubborn but lamentably tender heart.

Hodel felt the warmth of Chava's gaze upon her, felt her fingers entwine with her own in both helplessness and understanding.

"Well," said Chava, smirking, "one can hardly blame her."

"Oh, she is just so serious!" Hodel giggled at last, and Chava joined her as Hodel furrowed her face, impersonating Tzeitel's stern expression.

"I think she is just cross that we do not take life as seriously as she. Tzeitel has so much responsibility on her shoulders," said Chava judiciously. "Perhaps she is as cross with *us* as we are with her for being so solemn! Perhaps it is the same?"

"Perhaps . . ." Hodel understood but was still stung. "*Zol zein*—just let it be!" she cried, taking her sister up in her arms.

Everything Hodel felt Tzeitel did not do for her, she wanted to do and be for Chava. It was the greatest joy in her life.

"And Hodelleh? All I meant before about all the brothers was perhaps *that* is why she is so much crosser with you than the rest of us. It is as old as the Good Book. It is destined to be. It is not your fault."

Hodel nodded, holding Chava closer. "But Cain and Abel? You think Tzeitel and I are like Cain and Abel?"

"No, I'm just—"

"What? I should make certain Tzeitel doesn't invite me into a field and kill me?"

"I'm not saying that at all—and if you're not careful I might just beat her to it!"

"Oh, *shah*—quiet! You might try but I always come back stronger!"

"Only because you're a giant!"

"Remember that time I got her to chase me around the barn?" Hodel cackled. "In search of that awful dress drippy Motel the tailor had fixed *'espeeecially'?"*

"Yes," squealed Chava, "yes! I remember that look upon her face when she knew she had been beaten!"

Their sides ached as they buried their laughter in the pillows before slowly nestling into each other and falling asleep.

Hodel woke to a metal clang.

"Potato," the jailer called as he plodded back down the dark corridor.

Alone again, she held the dish and sat, unmoving. *Perchik,* she thought. *Perchik, I will find you.* Her mind filled with him, her longing for him constant, coital, and unrequited.

five

A clamor at the entrance of her cell revealed a man in a splendid high-ranking officer's uniform accompanied by the jailer and several officers who lined the corridor behind him. With an angular face accented by a thin mustache, the man walked with an elegant cane of dark wood clutched in his meticulously maintained fingers.

Hodel locked eyes with him and rose to her feet, resisting the urge to scratch at her skin itching from vermin and foul garments.

The man before her was doubtless a descendant from the peoples of the North, for he was implausibly fairer and taller than any man she had ever seen, with hair so light it was almost white, eyes like razors, and a towering presence that commanded respect, aided by the fine clothing that draped his treelike limbs. He wore a cape lined with fur tied with a purple velvet cord that fell elegantly along his wide shoulders, yet his grooming was queer, with a beard kept to just his chin like that of a goat, his mustache curled at the sides, kept in place by both the force of his will and a sour-smelling wax. His presence was also aromatic, smelling pungently of exotic spices she did not recognize (perhaps native to the not-so-distant Orient).

All told, the man was physically immaculate—everything except for his right trouser leg, which billowed oddly, hinting at a leg missing below the knee.

She now realized she beheld no less a person than the Chief Commander of Omsk himself.

At Omsk and Tobolsk sat the headquarters of the Commission of Inquiry and Deportation, whose business was to assign a definitive destination to each man, according to local convenience or the necessities of the public works. It has been calculated that at the time, the number of transported persons annually amounted to a little short of ten thousand.

The Chief Commander removed his cape, pushed the bars open, and with the aid of his cane, sat himself down upon a chair, which materialized as he moved.

"Who are you?" he said, to her shock, in serviceable, icy-voiced Yiddish, then signaled for her to return herself to the floor from which she had just risen.

"Hodel, sir."

"Hello, Hodel," he replied, emphasizing her name in a manner she could not detect. "So, your presence in Omsk has no other objective than that of joining your intended? This is your claim?"

"Yes, sir."

His gaze narrowed. Studying her, he proceeded henceforth to address her in Russian, lighting a cigarette as he did so. "Can you tell me the name of your leader?"

Hodel did not answer at once; her mind was calculating—he had switched tongues perhaps tactically and she desired to keep up. Her Russian was good enough but patchy, and this man was so grand.

"Leader?" she half asked, half repeated for the sake of clarity.

The man seemed very much impressed and intrigued at this capability, though very much annoyed at the fetid air of the room and turned to the high window several times, as if to breathe freely.

The man held up a familiar letter—the confiscated letter Perchik had written to her detailing his circumstances and whereabouts. "This leader."

"Well, Perchik Tselenovich is not my leader."

"Are you, or are you not, the intended wife of Perchik Tselenovich?"

"I am."

"Are you now, or have you ever been, aligned with any sort of Democratic society?"

"No."

"To your knowledge, is your intended husband a member of any such society?"

She troubled herself with her answer for a moment, then spoke again. "I know that my intended husband once formed a part of one at the university in Kiev, but withdrew from it long ago."

"Ah, then you yourself are also an emissary of that society?"

"Not at all, sir."

"Then in coming here you had absolutely no political mission?"

She stared hard at him without blinking, then said with total certainty, "I had none."

The Chief Commander took a final drag of his cigarette in contemplation. Exhaling, he spoke again. "Such assertions are not likely to improve your situation, my dear"—he glanced around the cell—"which, I grant you, is a very unpleasant one. Only a sincere and complete confession can diminish your troubles. Make you worthy of the indulgence of the tsar."

"But, sir—"

"I merely wish to know with whom you were acquainted."

"But I knew no one!" she cried.

"My dear," he said. "Be serious." His voice had turned to metal and grew firmer and more jarring as he continued. "The empire is rife with dissension and revolt. Wounds are festering, prisons filled to bursting with the filthy detritus of liberal thinkers. Do you not understand that?" She did not! "Or is that something that your little insulated communities of Christ killers take no notice of?" He flicked the stub of his cigarette toward her. "Your situation is most critical." He leaned upon his cane and brought himself to standing. "Improve it by making a sincere confession; I can intercede with the tsar."

"But, sir, my husband!" So much of this she could not understand.

"What of him?"

"I have come so far to join him—not yet even told of his whereabouts—his condition—have just been kept alone in chains!"

He towered above as he looked upon her with a certain gentleness. "You are weak, girl," he said, "and under misapprehensions. I do not ask for all your secrets—only the names of the persons by whom you were known. Their names are all that is required."

She began to weep.

"Now, now," the Chief Commander said, furrowing his brow in mock sympathy. "Women too can be courageous." He paused, eyeing her up and down. "You are young; you are not wanting in intellect. The course of your life depends entirely upon yourself. Even a concocted confession cleanses the soul. But you must keep your spirit, girl. It seems you shall be with us for quite some time."

He went out, stopped at the gate, and ordered to the jailer, "Chains off—and, for Christ's sake, bring her some soup. Jews love to eat. Though Lord knows this soup is the piss of gutters." He bowed and paused as if about to leave, then he turned back to her, smiling, his eyes making one last shrewd calculation.

"And shave her."

He knocked his cane against the bars as he turned to take his leave.

Hodel's dreams had become less frequent as the weeks progressed, but they were no less vivid or stirring. It was summer as she slept tonight, and she was bathing with her sisters in the secluded river just west of their home. Sheets had been hung upon the tree branches to preserve their modesty, and the sails of white danced in the gentle breeze, catching the flickering light off the rippling river. Hodel could not help but see every aspect of the scene as essential. It was a perfect day.

They had never spoken of it, but this was the activity they looked forward to the most, and they always enjoyed it together—tromping as a motley quintet to the banks, in a rare but blissful silence, then taking to the waters with abandon.

First, you must wash it.

Shprintze, the fourth sister, was a nervous girl and afraid of the water, always had been. As the others swam and washed and splashed, Shprintze would often dangle her feet on the shores and watch, reluctant to enter; washing hair seemed to frighten her with its full and repeated submersions.

Chava had a way of calming those around her, exuding an almost palpable warmth. She would distract Shprintze with little jokes.

"I have a joke," she said.

"Please, Chava, do me a favor—" said Shprintze.

"Don't do *me* any favors!" Hodel chuckled.

"Shah!" said Chava, smacking Hodel on the arm. "Shprintze, why do bees have sticky hair?"

"Bees don't have hair, Chavaleh." Shprintze scoffed.

"I know," Chava said with a smile. "It's a joke. Listen: Why do bees have sticky hair?"

"I don't know." Shprintze sighed.

"Because they use honeycombs." Chava's face sprouted a grin as she awaited her sisters' reactions. They were very quiet as Shprintze stared at her blankly.

"That is really terrible."

Chava's smile broadened as they all convulsed with laughter. It was Chava's soothing touch that allowed Shprintze the joy of freshly cleansed hair without a fuss; an image burned onto Hodel's brain in the colors of compassion and golden summer light.

Then, you must comb it.

The sisters often joined forces to attend to

Chava's hair before the Sabbath. The taming required to bridle the indignant, irrepressible mop atop Chava's head was astonishing.

"How do the *goyeshe* do it?" whined Chava, removing her headscarf, steeling herself. "Without this I'd never be able to leave the house. I would frighten people."

"Nonsense," said Tzeitel.

"Yes, nonsense," agreed Hodel. "You frighten them already."

And they all laughed together, even Tzeitel, after Hodel had been suitably smacked.

And don't forget: plaited is best.

They often plaited one another's hair before bed. At first Hodel was too vain to plait her hair at night, claiming it "crimped her natural curls" and that she preferred her hair "as God intended it to be" (at this she received head-shaking stares of disbelief). But once the very youngest, Bielke, was old enough to lure all her older sisters, they would sit upon the floor of their room in a tidy line—most often youngest to eldest, but oftentimes with Hodel at the back and Chava at the front (Hodel avoiding her hair being "bothered with" and Chava as clumsy with hair as she was with everything else).

Then, last, it must be scarfed.

The girls were taught about modesty, of course. But it was Hodel's least favorite thing.

The richer women in their community often

wore *sheitls*, or wigs, though there was debate around the issue. Some said wigs were the best option—headscarves always left at least a few hairs sticking out here and there. Others claimed a headscarf made it easier to see that a woman was married.

"According to Jewish law, we are commanded only to cover our hair. It doesn't specify how," said Golde under her breath. She would have died for the luxury of a wig.

Hodel sometimes had to be spoken to. She was curious and flirtatious and more than a little self-admiring.

"Hodel. My daughter. Listen to me. You are an attractive woman of great beauty, and beauty is one of the gifts the Almighty graciously gives us. But we must not be full to bursting with pride. Like every gift, it must be used wisely." Hodel would not meet her eyes, so Golde tilted Hodel's chin up and forced a look of maternal warning into Hodel's view.

"Hodelleh: your hair *is* beautiful. But it is intended for your family and future husband alone. You must find it within yourself to cover it as a sign of being a devout woman. I am not saying women should be hidden or unheard all the days of their life. . . ."

Of course you aren't, thought Hodel, rolling her eyes.

Golde continued, sterner than before, "But we

were given preventive measures against leading men into sin and women into vanity—a line you are dancing on, my dearest."

"But, Mama," Hodel protested, "how am I supposed to both stand tall and maintain modesty?"

"That," Golde replied, "is what true womanhood is all about. So. Find a way or I will find it for you." And with that, the matter was done with, and Golde gave her a newly handmade headscarf—the largest and dullest Hodel had ever seen.

She jolted. Looking down, she saw the headscarf sitting neatly in her hand, just as if her mother had put it there a moment ago. Sitting on the brink of marriage, she appreciated her mother's words anew. When she saw Perchik she would enthrall him—he would see her hair in all its wild glory and her lifetime of modesty would all be worth it. She lifted the scarf to her face, inhaling. It smelled of her home—the odors of brewing pots and feminine sweat and sweetened air. Her heart jerked and she began drawing the scarf around her head.

Suddenly, from behind, the scarf was ripped from her hands. Firm grips caught her arms and dragged and pinned her down as she thrashed against them, teeth bared and now wide-awake.

"Ooh! Ain't she wild?" an aide declared, gripping her tighter.

The jailer looked on as the aides held her down while she feverishly bucked and railed against the strength they possessed. The truculent woman held the razor.

Hodel shrieked, pleading.

"Keep her steady," the jailer muttered, no life in his eyes, the gaze showing neither mercy nor cruelty.

She was shaking when she returned to her cell. The cell itself had been purified too.

"Better, yes?" the jailer asked. He took a rag from his pocket and indicated that she could use it to improve the cell further. She felt a fondness for the jailer. The rag was brown with use, but the fabric was so soft it made her heart lift. Greater still was the fact that she was without the chains and thus felt she had reclaimed her mind!

Her legs were cut and bruised, but she stretched them, walking up and down her cell, the pain of the movement almost pleasing. She waved her arms about—she could not stop herself! She recalled the glories of basic motion, as perhaps a flailing insect might do when freed from a spiderweb. When she turned around, the gate was shut and locked, and there, before her, once again stood the upright figure of the Chief Commander.

"Well, hello," his said, his mouth dimpling.

"I've come with news of your Perchik Tselenovich." Hodel's heart leapt, but she moved slowly toward him, her legs throbbing from lack of use, her wits still wary of this unnerving man.

"My, my." He chuckled. "It really is amusing how only the most pathetic of revolutionaries end up here."

His gaze turned blacker somehow as he began looking her over in a particularly indecent way.

"Perchik Tselenovich is no longer a prisoner here, my girl," the Chief Commander said. "But I'm certain he'd be terribly touched by your mettle. He was exported over three weeks ago to which far-off location I just cannot seem to recall. . . ." At this, his dimpled mouth became a fully fledged curl of the lip. "Though I am certain I could be moved to remember if, of course, your memory improved as well. . . ." He turned to the jailer hidden behind him in the shadows and spoke to him in a murmur. Then the jailer handed Hodel a bundle—the fabric stained, wet, and heavy with its contents.

"For sentiment, girl. Consider it a wedding gift."

As she opened the bundle, she was surprised by a familiar color within.

It was her hair.

"We left you nothing but a short shave in the Jewish fashion. You are nearly a married woman, yes? And the married Jews wear nothing at all. Is that not so?"

Her hands grasped the nakedness upon her head a moment before her mind did. A groan of lamentation followed—nearly inhuman.

Then all went white.

Six

It had been exactly ninety-four days since she had heard Perchik's voice from beyond the bars, and, Hodel counted, well over seven months that she had been interned in Omsk. Days had turned to nights, weeks to months, and seasons had swiftly come and gone without a change to her captivity. There was an unrelenting wheel whirring in her chest—it churned within her ribs, exhausting her desire for anything but sleep.

She found that the unnatural silence of the night had cracked open, revealing with each fracture a kind of nocturnal cacophony—every creaking chain and stone and creature, the stomp of every foot, clicking of every clock, *thuds* of clubs landing upon bodies, shrieks and moans and cries for loved ones or sometimes simply of despair, and once, the lone voice of a man singing in an unfamiliar language, whose song was so bright, and the emotion within it so clear, it made her insides swell.

There were storms too, unlike any she had ever experienced. They would blow up around the place: ice would pelt; wind would roar furiously against the feeble windows and creep through the thickness of the walls.

She could almost see Chava before her: hair loosened around her shoulders, the whiteness of her nightgown rivaling the sky beyond the window, tucked warmly into the bed they had shared since the beginning of their lives, and the overwhelming emptiness of the spot beside her.

In the depths of the night, she could hear, as plain as day, the *Seyder Tkhines*, prayers in Yiddish sung and recited at home by women—in her mother's distinctive contralto, and she opened her eyes to see the familiar outline of the door she had so come to loathe during her incarceration.

But to her surprise, this time the door sat open, unhinged from itself. She grabbed the handle, pushed it, and was at once flooded with the sounds, smells, and lights of home. Her family was gathered around the Sabbath table, eyes closed in deepest devotion so that her tardy entrance went unnoticed.

It had been some time since Hodel had met her family in her dreams. She had reached the place she longed for when she began. At the cliff's edge of all she had known, accepted as true, or thought she could bear, Hodel, since her departure, had continued to take step after step into the abyss—only to discover that firmament would materialize beneath her, so that she might take even one more step.

She noted the cleanliness of their garments—the freshly laundered blouses and pressed hair ribbons—and suddenly felt so poorly dressed in comparison that she nearly turned on her heel in shame. But when she looked down, she noted that she too was finely dressed, her fingernails clean, her hair long and styled, and so she quietly moved to the chair that was always her own at the end of the table and slipped into the scene without a sound.

There were three women's commandments to be observed:

First, *niddah*, preventing men and woman from intercourse during menstruation. Second, the lighting of the candles on the eve of the Sabbath and on holidays. And last, the challah—the tradition of separating a piece of dough from the unbaked bread, which was originally put aside for a *kohen* in biblical times. She recalled her mother's words: "This custom of setting aside a part of the bread continued, which is why the separation and destruction of a portion of challah has become one of the duties incumbent upon us as women."

Associated with all these tasks were prayer recitations, at times in Hebrew, but for the more mundane affairs of the home, the women would spout Yiddish prayers, or *tkhines*, that addressed these everyday concerns.

Golde had a printed tkhine collection, which

she kept safely in a handwoven cover in a secluded corner of their living area, and Hodel loved to remove the sheath and quietly thumb through it. Each individual prayer began with a heading that described when and sometimes how it should be recited. She thumbed through it now. There was a thkine to say on the Sabbath and one to pray for your husband and children. There was a thkine for confession. There were thkines to say when the shofar is blown on Rosh Hashanna, on the eve of Yom Kippur, and when emerging from the ritual bath. There were thkines for confessions, for fasting, for the new moon, at weddings, when a baby is born, and more and more.

Delightful, she thought, grinning to herself as she wore the pages ever thinner with the truth of her devotion, thinking on how many hands and fingers, how many generations of women had graced the pages before her.

As she sat down at the family dinner table, she observed them all, their heads bowed as her mother prayed over the candles.

Devotion and faith were not the same thing. Hodel knew countless women who did not love their husbands but were devoted and obedient nonetheless. Was it not the same with faith?

Tzeitel accepted. Tzeitel's God was in the home. She had things to do, babies to raise, and the traditions of their ancestors to uphold. That meant something to her. Yet God's message did not appear to be a personal one to Tzeitel; it was shared, descending from a long line of biblical matriarchs upheld in the beauty of symbolic traditions.

Chava questioned. Chava's God was in books, in thinkers and kingdoms and imaginary worlds beyond. Chava went along, for there was no discernible alternative, but Hodel often looked at her sister and recognized the line between obedience and belief.

But Hodel truly believed. This was a difference between her and her sisters. The first thing Hodel ever remembered knowing was that God was present in her life whether she was always aware of it or not, and nothing in this world felt as though it was happening without His direct supervision and guidance. She did not fear God; she trusted in Him.

It was strange to sit at the table of her past so full of her present understanding. As she sat there she thought back on her sojourn, her torture, her isolated imprisonment, and on what it meant to be here: simultaneously both years before and beyond life's road. Harshness ventilates perspective, makes one resilient. The trials she endured were necessary— necessary to truly see the beauties and wonders of the past, to prepare for the trials of the future.

As the scene dissolved, as her conscious mind overtook the table like a burst of rising light, Hodel awoke to another morning in exile.

It was all part of the same path.

How long would any of them wait? Here, unable to go either back or forward, she felt herself rot day after limitless day.

Hodel lay atop a blanket of what was once her hair—cooing, stroking it mildly, nursing it back to life, encouraging it to thrive as she herself could not. The release of her chains was a great relief, yet despite her new physical freedom she remained almost always on the floor, rising only to pace or kneel in prayer for her survival, for Perchik's, and for what she had to believe was a reunion with him in a location she also prayed to discover. She seized a moldy crust from her secret storage and nibbled on it heedfully before turning her head to the wall once more and closing her eyes.

Guards came and went—some watched her closely, others slept, some thrust themselves at her with leering eyes, but more often than not it was the jailer with the marks of *VOR* upon his face, holding his chain of keys and aggravating her grief so. Her bare head lifted upward, tears falling silently onto the mass of her former hair.

Tonight it felt as if only she lay awake—or at least only she and the miserable jailer, for she heard him stir outside the bars. *What makes that man so restless?* she thought as the flame from his lamp blazed.

seven

The sisters lay in bed together as they always did—the windows of their room covered as they always were. Their warm breath flowed outward in billows as it struck the cold of the air in their bedroom; it was (according to the depth of the darkness) two, perhaps even three o'clock.

Chava was restless, and as a result Hodel was not sleeping well either, for the bed they had shared all their lives was beginning to feel smaller.

"Hodel," Chava whispered, careful to shake her sister just enough to rouse her without her starting or making too great a noise. Hodel half woke and nudged her sister with her leg—she was so very near the edge of slumber.

"Hodel!" she whispered again, this time more insistent.

"What *is* it, Chava?" Hodel replied, not moving from her position, her tone unmistakably put out. Chava had a tendency to be full of talk at very late hours, and Hodel was always the bearer of her chatter, whether she liked it or not.

"Well, Bird?" Hodel bit into the darkness.

The little bird. That was what they called her. Chava would flit around the house, the barn, the fields, the town, leaving her "bird droppings" everywhere. Handkerchiefs, books, apple cores, bits of glass or string or pretty stones she had collected, then lost within a day. She was an innately childlike presence in their household, a *luftmensh*—a dreamer with her head in the clouds—her wide-open mind preoccupied with other things. Books, mostly. Dreams.

Chava was clever and could not stave her appetite for reading, for any kernel of information she could collect from a world beyond their own. Even her appearance was birdlike: delicately framed, enviably long hands, a small bust, a milky-pale complexion, and an open face with two of the sincerest eyes one could ever gaze upon.

Having spent so many of her earliest years as the youngest child, Chava quickly grasped a sense of her headstrong family and went about catching her flies with honey; she was mild and genuine, the baby, endowed with an irresistible disposition.

"What in the world *is* it, Chaveleh?"

Tonight, apparently, was a poor example of that.

Chava hovered above her sister for a moment, then uttered a swift, "Oh, nothing."

"I hate you; I really do," grunted Hodel, returning to her pillow with new purpose. "Go to sleep!"

"It is just that," Chava said, her voice fragile, her breath against her sister's ear. "I dreamed . . . I dreamed we were both sent very far away."

"Well, I suppose some day we shall, all of us, be sent away from home. To join a husband."

"Shall we?"

Hodel turned her head and sighed. "Well, of course. You know we shall."

"Yes, but must we? Can we not stay like this in this tiny bed for always?"

"Chaveleh, you know we cannot stay here for always; we should become very cross with each other if we were to grow old and gray and still be in this bed. Besides, I would sooner marry Reb Avrahm's hideous boy or that invalid son of the innkeeper than remain in a bed with my sister into eternity. Now, go to sleep."

But Chava could not. Hodel felt her lying there, still but rigid. She could feel the beating of her sister's heart.

"Hodel?" Chava said, this time her voice so full of anguish that it woke Hodel fully.

"Oh, Chaveleh. What is it?" She reached for Chava's open face within the darkness, cupping it between her hands.

Chava spoke again, her voice even fainter. "Hodel . . ." Then she stopped.

Hodel could feel the moisture upon Chava's cheeks. "What on earth is the matter, Bird?" she asked.

"Hodel," Chava continued haltingly. "Do you—do you think I am a fool?"

The question unsettled Hodel. "A fool?"

"Oh, then you do," Chava said woefully.

"No!"

It was difficult for Hodel to be objective; they had been reared so closely, born practically on top of each other. At times, it felt as though looking upon Chava was rather like looking into a glass.

"I want—I so want to be worldly. Discerning," Chava said.

I want to be asleep, Hodel thought but refrained from uttering aloud. Instead, she tried to comfort her sister. "A clever girl like you, who has read all those books?"

"Hodel," Chava said. "I wish you would tell me—"

Hodel could feel her sister steadying herself to broach some dreadful thing as Chava held her breath. At last the words poured from her, as if a final drop of torment had made her heart overflow.

"I wish you would tell me," Chava said, "what you thought of Fyedka."

At that, Hodel flushed. Perhaps Chava flushed too; she could not know, so dark was the room. Heart pounding, Hodel was rigid, her stomach tight and lurching. "Fyedka?"

"Yes," Chava said.

Hodel should have known it; Chava must have been getting up her nerve to ask for several weeks. "The young Russian man who is so often in the bookshop."

"I think . . ." Hodel said simply, "I think him very kind. And very . . . considerate of us. Of our ways. I like him." She hesitated only slightly before adding, "I do."

"You do?" Chava's voice lifted.

"I do."

Chava relaxed within her grip, the tears upon her cheeks coming harder now, but in relief perhaps. "And do you think I shall be sent far away like in my dream for so looking forward to seeing him in the shops every day? Am I a fool indeed?"

Hodel rose from the pillow and took Chava up in her arms fully, her closest sister, her soul's companion. "We shall all go away someday," she said. "How far is up to us, I suppose."

Chava nodded, wiping her eyes, enveloped there in the arms of her sister. "Yes."

"Now, for goodness' sake, do go to sleep, Bird, before I squeeze the talk right out of you."

"Yes, Hodel. Good night."

And just like that, they slept.

eight

Just after dawn, Hodel was escorted into a room filled floor-to-ceiling with files, bookshelves, and cabinets, as well as a great number of tall desks, where several prisoners sat writing upon high stools while overseers paced lazily, keeping loose eyes upon the workers. This was administrative exile: the punishment of pushing papers, which required no trial or sentencing procedure, ideal for insipid, nonviolent, or academic-minded political prisoners so often useless for hard-labor sentences.

All the eyes in the room darted toward her. They knew who she was. Once the supervisors were out of view, they approached. These were the sentenced Jews—some from as far as Lyubavichi and Slabodka, even a handful from Zolodin, Kasrilevke, and Rabelevka, near her own Anatevka. They held out their hands and quietly addressed her in Yiddish.

An overseeing commandant entered, and the men scurried back like mice. One of the men in particular caught Hodel's eye; she could see him watching her eagerly, even as he pretended to continue his writing. When the commandant was out of sight again, he rose, tilted toward her, and bowed with his cap.

"You are the intended wife of Perchik Tselenovich, yes?"

She nodded.

"I am an ally," he whispered urgently. "Listen closely to me: they have scheduled your hearing before the Commission of Inquiry and Deportation." He continued, "I have been keeping watch for your name, attempting to hold them off, but last night your case arrived on my desk. I filed the papers myself this morning. You require a strategy, ma'am." He explained that this place was the seat of government in the region, the artery for all other encampment points eastward. He looked over his shoulder, hands shaking. It was here, he whispered hurriedly, where most political revolutionaries were received. "All the wives are processed and assigned to the future destination of their husband," he explained. But because Hodel had made the journey in her own right and was not yet the legal wife of Perchik Tselenovich, she was therefore in a most precarious circumstance.

"Wives are practically obliged to follow their husbands to internment," he said, taking her hands in his. "But they have a tight leash on Perchik and thus have many reasons to keep you close. You are suspicious—you may be his conspirator. And you are valuable collateral. Perchik may be moved to talk if they threaten him with harm to you."

"And when I am no longer 'valuable'?"

He tightened his grip upon her hands. He explained that the Chief Commander would determine her fate. "They have the authority to make it appear as though you never existed at all!" he said.

It was worse than she feared.

"Give them anything they ask," he urged. "They shall sentence you regardless. Stay alive. You must. Perchik held out hope for you even as he was being carted away."

"But where is he, friend?" she asked, quaking.

"East. A labor camp—that is all I know. I deal only with hearing papers—deportation documents are accessible exclusively to those with the keys! So that's most important: befriend anyone with keys."

"Oi! Seven eighty-eight!" a commandant shouted from across the room. "Back to it!"

The man put his hand upward in apology and turned back to Hodel. "Go with God," he said, bowing once more, and then returned to his post.

"You!" the overseer called to Hodel. "Come, girl. We need you on the books at last. Your prints and things." She was carted away into the processing office.

nine

For three days, Hodel convinced herself that she would resist the stranger. She may have succeeded had it not been for her sisters.

"What is he even teaching you?" Hodel asked as they cooked together, dismissing the stranger with each angry flick of potato peel.

"Yesterday we learned about Psalms," replied Bielke. "It's a part of the Bible."

"I know that," Hodel replied, with another flick of potato. "What about Psalms, then?"

"About giving—and fairness and things," said Shprintze, a little pensive. "It was all things we already knew about the charitable giving of *tzedakah*, but this was for many people, rather than just a few. 'He has distributed freely; he has given to the poor; his righteousness endures forever; his horn is exalted in honor.' "

"That is from Psalms," Bielke whispered to Hodel, at which Hodel smirked and threw a potato peel at her sister.

"I will say," said Shprintze, "for someone so concerned with giving things away, he sounded very . . . cross."

Chava laughed below her breath.

"What, Bird?" Hodel demanded.

"Nothing." Chava put her hand to her mouth,

as if to keep the laughter from spilling out. "I just thought you didn't care about the lessons."

"I don't!" Hodel replied. "I'm just trying to protect my sisters." She threw her head back in defiance.

"From what?"

"Why, from stupidity," she sputtered, "naturally."

The others stared at her, still and blank.

"Right," said Chava with a little raise of her eyebrow, "naturally."

The next morning, Hodel watched the stranger as she cleaned and re-cleaned the milk pails.

The lessons had not yet begun, and he was washing himself by the well. Hodel studied him as he did: the particular angles of his neck, the way his hair fell into his face when his head was uncovered, the arch of his brow, the natural openness of his face, the pure, undiluted brilliance and distinctive sadness in his eyes. Her breath caught, and she was all at once quite faint, and as her head fell heavily upon the wall of the barn, she reveled in its roughness. It felt accurate, deserved—the thought of him leaving her weak with something she had no language to express.

She gazed at the scene laid out before her: Perchik and her little sisters poised like figurines, acting out a kind of parable. She jolted as the lesson ended.

"It was a very interesting lesson," she said.

"Oh?"

"Though I'm not sure that the rabbi would agree."

He kept his eyes intent upon his reading and did not look at her; he spoke laconically, as if he expected her to be there and that fact was far less interesting than his book. "And what about the rabbi's son?"

Hodel spun on her heel—*you little snitch*—her eyes raged at Chava, and she chased her out of the yard.

At this, Hodel fought with him. He was smart, arrogant, insufferable. With every sentence from his mouth she longed to burst his logic to dust, and she might very well have succeeded had the next sensation not been the rough, bare skin of his hands against hers. The vine of tendons creeping from his arms and down through his fingertips sent a surge of indescribable heat straight through to her own, and neither dared to breathe. At last she inhaled sharply. *What if someone saw us touching! Alone and unchaperoned, out here in the open daylight!* But she did not release her grip. She would not move until he allowed her to.

Before she knew it, they were dancing. *This is a sin,* she thought, her head swirling with fear and consequence. *A sin beyond forgiving.* She encountered the faint rustle of her underskirt as she moved, and it made her conscious of the heat between her thighs. With his hands upon her spine, she shuddered; her face was closer to his than it had ever been to any man, so close she could almost taste the moisture of his breath.

"I learned that dance in Kiev," he said. "What do you think?"

She felt an intense aching rise from deep within her; an urge so vast, so keen, she feared it would pulse and pulse forever, smothering her utterly. She was wide-awake for the first time in all her life. But as her pleasure mingled with fear, her hands turned to fists as she pushed him from her shuddering body. She turned abruptly and sprinted away from him and all that he had done to her. Perchik had set alight a beacon within her—her lifelong emptiness the aperture, his mind the shaft of light cascading through into a darkened room, illuminating all.

Who was this man? Where had he come from? Would it change him and all he was? Would it matter? *No,* she thought. She did not need to know.

She could feel his eyes upon her as she ran up the path.

She did not look back.

ten

Hodel was still convinced she would be released. Even after so great a number of weeks had passed that she could no longer account for them.

She sent letters to her family—the prison allowed her that brief luxury. The pain in her hands was terrible as she worked them to write again. *He sits in prison; I work,* she would scribble, hands weak and unpracticed. She gave the letters, thick with intimacy and lies, to the jailer, and she had to trust they would reach her family as the jailer slipped her words into the void of his deep-set pockets. She prayed the letters would find them and give them solace.

The full force of winter's anger had bellowed in, endless and wretched, and as a result her food was even less wholesome, the room caked with frost, and the want of air, of physical movement, and an isolation as profound as any hunger had completely drained her of her sanity.

One night, unable to stand the silence any longer, she spoke into the darkness.

"You!" she said abruptly. "You there!"

The jailer made his way to the bars, holding his lantern with his usual detachment. She pointed to her cheeks to indicate the marks upon his own.

"You are a criminal." He made no movement whatsoever. "And now you are in their employ?"

The jailer stepped away from the bars in what Hodel thought at first was an attempt to ignore her, but he returned momentarily with a chair and sat down upon it, placing the lamp near enough that she could feel its warmth.

"When I first arrived here," he began, most solemnly, "I was taken to a station house full of Poles who had fought in the war of independence."

"The war of independence?" She had not heard of any war referred to in that manner.

"Ah, Tygrysek, you have found me out." He grimaced. "I am a Pole."

So this explained it. His foreignness. His mysterious, particular misery.

"Their staffing is low, and I am not violent. I have been assigned to serve for life on this side of the bars. No matter." He paused a moment and shrugged. "Russia has seized Poland's most devout women and most charitable sons for nearly a century. "Most of the prisoners here are from what is now left of the town of Lodz."

He looked away.

"Poland. Our own land. Our people. In the beginning we hoped revolt might save us. We all detested the occupation, and many lost their jobs in the great recession—was it five years ago it began?" It was clear time had run away from him.

75

"They let the oldest go first. My two young sons stayed on for three more years, supported our family. Fine young men. Hardworking. Bright."

Hodel could not believe how beautifully he spoke—his voice was bell-like.

"By winter, over one hundred thousand workers across Poland had lost their jobs. Japanese War. A ravaged economy. But then came the conscriptions to the Russian army, the never-ending Russification, the lowering of wages and working conditions. We only wanted our freedom."

She thought of her own people in Anatevka. Before she left, there had been whispers of Jews dislocated from their villages by the tsar, entire townships being emptied of their people. She thought of the pogroms—the governmental demonstrations her father swore were nothing more than rumor. She adored him, but Tzeitel's ravaged wedding was too close for her father's gleaming optimism. Her papa—a father just like the jailer.

"What else could we do?" Obviously the wound still festered, for his face was full—full of an emotion no longer available to him. "In June, Russian police opened fire on the demonstrations, killing ten. Among the dead was my son. The elder: Krzesimir is his name. Was his name. So young. Not even your age I would think. They buried the dead in a mass grave. It was all any

76

of us could do to contain our fury, and thus the funeral escalated into an even greater revolt met by the Cossack cavalry. We threw stones— they were all we had. They returned with guns, killing twenty-five. Among them, my other son. Jerzy."

This man had once been human after all.

"I threw myself upon his body and held his head as the life left his eyes. He was so afraid and left this world so angry. When the fighting ceased, I took Jerzy up into my arms and carried him on my back toward home. I did not wish for them to take my boy, to watch another son buried in a pile. But they seized me, shouting that I had stolen property of the empire and that I was now a criminal. I watched Jerzy's corpse crumple as they carted me away. . . ."

He stared at the light upon the floor, his eyes dead from deep within.

"We wished only for fairness. We thought our voices could liberate. But no, the only thing our voices liberated was savagery."

The reflection from the lamplight danced in the wet blackness of his eyes.

"I was brought straightaway to this place, *thief* directly burned upon my face. I am happy they have marked me. For now it is not merely I, but they, who shall never forget what they stole from *me*. . . ."

The light briefly flickered, making the mark of

his branding seem somehow more wicked than before.

"There is an expression in Polish: *my nigdy spotykają znowu*—never we meet again. This is the way it is for those of us left behind in grief. In any exile. Siberia never relinquishes her prey." That conviction seemed to run deep. "The only way to find ourselves once again among those we loved would be to meet them in this place of torment"—his throat caught—"or in the kingdom of heaven."

She stared up at him, his face starkly illuminated by the lamplight waning from below.

eleven

There came, in the murky world that was her recurring dream, a great knock, abrupt and horrible. Then came another.

"Hodel!" a voice cried out.

The knocking was upon a door. The same impenetrable door that had been before her for countless nights of dreaming now.

"Are you there?"

She was! Her hands fumbled in the darkness—for a wedge, a handle, some means of opening the door to the voice behind it in any way whatsoever.

"Hodelleh! Open up!"

"I am trying!" Hodel wailed in desperation to the unknown voice.

Mind throbbing, her fists beat against the door with all that was left of her spirit. At once she felt it shift. The door jolted. Light flooded her feet as the door began to open from the other side.

"Hodel!" the voice rang from behind the door.

The light grew stronger with every jerk of her shoulder, every push from her own body as she felt hands tugging from the other side.

At last it opened. She could not believe her eyes. Standing before her, quite calm, and as if no effort had been exerted whatsoever, was Tzeitel.

"Hello, Hodelleh."

"Tzeitel!" The joy in her heart could not be measured! Her own sister! And in so queer a place as this!

"How are you?" Tzeitel asked brightly from the doorway, as if this were no great meeting at all.

"I—" Hodel could scarcely get out a word before her sister reached for her shorn head.

"Your hair . . ." Tzeitel whispered, fingering what were now softly forming curls at the base of her neck.

"I know."

"It is . . ."

"I know."

She noticed a scurrying beyond the door frame, and she cocked her head to see: inside were figures moving through a familiar kitchen. The room was steaming from the blazing oven, and now she could make out every recognizable member of her family going about their noisy business—how wonderful a thing to see them all again! A heavenly scent of meats broiling overwhelmed her. "*Vos kocht zich in teppel*?" she asked. "What is cooking?" And she moved to enter the room.

"No!" Tzeitel cried, her arm extended between them. "You may not come in, Hodel." Her words were so firm, her expression so dogged as she blocked the door and looked behind her nervously, steeling herself. "Not right now." The sisters exchanged a look of mutual desperation. "I am so sorry."

Hodel felt a prickling furor in her eyes. She blinked. The room behind Tzeitel began to blur and dissipate. Hodel felt her legs shake, her soul weeping—trapped between—so close to heaven and yet so barred.

"Take this." Tzeitel reached behind the door and pushed a small, hot roll of bread into Hodel's chest, the heat of it so unfamiliar that it shocked her. Tzeitel shook her sister and, with a gravity upon her normally composed face, spoke severely. "Go with God," she said before shutting the door.

"Tzeitel!" Hodel wailed. *"Tzeitel!"*

Then she was once more alone in the darkness. Upright in her cell, she inhaled abruptly, her eyes wide.

A great clang rang out from beyond—a prisoner was being carted away, having been snatched up from eating his dinner.

"Little bitch!" he screeched as the guards dragged him along. "You dare look at me!" Throwing scraps at her, he roared, "I'll choke you with that hair they cut from your rotting head!"

Not once in all her time here had Hodel ever been this afraid: afraid that her family had forgotten, afraid for Perchik's life, afraid for her own, afraid that the roll would choke her.

Afraid the darkness might snuff her out altogether.

Bread had always been a point of light in Hodel's life, since the day Hodel and Chava had received the ancient family bread-making traditions. This was a very special moment in the lives of all the women of Golde's family, a tradition passed down for six generations. Tzeitel had received her lesson just a few years earlier, and although Hodel and Chava were admittedly far less interested in the import and mechanics of bread-making, they nevertheless were thrilled that their moment had arrived at last. They stood on either side of their mother in eager anticipation.

"Bread," began Golde with a little preparatory cough, "is life. Everything in life is braided together like the very plaits of challah itself."

The girls sat in wonder. Never had Mama appeared so majestic. Golde presented the ingredients carefully upon the tabletop before them.

"According to our traditions, the three Sabbath meals and two holy meals on holidays each begin with two complete loaves of plaited challah bread. This custom pays tribute to the manna—the name of a food that God provided for the Israelites during their travels in the desert when our people wandered for forty years. It was said to be sweet to the taste, like honey that fell from heaven."

"After the Exodus from Egypt!" Hodel exclaimed, very smug about knowing the answer.

"Yes, Hodel."

"The bread fell right out of the sky?" said Hodel.

"Apparently," Golde said dryly. "In any case, the manna did not fall on the Sabbath or holidays; instead, a double portion would fall the day before the holiday or Sabbath so that the Lord could rest—just as He commanded us to do."

She looked hard at the girls, making certain they followed.

"So. Hold your hands together as if you are going to drink from them. That is a handful. Yes?" They nodded. "So. Three and a half handfuls of grain—that is important, the three and a half handfuls per loaf. There is a reason we do not begin to teach our daughters the secrets of dough-making until their hands are grown enough to make the proper measurements! Well, go ahead and do it, girls; we haven't all day!"

Chava moved to the bowl of grain and cupped her hands obediently, looking to her mother for approval.

"That is it, Chaveleh, very good." Chava beamed. It was not often she received praise for her work in the kitchen. "One handful of water. A cooking spoonful of oil. A fistful of sugar if you have it."

The sisters placed the items on the long wooden baking tray their mother had used all their lives, but not until this moment did they understand what went into the golden loaf that always emerged as if by sorcery. "Two large pinches of yeast, and now the secret." The girls leaned inward to take in Golde's measured whisper. "*Three* eggs. If you can spare them, use three. Save one yolk and place it aside for glazing the top. But in the dough, use two full eggs and one white. It will give your challah, and all the challah this family makes, an additional something." Golde smiled broadly, and Hodel realized her face hurt from smiling back.

"Gather it all together, fold it upon itself . . . over . . . and over again . . . once more now. Yes. Now it looks very much as it does when I have you take over, yes? Next give it a good long beating."

Hodel and Chava, both covered in specks of ingredients, exchanged a look and a chuckle, pounding the dough as their mother continued.

"Abraham had his wife, Sarah, bake bread for the visiting angels as a sign of hospitality. Because of this, God not only made their loaves fresh for an entire week, but He also made certain that Sarah's bread would always satisfy all who shared their table—no matter how little they ate.

God commanded Adam and his family to eat bread gained "from the sweat of his brow" in the book of Genesis. Bread nourished the Jews in the desert in the book of Exodus. Bread was one of the grain offerings sacrificed on the altar at the Temple in Jerusalem, and was later on the family table as a symbol for the altar."

Hodel's arms burned from the exertion, and her pace slowed.

"Now we allow the bread to rise for a while before we knead it once again." The girls looked relieved, and Chava even wiped her brow with her apron. "Sometimes it can happen very quickly, and sometimes it takes up half the day. That is why it is always important to make certain the bread preparations are done early. But I have prepared a loaf ahead so we may continue on."

The girls looked spent.

"Once the dough has risen a little, puncture it and knead it once more, adding a splash of water if need be." She watched her girls, smirking a little. "And perhaps take turns kneading this time." Golde handed the duties over to Hodel first. Chava threw her sister a smug glance of victory. "So, you know of course about the good deed, the mitzvah, of what is called *hafrashat challah*—separating a portion of the dough before the braiding. This term is where the name challah bread comes from, of course. The term *challah* also refers to the one-tenth portion of

85

dough that we set aside for the kohen—the direct descendants of our biblical Aaron, who were commanded to give this piece as a sacrificial offering to God. This custom of the separation and destruction of a portion of challah has become one of our female duties."

Hodel nodded. She was filled with an unanticipated sense of pride.

"Now, my girls, it is time to plait the bread."

Chava glanced at her sister eagerly.

"First, separate the dough into six pieces." The girls obliged. "Some women prefer four strands, some five, others three," Golde continued, her voice suddenly stern. "But the women in this family have always done six. Proudly."

The girls nodded. Proudly.

"Sprinkle your baking tray with flour. Rub it well into the wood. Then take each of the six pieces and roll them between your hands briskly until they are nice long strands. It may be sticky, so use a bit of flour to keep it clean. Good." She smiled, watching them together. Hodel's eyes were ablaze. Chava's tongue stuck out slightly as she concentrated; she looked perfectly childlike. "Good. Long and lean—just like Hodelleh, eh?"

Hodel smiled, rolling her eyes.

"What?" Golde said. "It is no bad thing! All my girls are *shain vi der lavoone*—as pretty as the moon. And who is ashamed of that? Not me. Now, on top of the baking tray, attach the strands together at one end by giving the ends a little pinch."

They did, Chava pushing Hodel out of the way a little in her excitement.

"Now. Divide the six strands into three sections—one on the far left, one on the far right, and four in the middle with a space in the center. Take the strand at the far right and bring it all the way over to the far left side, being careful not to break the ropes of dough."

Describing the distinct family plait so sacred to her, Golde beamed, her face alight.

"Take the remaining egg yolk and lightly brush the top of the loaf to give it the golden color, and then place it in the oven."

Hodel had never seen Chava so keen to participate in the kitchen, so she allowed her the honors. They closed the oven door and sat down before their mother again.

"Bread has always been linked to the cycle of life. Fertilization, growth, and death of the plant. The process of kneading, baking, and eating. It is believed that bread is so complex a creation, man could never have thought of it alone. Bread reminds us that God is taking care of us."

Golde looked at her girls. From one to the other: her string bean and her little bird, growing into women. When she spoke again, it was plain but genuine. " 'Like the birds that fly, even so will the Lord of Hosts shield Jerusalem.' "

"Isaiah," said Hodel.

Mama nodded. "Good. And because of this very passage, challah loaves originally were baked with the shape of a bird on them. Some people even call the challah a *feigel*, which of course means—"

"Little bird," Chava whispered, her eyes lighting up with sheer, unbridled joy.

"Yes," replied Golde, smiling to herself. "I thought you'd like that."

Chava smiled in return, overwhelmed by how special this made her feel.

"Now we wait—and clean in the meanwhile."

The final speck of flour had long been swept away when Golde at last reached into the oven, carefully removed the golden loaf, tapped the bottom to make certain it sounded hollow, and placed it onto the table.

"So you see, bread is not just nourishment for our bodies but also for our spirits."

They beheld their creation. Golden, warm, and inviting. The aroma of it beyond description but evocative of home and comfort. The smell of this moment would remain with them throughout their lives.

"Now, just as God told Adam in Genesis, 'By the sweat of your brow will you eat your bread.' Delicious, yes?"

Never, not ever in the history of the entire world, could bread have tasted so good.

• • •

Hodel would have given anything for the smallest piece of that fresh bread now, as she sat on the floor of her cold cell. She was motionless, facial muscles twitching slightly. Flies buzzed, landed lightly on her face. She found them oddly comforting—specks of affection. Besides, she could no longer afford the energy required to deflect them, nor did she see the point. So much of her daily existence was spent with her eyes closed, envisioning herself somewhere— anywhere—else. At last she opened them. The crust around her eyes cracked, clouding her vision.

She lived to sleep. Despised being awake. *But until the moment we do not,* she thought, *we must always wake.* So she lay there, her milky eyes fixed on the floor, seeing only the dust, the mud, the flicking of shadows, and the unmissable lesion-colored night.

She was in exile. From herself. She was more roiled with hunger than she had ever been.

She moved in hysteria to her secret hoard behind the stove. She plunged an arm in to retrieve a scrap from her stash. It did not matter that they were rotten—moldy and half-devoured by shadowy critters. Even a rotten roll is food when you're starving. *That is true of souls, too,* she thought.

She swept her hand back and forth in the small

space, unable to reach her prize. Then suddenly, the horror of nothingness settled: her storage of bread was completely cleared away.

The jailer, she thought, defeated and raging. *This must be his doing! What humanity I thought remained within him, the goddamn scoundrel!* In her rage, she tried again. The last search. Which one does when they cannot bring themselves to quite believe what they already know to be true.

Then her frantic hand came across something at the far back.

Hodel stopped dead. *What is this?*

Her hand grazed what indeed felt like another roll—*what joy!* She wrestled it out, hid it beneath her skirts, and returned to the corner of her cell, buoyed instantly by her guile.

All suspicion, Hodel inspected her loot. It was smaller, harder, lighter too. *My God,* she realized. *This is one of Tzeitel's rolls, the very same from my dream!* So new and fresh it seemed, dishonest even. But starvation got the better of Hodel, and she revealed its guts as she ripped it open, mouth attacking like an animal. But before she could devour the bread, her eye came upon something more miraculous: a roll of paper, small and tight. She looked around. *Who would leave so covert a note? Who so artfully?* But no one was there. She reached inside and pulled it out in careful stillness. Hodel held her breath as she unrolled the scroll in total silence. She gazed at the words: *Further in.* That was all it offered her.

Hodel returned to the pipe and at once laid her body upon the ground. Her arm throbbed with urgency as she reached and reached to the very back—this was the kind of search distinct to deprivation, the reach of yearning; a search for light beyond the darkness when all you saw was snow and shadow. Or perhaps snow was shadow now, black now white—no reason sound, no sanity pure. Ever deeper in, her arm all torment, Hodel no longer cared to disguise her movements. *Lord,* she thought as her fingers came upon it. Fist tight, she wriggled out the paper and dashed back to the corner of her cell; her eyes found light just as she unfolded the crumpled page. *Steady, steady, take it in.* Could her heart believe it? It could not be. It was an official transfer form:

Perchik Tselenovich, Prisoner No. 937
Crime: Political
Sentence: Labor, 24 to 48 months
Location: Nerchinsk Katorga
Prison Camp
Town: Nerchinsk, Transbaikalia,
Eastern Siberia
Note: High security
Signed: Sergei Konstantinovich Dubov,
Governor General of Omsk

At long last.
She knew.
In the city of Nerchinsk.
She knew where Perchik was.

twelve

S he knew where he was. *Nerchinsk Katorga Prison Camp in Transbaikalia, Eastern Siberia.* That was something.

She lay on the damp, bare floor, grateful for the clarity, the sobering effect it provided. Earlier in the night, the jailer had appeared beyond the bars. She could not help but notice that he held her gaze a little longer than ever before. She understood. He merely bowed his head and, in his retreat, left a lamp. . . . She knew. Somehow. She was going to be free of this place.

Her fate was being determined in the nearby room where the Chief Commander's council was sitting. Her hopes were pinned upon it. The Chief Commander might indeed send her to Nerchinsk alongside Perchik. He might assign her to serve out Perchik's penal sentence in any of the government work camps. He might send her to a remote settlement to expand the female populace. Or worse than all of these, he might simply send her home again.

But she knew where he was. That was something. Wasn't it? Slumber hovered over her like an incessant song—a constant melody that would not flee her brain. Squinting against the feeble light, she saw, for the first time in months, her face reflected in the many surfaces of the lamp: a horrific face it was—pale, hollowed, with crust along all the moist places, all health and hope within it melted away like wax beneath a flame. She gazed beyond the image, deep into the unknown emptiness that called her away from beyond the prison gates, into an endless, ineffable night that also held Nerchinsk within it.

Despite her horror, she could not help but look. In some corner of that darkness, Perchik lay. Perchik—growing nearer and more tangible. Perchik, in some unnameable shadow, his arms empty and awaiting her. . . .

There was a great deal of work to be done before the Sabbath—the laundry, cleaning, and all food preparation had to be completed before sunset on Friday afternoon, when the Sabbath officially began. The Sabbath may have been a day of rest, but the hours leading up to it were fraught. No matter how much preparation went into the task, the Sabbath always threw them into a frenzy.

"It's important all of us pitch in," Tzeitel announced far too near the sunset on this particularly stressful autumn day (impending sunset loomed more severely than in summer). The girls internally groaned. "The incredibly important work of a woman is as the spirit of the home." Here she was: Tzeitel the boss. "Mama dashes madly from Friday morning till sunset to get this or fetch that for all of us, or for the guests who sometimes are invited—"

"—or unexpected," smirked Hodel, referencing Tzeitel's wide-eyed, oft-visiting childhood playmate Motel.

"We must aim to appreciate this struggle," continued Tzeitel, ignoring her. "Someday soon we shall all be on our own. We cannot thrive in a pigsty."

Hodel retorted coyly, "I thought the main purpose of Shabbat was to rest."

Tzeitel sighed and her face tightened as she laid out cooking pots, trays, and knives.

"Shabbat is supposed to be entered peacefully," she said as she shot Hodel the black look. "*Not* in total exhaustion." Tzeitel clanged the pots with an audible sense of purpose, punctuating her sentence.

"This is throwing me into total exhaustion," Hodel muttered under her breath to the others as she threw Chava a look of her own. Chava couldn't smile. She was too tense.

"Shprintze, Bielke," instructed Tzeitel. "Please recite to me the thirty-nine categories of endeavor that the sages specified are not allowed on the Sabbath while you scrub these potatoes," she said, placing them down.

The little ones took up their brushes and obediently began.

"Cooking and sewing of course," said Bielke,

the youngest, hesitantly. "Then carrying." She paused, stumped.

"Burning and extinguishing—must these all be in a special order?" asked Shprintze apprehensively.

"Oh, burn first, extinguish second, no question, particularly if Chava is doing the cooking," retorted Hodel.

"Hodel, please!" barked Tzeitel, and Hodel sulked away, iron pot on hip. "You are doing very well, girls. Continue."

"Finishing, writing . . . Those are all that I can remember. . . ." Disappointing Tzeitel caused Shprintze such anxiety.

"My head is sore," muttered Bielke.

Everyone's head is sore, thought Hodel.

Chava resided at the far end of the kitchen, hopelessly peeling at carrots for stew. She was stewing in her own right—painfully aware that her eldest sister harbored her most humiliating secret. Though Chava herself might characterize her attitude toward table-setting, laundry-folding, and corner-dusting as *free-sprited,* others might descrbe it more plainly as *disasterous.* For all her good intentions, Chava truly was a hopeless homemaker. She could not, at any acceptable level, sew, fold, or dust, but she was was particularly calamitous in the kitchen, having once started a stove fire when attempting to dry a dishcloth and another time mistaking salt for yeast. And, above all, she was utterly unable to properly peel a vegetable. Tzeitel had spent a lifetime nurturing Chava, keeping this devastating fact from everyone else.

Whenever Tzeitel was placed in charge of Sabbath delegations by Golde, she would see to it that Chava was often given tasks she could handle without too much of a fuss. Scrub. Perhaps peel. Stirring had consequences. Even folding had the potential to be sloppy. Instruction was of no use—it never seemed to make a dent in her proclivity toward disaster.

So, while Shprintze could genuinely cook, and Bielke was a fastidious cleaner, and even Hodel possessed real potential if she simply applied herself, things were different with Chava, and Tzeitel knew it.

"How old is the Sabbath?" Tzeitel continued, one eye on the disquieted Chava in the corner.

"As old as the creation of the world!" Shprintze exclaimed.

"And why do we refrain from work on the Sabbath?"

"I—I am not certain," said Bielke, "but I do like taking so long to eat. That is my favorite bit."

"I like the eating bit too," whispered Hodel, sneaking in a wink across the table toward the little one.

"Shprintze?" prodded Tzeitel.

"Because, on the seventh day, God rested from all the creation that He had done. So God commanded that on the seventh day, we were to rest as He did when He created the earth. And God blessed the seventh day and made it holy, because . . . because that was the day He rested?"

"Exactly," said Tzeitel. "But also to refrain from work, giving us time to enjoy our families, rest from the honesty of a week's labor, as well as take time to reflect on our relationship with God."

Tzeitel glanced over at Chava. Although she was tough on the others, Tzeitel never outwardly scolded Chava. In private she would take her aside and force her to cut what felt like thousands of vegetables (each with a thousand rules), to sew and resew seams, to scrub and re-scrub the floors. Tzeitel felt sorry for Chava and encouraged her to dig in.

"It will become easier once you *accept* the work. It can be joyful. But the more you continue to despise it, the less you will want to perfect it, and your spiral begins. Some things take practice. Not everything can come easily."

Tzeitel was genuinely concerned for Chava's future, for her welfare—not merely as a home-maker, wife, and mother, but as a functioning person. She pictured fingers sliced and bloody from rogue knives, stabbed with needles. In her mind, she could see Chava engulfed in flames due to yet another accidental kitchen fire. In discussing the Sabbath traditions, she was hoping to encourage a rise in Chava's bookish passion for full understanding.

Tzeitel asked, "Do you know the Hebrew word used to describe work?"

"*Melakha*?"

"Very good, Shprintze! But the word means more than just labor. In fact, we must refrain from any creative activity because this is the day we honor when God rested from His creation." She handed Hodel a pot of potatoes to peel. "And how does God feel about the Sabbath?"

"He . . . He likes it?" asked Bielke.

"Oh, He sure does," answered Hodel, smirking.

From the corner, Chava sighed deeply. She had missed bathing before the busy Friday afternoon preparations because a batch of rugelach had gone all wrong. Forbidden to do any form of work after sunset on the Sabbath was God's law, thus heating water to bathe in so close to dusk was asking for trouble. Cold water it was.

"A rude reminder you were not thinking of God," Golde said as she hurried back into the kitchen. Shivering but clean, Chava began preparing herself for dinner.

She attempted to smooth out her fluffy mess of hair with her hands to no avail. There was something poignant about her hair in its natural state of misfortune—something that symbolized every other shortcoming thrust upon her by God in comparison to her sisters. The insufficiency of her hair in this moment hurt so greatly, for it carried within in it every other disappointment she had ever felt about herself. She returned to the kitchen frozen and brittle, only to find Tzeitel talking like a rabbi. *Wonderful.*

"The Sabbath is probably the most important of the *moedim*, or God-ordained appointed times," Tzeitel continued, making her way over to Chava, who had picked up a peeler and begun to do a dismal job. She had to step in, patiently demonstrating a technique that would prevent the minuscule chunks of vegetable from flying everywhere but into the pot.

Chava kept her eyes downward, as though her head were splitting in half. She shook it abruptly and stabbed at the vegetables as though they were Tzeitel's eyeballs. Tzeitel lifted her finger and tapped it sweetly upon Chava's perfectly button-shaped nose, identical to Tzeitel's own. This was a gesture that was theirs and no one else's, and in its wake Hodel felt a pang of jealousy, for she knew Tzeitel adored and expressed her love for Chava in a way Hodel had never felt. But beyond that, Tzeitel and Chava possessed a closeness that required no language, no proof or articulation. Hodel drowned in the tidewaters of her covetousness—for Tzeitel's regard, and for her challenged rank as Chava's closest sister.

Tzeitel instructed Chava under her breath. "If you peel in long strips and not in little bits, it preserves more of the vegetable." Chava attempted this, but her hands were unpracticed and her mood foul. Tzeitel watched—and watched again—in disbelief.

"Well, I suppose it is easier with carrots," she said. Chava tried again. "That's better," Tzeitel said, though—quite clearly—it was not.

"You baby her," Hodel said under her breath.

Tzeitel shot her a dark look in response.

"Well, you do!" Hodel insisted, and sulkily pounded her fists into a mound of dough.

"So creativity is why we cannot cook on Shabbat?" asked Bielke, always in the mood to discuss food more.

"Yes, nor can we light fires or prepare for the upcoming week, which means that we cannot plan for tomorrow or the week ahead," said Tzeitel.

"So what *can* we do?"

Chava's voice cut, sharp and vexed, through the air from across the kitchen. "Nothing," she said.

They all turned.

"Not nothing—we read; we pray; we walk," said Shprintze. "And everything is so still and quiet. It is my favorite day of the week."

"And eat! In such a nice, slow way!" piped up Bielke. "Plus meals on Shabbat are so much fancier than normal. And, oh, the sweets . . ." Her eyes glistened. "The sweets are the very best part. The mandel bread, the rugelach—"

"Unless of course it is Chava's rugelach!" Smiling, Hodel danced over to her sister; she wrapped her arms around her waist and kissed her troubled little face. "Then there shall be no rugelach at all! A lazy person must do a task twice!"

That was it. Chava broke free of Hodel's arms, flung her knife down onto the table, turned the bowl containing the potatoes on its side, and stormed into the bedroom. She'd had enough.

The room went very still. The only sounds came from the bubbling of broths and the wind rapping on the windows. The little ones squirmed. Tzeitel turned her head toward Hodel and gazed at her in a manner far sterner, far more saddened, far more heartbreaking than any look she had ever thrown at her before or since; she closed her eyes, exhaled deeply, and left the room shaking her head. Hodel was horrified—what had she done?

"Chavaleh?" Tzeitel said in a hush as she entered the bedroom. Setting herself down gently beside her sister, she put a hand on Chava's trembling back.

"Tzeitel, please. Go away."

"Chavaleh . . ." She began gently untangling the ends of Chava's knotted hair.

"Go away. I am so weary of your bossiness and your pity!"

"I do not pity you, Chava," she said. "Not in the least."

"Fine. Then please just leave me alone—and tell wretched Hodel to stay away. I want to be by myself."

Hodel came rushing up to their room and stopped short in the doorway when she heard Chava's cry. She lurked there, holding the door frame, listening.

"Chavaleh, there is so much still to be done. . . ."

"To think of all the things I am squandering by learning to cut vegetables and clean floors—"

"It is our God-given role, Chava. A beautiful one," said Tzeitel. "And I do not think I should feel guilty for cherishing our home, for making it the focus of my life, energy, and creativity. No woman should feel useless because she chooses to honor God, to make the home her first priority."

"Well, how wonderful for you, Tzeitel! Perhaps it is your role. You are a natural!" Chava wanted her words to sting her sister. "Why couldn't God have given me a role I could be good at?" Chava heaved sobs of utter despair. "Tzeitel!" she cried. "It is mindless, frivolous work, and no one will ever appreciate it or care if it is done well or poorly! Why must it be the only measure of our worth as women? As people?"

"Now, see here," Tzeitel said, her voice grave. "Women are not mindless, frivolous creatures. Nor is their work. You can be good at it, Chava, and you will be." She reached out and touched her sister's arm, more gentle now. "We know God sees what is right within our hearts, and therefore, as long as we offer our work to Him and to those we love, we needn't worry."

And then it happened. Standing in the door frame, Hodel finally understood. Tzeitel believed her home to be a symbol of her devotion to God, a testament to her faith and feminine spirit. Hodel saw it through her sister's eyes: women were created to be in every way partners, not mindless slaves or brainless doormats, but helpers, collaborators, equals. And that was a thing of great beauty. Meanwhile, what Chava longed for was a place in this world where she could be an individually gifted, impassioned expert, rather than the hopeless one. Chava felt diminished here; the little bird yearned to spread her wings. Hodel felt as if she were seeing her sisters for the very first time.

Tzeitel exhaled deeply. She lifted her finger and tapped it once more upon Chava's nose. She saw Chava soften and begin quietly to weep. Tzeitel held her closer and spoke quietly from a place of great depth. "When you're on a long journey— and life is most definitely such a journey—don't you want a companion ready to give counsel, support, and encouragement?"

"Yes," Chava whimpered. "But who will be there to help me?"

"Oh, Chavaleh, my darling one, shh, shh, shh—there, there, now," Tzeitel cooed, taking her sister firmly in her arms. "Chavaleh, you shall always—*always*—have me."

"And me," whispered Hodel from the doorway.

She climbed into bed beside them. And there, wrapped around one another, they nestled like doves.

The cell was too safe. That was the trouble.

She did not see the small flame along the corridor, nor did she hear the sound of uneven steps punctuated lightly by the click of a cane. She sensed him only when he was already inside the bars designed to keep things trapped within. Even at this hour of the night, he wore his fine, immaculate clothes. He removed his cape, which revealed the brutality of his arms and shoulders as well as the ever-haunting absence of his leg. Presently, he lifted his cane, held it menacingly upon his shoulder, and leaned against the back wall of the cell.

The Chief Commander stood looking at her, gaze unwavering, betraying an arrogant cruelty that could not be controlled. She felt the heat of his glare from his stance high above her in the raging muscles of her legs, in her spine and hip sockets, and waited—with the febrile acuteness of a needle. With his steel blue stare, he watched her wait. She stared back. In all her frailty against his height and power, she stared, the room thick with their antipathy.

"Hello there," the Chief Commander said, his voice grimly hushed.

At this, she stood to meet his gaze, head high, her body pressed against the farthest wall in a terror so pure, it sterilized her mind—terror matched with a loathsome curiosity she knew in that very moment he was depending upon. A flash of something came across the Chief Commander's face—something that could be mistaken for strength and swagger, something akin to laughter, though he made no sound. Then at once, he lifted his cane and used it to pin her hard against the wall, using the leverage to force himself upon her with the power of his three remaining limbs.

Hodel fought like a savage. It was no use trying to claw herself away, for the gripping arms of the Chief Commander engulfed her fully. She scratched and jolted in furious anguish, her mouth flooding with the metallic taste of blood as she sank her teeth into the bits of his flesh she could attack. But despite succeeding in breaking his skin, one of his massive arms pinned down both of hers; the other forced her head back, and he thrust his mouth upon her. He turned her around and threw her hard, face-first against the wall, foisting himself in violation. Her pulse throbbed all the way to her horror-laden eyes in hatred and ferocious helplessness, fighting to the last.

Her self had split open—clear in half. Within the shell of her person lay not hollow absence, but a black water, prepared to flood the cell with its density. She could almost hear the swoosh of viscid liquid as her hope drained, emptying onto the floor of the prison and beyond into the night, rippling like laughter.

thirteen

There is something that happens to a person when everything but the pulse has been taken—when their psyche has been scrubbed clean, their life force further burgled with every scrap of identity torn from them like ripping skin. For Hodel, what happened was a white-hot, sleepless stillness more terrifying than reality.

She could touch nothing in the cell after that—the walls, the floors, the stove, and the useless window had seen it all and done not a thing to stop it. But perhaps a week later, at a very late hour of the night, four soldiers bid her to rise, nodded to her knowingly, and she was shocked to find herself throwing a glance around her cell in something of a farewell.

Holding her arms, they escorted her into the briskness of the night. The sky was very dark, and snow creaked under their feet as they moved across the great courtyard. She was no longer accustomed to the freshness of the air and relished the wind as it cut into her lungs, sharp and pure, cleansing her from within.

Before long, she was led into a large, faintly illuminated room, where a dozen high-ranking officers were seated at a round table covered with a dark blue cloth. They were eating, coughing, playing cards; many smoked cigars, and they spoke in loud voices, laughing broadly among themselves while a pack of sturdy hunting dogs waited eagerly for bones from their meal.

But as she entered the room, all went quiet. The men turned, their eyes meeting hers with leering curiosity through the haze of smoke and feeble light. They were huge, formidable figures— one quite stout, another with the face of a toad, some with bearded faces, some deeply scarred with battle wounds, and one bulbous man with a set of piercing blue eyes who sat apart from the others and looked on thoughtfully. Swarthy and all of varying shapes, they looked like the last remaining potatoes at a market stall.

This was the Commission of Inquiry and Deportation.

"Guards," said the unmistakable voice of the Chief Commander. "Escort her to the security cell. We must decide what to do with her."

Hodel suddenly had the shape of a woman— far before her mind could catch up, leaving her open to a throng of unwelcome taunting. Walking down the main thoroughfare in town, a collection of young yeshiva boys skulked behind her thoroughly fascinated, observing her walk and her curves and calling out names.

That day, a boy named Dovidke had followed her to the livery from the schoolhouse, filled his hands in the trough of cold water, and when Hodel exited, threw the water in her face. She returned home soaking wet, red-faced, upset for the rest of the day.

Later, Tzeitel came to ask what was the matter.

"They were filthy things, the words they cried at me!" Hodel wept. "Horrible, petty street urchins. I will never forgive them!"

Tzeitel was furious, insisting Hodel name the boys.

The following day, the boys came all the way up to their house. They asked Golde for permission to see Hodel, and in a gallant voice, Dovidke said that they were all terribly sorry for using such harsh words with a lady. He was remorseful for being cruel; it would never happen again, and if anyone else ever bothered her, they would personally take care of them for her.

It wasn't until many weeks later that Golde said Tzeitel had gotten herself into serious trouble with the yeshiva.

"But Tzeitel doesn't even like me," said Hodel. "Why on earth would she do that?"

Hodel recalled that memory as she stood high above a mass of carrots in their low-ceilinged, aromatic kitchen, immersed meditatively in a repetitive task: scrub, rinse, peel, chop, and then again. Billows of steam swirled upward from large pots, filling the room with the hearty fragrances of cooking, not to mention the oppressive moist heat. No matter though, this was commonplace. This was the atmosphere of home.

A few weeks after the incident with Chava on the Sabbath, things were different. Calmer. The girls were kinder, gentler with one another, though it was hard to articulate why or how.

"*Oy, Mame, bin ikh farlibt*," her mouth quietly sang. Her hair lay in tousled plaits beneath a long headscarf used expressly for work, the sleeves of her blouse rolled neatly above her elbows, her tidy, high collar unbuttoned to keep her cool. Despite the impending cold, the heat of the kitchen required open windows to let in the refreshing cool of the autumn breeze.

Looking up, she noted that she was quite alone.

She laid down her peeling knife, wiped her hands, and moved to the door to see her mother, wrapped in a shawl against the cold, waving to the village matchmaker, who was slowly walking down the path away from their house.

Why did she not invite the woman inside? Hodel thought.

In the distance stood Chava and the little ones, watching giddily from the barn, barely visible behind the swinging door. Golde looked intrigued as she made her way around the back of the house. Hodel moved to the door and then stopped—she heard something.

Over the quiet bubbling of pots was an

unfamiliar rustling. Ears pricked, Hodel followed the muffled sounds into the hall. When she reached their bedroom, she could distinguish the distinct sound of crying. Careful not to disturb, she withheld herself silently at the door frame for a moment, observing.

It was Tzeitel.

Strong, indestructible Tzeitel. She sat upright upon the edge of her bed, face toward the wall, her back so rigid that Hodel could tell it was only this posture that kept her from losing herself in the emotion altogether.

"Tzeitel?" Hodel asked softly.

"Oh, Hodel," Tzeitel said, her voice stiff. "Hello." Turning farther away, she tried to hide her face but was unable to disguise her tears. "I was just taking a moment for prayer. I was working in the kitchen and suddenly found myself very, very tired and—" Her voice broke as she wiped her face in panic. "And, well, I decided a moment or two in prayer might serve me well, and I could ask God for—for *strength,* I suppose, to continue . . . to continue on with the work." Tzeitel looked at Hodel with anguished eyes, and they stared at each other in silence.

The image was devastating. There she sat: the constant leader, the example, the one who cared for everyone but was never given care. She did not appear to need it. How strong, how selfless, how gifted a woman she was.

"Oh, Tzeitel," said Hodel so quietly she was not certain she had said it aloud. She could not help herself; her body ached to hold her sister, but a lifetime of resistance lay between them. Hodel approached steadily, sat beside Tzeitel, and clutched her hand without taking her eyes from her face.

Tzeitel's expression was limp but for her brow as she gazed at Hodel's hand upon her own. Suddenly, she looked up at her sister—eyes wet, brittle, and searching—and without any warning, Hodel felt Tzeitel's hand respond beneath her gesture, clutching at her fingers with what she could not yet determine as relief, gratitude, or desperation.

"I cannot," she whispered, as if in whispering it might not be real. "I cannot." So hushed a voice that her family, the matchmaker, her sisters, and God Himself might not hear her. "The responsibility—" Her voice choked. "It is so hard to be the very first . . . to never really be a child!"

Hodel watched, eyes wide, her forehead wrinkled and heart swollen as her elder sister shook.

"I have loved him all my life, Hodel. Love. Not affection, not familiarity. Motel and I are one. We have been cut, like cloth, from the same bolt of fabric. We have grown up; we have become ourselves beside each other. I cannot imagine a life without him by my side! When I look at my hands I am certain they are mine. Look at your own—look at any part of you—aren't you certain they belong to you? That is the same certainty with which I know he is my husband. I more than love him—that is an easy thing to say—no. We are sewn together, inextricably. Don't you understand, Hodel? The old way will end me, end us both. For there is no Tzeitel without Motel Kamzoil—I must be with him or perish!"

Tzeitel's cry, and the sorrow that emitted from within it, was like nothing Hodel had ever witnessed. "I am so frightened, Hodel, so frightened. And I need sisters too! I need you too!"

Hodel grasped her in the sweep of her arms— arms granted to her to seize Tzeitel in this pivotal embrace—and she felt Tzeitel release there, for perhaps the first time in all her life.

"*Ich hob mir fer pacht*, Tzeitel," Hodel whispered. "I know you for what you are." Hodel gripped Tzeitel fiercely, with the strength and steeliness she had learned from the sister she encompassed. "Ich hob mir fer pacht."

fourteen

Dreaming again, Hodel faced the strip of light below the base of the same forbidden door. She gazed down at her hands, illuminated by the light from beyond: the grime between the webs of her fingers had an oily crunch, and her mired skin was caked with more blood than she had thought. *This door*—her body ached with the thought—*this door might be a portal into heaven itself.*

Had she not sacrificed? Had she not left all she had ever known and traveled to so foreign a place on faith alone?

A Torah passage slipped into her mind: "Now the Lord said unto Abraham: 'Get thee out of thy country, and from thy kindred, and from thy father's house, unto the land that I will show thee. . . .' "

She had trusted that God would guide and care for her. Was that not faith? She yearned to know. But she felt quite incapable of serious thought. She squeezed her eyes, body shuddering as she exhaled a breath so deep, it nearly woke her from this stupor.

She thought of the rest of the Torah passage: "For I, the Lord your God, hold your right hand; it is I who say to you, 'Fear not; I will help you.' "

Had her moment arrived?

Thoughts of Perchik turned her vision turbid, as though she were beneath fathoms of murky water. She was not alone. She had never been alone. Despite it all, she still had faith.

Hodel could not say exactly how long she and Perchik had been walking, but she was conscious of how long they had been alone, for when she looked at the sky again she saw it was very dark. These walks of theirs had become a daily practice in the last few months since he had arrived in Anatevka, and on them he told her of life in the cities, teaching her all about politics, economics, and the needs of the people. He spoke not of dreams but of what he would do— and in challenging him she made his thoughts stronger, his plans more vivid. She felt terror at the thought of losing him. Perchik would often just gaze at her silently, allowing no hint of ardor to grace his face but looking straight into her— his understanding so intimate, she almost could not bear it. She would stand before him, open and exposed, slightly faint. She had never met a man like him—she did not know there were men like him. She was enthralled by his character, his dreams and values, his sense of life, the way in which he confronted existence.

"You will follow me, Hodel?" he asked, clutching her hair and holding her close.

She pulled away to look into his eyes, then answered without smiling, "Forever."

Flickering lights from the dying fires and candles in distant homes dotted the landscape like sprinkled stars. It was hours before dawn. The train was to arrive in minutes. They waited there together, feeling the warmth from within those homes: children fast asleep, families together, bodies weary and resting.

There was a feeling in the air—every gesture, movement, slash of light, and roar of wind was charged: the way he gathered his belongings into a satchel; the way he held her hand, caressing her fingers with one thoughtful stroke of his thumb. They sat in silence, side by side, waiting. The sounds were those only ever audible in stillness: breathing and the synchronous beating of their hearts. The sky was cracking in its clarity.

That morning Hodel saw nothing but the radiance of a blend of different lights: the reflection of sun upon the earth, the bright orange of the sky, and the light from within him—the amalgamated glow of that particular morning shone so tenderly upon the earth, she felt as if there were nothing beyond this scene—nothing beyond Perchik at all.

Hodel glanced over at him: his gaze was outward, his face calm. The train was approaching in the distance. He must have felt her eyes upon him, for he moved his eyes from the horizon and looked deeply into her.

"It is time."

"Yes."

"Believe me, Hodel," he said. "This is easier for me."

"Oh?"

"Yes. It is so much harder to be left behind."

The space between them was suddenly heated, ablaze with intimacy.

She could not stand it a moment longer—she rushed toward him, burrowed her head into his shoulder, fiercely wrapped her arms around his body in an act of both complete adoration and anguish. With one arm around her frame, he lifted his other to cradle her head and draw her closer, inhaling deeply the scent of her hair, along with her very essence. It was an exhilaration almost too great to bear.

"Oh, Hodel," he said, voice flooded with love. "We cannot be stopped."

"Your revolution?" she cried.

"No," he said. "You and I."

She walked home in silence.

Hodel leaned against the window, gazing out at the horizon. It was very early morning—the late-autumn sun was slowly climbing over the rugged beams along the roof of the barn and tumbling across the house, cascading through the windows and into the kitchen. The dark orange light glowed on the infantry of last night's pots, which had been filed in neat rows along the warmer of the earthen stove to dry. It was a cozy and pleasant kitchen worn into comfort by generations of women. Like her mother and sisters. Like her. As the dawn crept on, noises emerged from the outside. The milk cows groaned. Chickens cackled. The heavy-eyed horse snorted sleepily in his stall, and their always-tardy rooster crowed even though the sun had long ago arrived. Hodel had been awake all night.

She stared at the letter in her hands, and a sense of excitement blazed within her.

The day before, Tzeitel had hurried up the road, her heavily pregnant body gasping for breath as she ran up to the house and delivered the letter directly. Her strong, familiar arms clutched Hodel fiercely as they read and reread the message together:

30 October 1905

Hodel,

There has been in a violent pogrom in the city of Kiev. A city hall meeting collapsed and a mob filled the streets. The perpetrators claim that Russia's troubles all stem from the machinations of Jews and Socialists. There was wild looting, rape, killing—all directed at the homes, factories, shops, and persons of the Jews. Approximately one hundred were massacred. Serious injury done to at least three hundred more.

This is what we spoke of, Hodel. The events building up to this included what happened at Tzeitel's wedding—a wave of anti-Jewish demonstrations across southern Russia. Not only here but in Elizabethgrad, Shpola, Ananyiv, Wasilkov, Konotop. They are being followed by massive deportations of the Jews from their villages. Be careful. Warn your family. These demonstrations and relocations are premeditated. Everywhere, there is hatred.

Of course, I could not remain silent. I have been arrested and will be sent to a prison in Omsk until further notice. I am sorry, Hodel. Despite this setback and these hardships, I still believe I am participating in the greatest work a man can do. The work of freedom.

Burn this. Do not wait for me. I love you.

Perchik.

Hodel froze.

She knew this moment's decision was the pivot of her life's path. This or that. Yes or no.

In Anatevka, decisions were often made for her, deference a virtue. She had been taught to see the world in the prescribed ways of her people—ways she deeply valued and respected, ways she felt had always served her.

She prayed for guidance. But today, in the silence of her invocation, the voice she heard responding did not belong to her father, to the rabbi, or even to God Himself. This voice did not lecture, explain, or even elaborate. This voice was clear and calm and certain. It was intuition.

This voice was her own.

The choice was simple. She loved Perchik so deeply in her tissue, bones, and flesh that her thinking mind could not comprehend it. She felt it acutely. It was lightning. It was tremor. Perhaps belief in her purpose was a new kind of faith.

She would go to him. She had to. She would leave all she knew and had ever known and loved in this world behind her. She would find him. Go to him. Even if it meant she perished in the process.

Hodel stood now before the collection of men, drenched in chains.

A stack of papers before the Chief Commander looked as crisp as he. Hodel could feel the contempt buried deep within him. She thought she would be glad to leave a world filled with people like this.

"Really, girl," the Chief Commander said, in a voice dripping with disdain. "Really, it is to be admired. Your simplicity."

She grimaced inwardly at the insult, but denied herself the reaction she knew he desired.

"The tsar fears your people contemplate some kind of uprising," he continued.

She remained perfectly still.

"For the sake of God, put such thoughts out of your mind. Many of your comrades have tried; all have failed. Your movements have been watched, your actions and even thoughts tracked on every side. None have been able to escape the misery." She watched a vein in his neck beat silently. "I can only assume you are acting on behalf of your *sweetheart,* this"—he tossed a glance across the papers—"Perchik Tselenovich, is it? Now, whatever could Perchik have done to incur so harsh a watch upon himself?" He glanced up at her. "Or perhaps he was simply caught? Disgraceful, really, the carelessness." The Chief Commander rolled his eyes. "Revolutionaries . . . good God. Join a youth group."

He leaned back in his chair and stretched for a moment. "*Dobrovol'nye.* Do you know that word in Russian, girl? It means 'voluntary.' It is the word we use for those who accompany or follow their men into exile. The dobrovol'nye are the unfortunate idiots who voluntarily choose to march thousands of kilometers into frozen hinterlands to share in a criminal's hardship. I believe someone here falls into that category, do they not?"

The Chief Commander continued, "Your situation is complicated by the fact that you are not legally married to your criminal, and therefore we have had the most difficult time deciding what to do with you. As a legal wife, you would have been sent immediately to join your husband. But without a marriage license for your union, you are simply revolutionary fodder. So. Do we keep you here for our amusement? Perhaps we send you off to Irkutsk to become a Siberian baby factory? Or do we kill you for treachery? Or deem you innocuous and simply allow you to join your Socialist beau? Ah. Decisions. Your little boyfriend has been impressively weasel-like in his political life that we've had to keep an exceptionally close eye on him and upon those he has feelings for. You realize of course that you have had a terrorist in your bed, my dear, yes? Or"—he smiled—"has he not yet had that pleasure?"

She ground her teeth so ferociously that she thought they would crumble to dust. Yet Hodel remained rooted, her upright posture almost statuesque.

"What have you to say, girl?" the Chief Commander bit. "Just silence? Well, then. I must withdraw any influence of clemency that might have mollified my judgment. I sentence you to eight years labor in the Irkutsk *katorga* in whichever capacity the authorities there see fit."

All she could think was that her journey could not end like this.

"You do realize," he snarled, "you are going to die out there, my dear?"

What happened next shocked them all: from the depths of herself came a laugh—one that seemed ancient in its bitterness. The sound astonished her as much as the sensation, and when at last she quelled it, she spoke.

"Well," she said with a light laugh, her eyes glistening with unshed tears. "I'm not dead yet."

fifteen

"Tygrysek!" called the now familiar voice of the jailer. "Tygrysek, you must wake."

She lifted herself from the ground of this new solitary cell, which was even smaller and more miserable than the one she had occupied before. Her head was pounding, and her eyes were cloudy; she lifted her hands to her eyes to stop their incessant throbbing. Her stomach raged from within her as she began to move. She sensed she had been lying dormant for a long while.

"How long have I been asleep?" she asked the jailer.

"Few days," he said.

She noticed then that he was eating a slice of something on a tiny tin plate. Hodel felt her mouth fill with saliva as her stomach churned with want, and she could not help but stare.

"Why have you not woken me for meals?" she asked, her voice slightly desperate.

"We have been fasting, Tygrysek."

"Fasting?"

"Why, Christ is born. It is now Epiphany."

"Epiphany?" she repeated, stunned. *It cannot be,* she thought to herself. It meant that well over a year had passed since she had come to this place.

"The other guards are marking the baptism of Christ—priests are performing the Great Blessing of Waters."

Hodel remembered the Christians who resided beyond their shtetl boundaries engaging in this water ritual. Apparently, all over the country, people spent Epiphany cutting holes in the shape of the cross in the ice of lakes and rivers then dipping themselves three times in the freezing water to honor the Holy Trinity. Whether to symbolically wash away their sins or to experience a sense of spiritual rebirth, she did not know or understand.

"Back in Poland we call it *Trzech Kroli*—Three Kings' Day," he said. He brushed off the crumbs that had gathered on his shirt and trousers. "Huge parades are held." He wiped the corners of his mouth with his sleeve. He must have caught Hodel's hungry glare upon him, for he paused, taking a moment to swallow properly.

"Polish-style Three Kings' cake," he said, gesturing to the now clean plate. "Made with a coin baked inside. The one who gets it is king or queen for the day. They will be lucky in the coming year. Some lady in the village makes Polish pastries if you request. She's taken a terrible fancy to one of the guards. Delivered it yesterday. Stale." He shrugged and placed the tin plate at her feet. "Anyway, farewell. Tomorrow you are to be taken to Irkutsk. I wish you health."

He licked his fingers and stood staring at her. They both knew full well that this was to be the last they ever saw of each other. "As they say in the homeland, Tygrysek: *szczesliwego nowego roku*—happy New Year."

Hodel looked down at the empty tin plate. Settled among the flakes and crumbs lay the coin.

What luck.

sixteen

Hodel heard someone approach. A pair of footsteps stopped before the bars. She lifted her head to see to whom the feet belonged.

"Hello," said the man, his voice so gentle, it was almost hair-raising in a place such as this.

Before her was not a new figure but a man she had seen once before: it was the bulbous man with piercing blue eyes from the Commission of Inquiry and Deportation so quietly present at her sentencing.

This very large man looked upon her, the hint of feeling emitting from him strange after all the severity she had endured. Kindness, it seemed, was a language spoken long ago, but now unpracticed, nearly forgotten. A ring of what must have been hundreds of keys was clasped in the fat bulges of his hands. Smiling, he plucked the correct key from the ring and unlocked the cell. He slid the gate open with a single lurch of his tremendous arm, his movements clumsy, though not completely without grace.

"Come with me."

She hesitated but obeyed. The man smiled again and led her through the ghostly rows of solitary cells, shafts of moonlight slashing their path as they made their way down to the end of the long corridor, the ring of keys still clasped tightly in his hand. When they reached the end, he turned the corner and gestured an *after you* before the entrance to a set of steps. She climbed stair after painful stair toward a light coming from above.

The room at the top of the tower was fashioned to serve as a kind of office. The man coughed hard as he caught his breath, and she looked about, noting the fineness of the large wooden desk, the ornate clock upon the wall with a slouched, woeful wallpaper stained with yellowing watermarks. The clock emitted a sonorous tick that disquieted her even more than the horrible howling of the wind, which was rattling the window. The man walked toward the window and gazed down at a sight below them. She made her way to join him and saw, through curtains of churning snow, a cluster of men.

Prisoners: plodding methodically in a circle, each man following the footsteps of the man preceding him. Their faces cast down, they appeared to move as one cog in a far larger universal machination. She moved her eyes from the men below to the man beside her: he was gazing at the prisoners with a kind of reverence.

"How solemnly they march," he said.

"For how long must they circle in that way?"

"For a quarter of an hour, after which time they change directions. If the weather is poor, then they go without the exercise," he replied, eyes fixed upon the sight beneath. "Those are very bad days."

They stood in silence for a long while. Then suddenly, he spoke. "What is your name, my dear?"

"My name, sir?" She was certain he must know the answer.

He nodded. No one had asked for her name in all the time she had been here. She wondered if she even remembered it.

"Hodel," she replied, startled by its simplicity.

"Hodel," he repeated, his gaze still locked upon the prisoners. "Yiddish."

"Yes, sir."

"Hodel: from *Hode*. A derivative of *Hadassah*. Meaning 'the myrtle tree.' " His face was flushed. The exertion of the climb had caused him to overheat inside his thick uniform, which, despite this, he wore very well. A gold medallion pinned to his jacket indicated his rank and position.

The man turned to look at her. His face was wide and pocked and buttery, his piercing blue eyes filled with the first true expression of regard she had met since her time here began. His face revealed an understanding, a look that recognized without pity that she was still a very young girl.

"You really know nothing of politics, do you, my dear?"

She shook her head. The rush of deliverance that came over her at this was euphoric.

"I thought not, Hodel. It is evident."

To be believed! To feel some semblance of sanity in this belief. She felt her eyes prick with tears of enormous relief; she nearly wrapped her arms around him.

"Do you know who I am, Hodel?" he asked.

"No, sir."

"I am a gentleman." His voice had an unaffected ease.

A gentleman? Now that she could truly gaze upon him, she noted that everything about his temperament, grooming, and manner appeared to be nothing short of exact; a clear manifestation of not only his upbringing but also his will.

"I govern a camp much farther east of here. Our post specializes in silver and salt mining. It is located in the village of Nerchinsk."

Nerchinsk. The camp where Perchik was! Oh, sweet Nerchinsk! The paper she had discovered said that he was there, and thus the word itself made her churn. Nerchinsk—this simplest of utterances—inspired in her such a feeling of yearning that all she could say was: "I have heard of it, sir."

At this, The Gentleman clasped his hands

131

behind his back and made a clean quarter turn toward her. "I have a daughter, you know. About your age, so I do understand. I can see through a young woman—whether her motives are tarnished or clean. I see purity in you." He planted his feet in a tidy parallel. His boots were spotless. "I already know much of your situation," he said. "But I suppose you already presumed that."

She nodded, eyes wide and body rigid, her mind alert for the first time in uncountable days.

"Hodel, I believe we can come to some kind of understanding."

She was not in any way braced for kindness. Her mind whirled, circling around and around like the prisoners who marched hundreds of feet below them.

"Mother Russia is playing catch-up with the world. The tsar can see that potential lies beyond the Urals. We already have thousands flocking to our mineral-rich settlements." He leaned forward in his enthusiasm, teetering on his perfectly placed feet.

"Flocking, sir?"

"There are indeed the convicts serving sentences. But of far greater economic importance are the settlers, some admittedly forced, who live in developing Siberian communities—though not in prison! They reside in underpopulated regions of the country chosen for their economic potential. Many do not understand, but there are those of us who see that Siberia is merely a tool being used in the inevitable triumph of our people. I like to think of it as a . . . beneficial instrument."

For so many weeks now, she had been prepared to rebut any attack and thus was armed with rage to defend herself. In the tranquility of this tower, she was off-balance.

"But there are very few women," he continued. "Their numbers never manage to exceed fifteen percent. There are even fewer books, limited access to food and alcohol, beastly weather. Nothing to do but work. Hodel, we in the East truly have many noble uses for strong women such as yourself. The female populace in the East is in dire need of expansion." With hands still clasped behind his back, he took a few assured steps closer. As he looked deep within her, she could feel him almost cupping her heart. "And I think you would agree that Nerchinsk has certain qualities that *you* would find . . . irresistible, yes?"

Hodel caught her breath. This new hope was quite a shock to her system.

"I would like to request that you accompany me to Nerchinsk. Would you consider this proposal?"

Her heart leapt. Tears fell hard, silently flowing

down her hollowed face. "I would, sir," she said.

"I will of course have to use my influence with our friend the Chief Commander of Omsk, with whom I believe you are already a little too familiar. But I am confident I can make a persuasive case in the morning." The Gentleman paused, his eyes bluer and more piercing than before. He spoke again, his voice filled with a surprising degree of tenderness, "I will personally see to it, Hodel, that no harm comes to you. Do we understand each other?"

She nodded in disbelief, quaking with the mere thought of her deliverance.

"For our greatest rewards, Hodel, sometimes we must endure."

Yes, she thought. She had endured long enough.

Located in Eastern Siberia, the village of Nerchinsk is in the Russian province of what is now the mountainous region of Transbaikalia, or Dauriya. To the east is majestic freshwater Lake Baikal. To the west and to the south is China; it is nearly a straight shot as the crow flies to Beijing. Nerchinsk sits on the left bank of the Nercha River, which flows into the great Amur River, which then empties out into the Sea of Okhotsk. In addition to agriculture and silver mining, there is a modest trade in fur and brick tea from

China, but the major business is salt. The vast numbers of workers within the salt mines create a humming sound, like bees at work in an apiary. But Nerchinsk is so bleak a place, it is almost entirely made up of workers forced to reside there.

Those are the facts.

But the facts could never capture Nerchinsk's poetry. How exquisitely Nerchinsk sulks upon its gray and sorrowful bluff. How shafts of sun burst through the thick, low blanket of cloud above the village like stabs of hope from heaven. How the entire town seems to sigh as it overlooks the river and the bleak, endless flatlands. How a southern breeze carries odors in from Beijing: duck fat, tangerine peels, industry, and opiates. How the washed-out colors of Nerchinsk are more beautiful than they should be: the land the gray of a gun, the sky a leaden violet, the shadows of the cavernous mines as dark and forbidding as the holes within them. How the mud-soaked roads are dotted with meandering cows and wild dogs, with no visible signs of human life save the prison in the distance, with its barracks, officer residencies, and dilapidated local shanty huts made of clapboard. And all of it sitting on top of the salt that lurks within the depths of the soil, fathoms beneath the ground.

This land contained Perchik and that was a

beauty unlike any she had ever known. Nerchinsk was beautiful to Hodel from the moment she first laid eyes on it because, for Hodel, that's where Perchik was.

Hodel had already traveled 3,500 kilometers by prisoner train from Omsk, a few hundred more with other convicts and wives by carriage, but now they drove east, farther than she believed was possible, through the low, undulating taiga, past endless miles of feral country. At ten o'clock on this particularly cold morning, the carriage crested the rolling hills of the country, and Hodel—who was chained to the prison carriage that had brought her from the train station—laid her eyes upon the village of Nerchinsk for the very first time.

She saw before her the outlines of a village composed of perhaps two hundred ramshackle dwellings, all built of damp black wood, hunched beside the river along the vast open land. Far off, the mounds of the mining assembly were just barely visible.

The carriage halted—horses blustered, clouds of exertion puffing from their mouths, hooves sticking into the frozen mud. Foreign-faced workers entered and removed her chains.

"Now, now, steady, all of you," said one of the men. "Nothing to get excited about."

But there was.

Hodel emerged from the back of the carriage

rubbing her newly freed arms with relief. She kept her eyes upon the horizon, searching wildly for his form and face.

Then, revealed from the mists of the morning, she saw him. Their eyes locked. "Perchik!" she called out.

They ran, tearing toward each other, across the bluff, the ice and wind and frozen mud.

They knew that all the days behind them had merely led to this very moment. They had gone forward in the trust that they would be reunited somehow in one world or another. It had been close to eighteen months, and now, at last they had found each other.

"My girl!"

They were free. Finally, they could live together in the present. This was a release from every kind of prison.

"I thought you were dead, my beloved," she said as Perchik swept her into his arms.

There would come a day when Hodel would have names for every color of sky and mud, knowledge of every scent of rain or road or mineral that came from the horizon. She would know where each dog slept, and how to read the clouds, the waters of the Nercha, the scents that wafted upward from the Orient. She would have carnal knowledge of every quality of earth beneath her boots, and know the color and angles of every ray of exquisite, spectral

Siberian light. But today? Today, there was only him.

She lifted her head. Beheld his face. Touched the soft place beneath his eyes. Vowed never to lose him again.

Through the darkest days in prison, through shorn heads and hunger, through violations, abuse, hopelessness, and deepest despair— through all of it, they had been moved by the power of their belief that they would have this moment. This singular moment of unparalleled joy.

"Perchik." She wept, her head pressed against his like two hands in prayer. "Perchik."

Nothing in this world was worth having that had not been so fought for.

And there, with no division between his spirit and her own, she felt the pounding of his heart as he felt her quiver in his arms, responding in the same instant.

He leaned farther into her, his arms wrapped around the entirety of her frame, enveloping her as if to fuse with her being for eternity—as indeed they both wished to do in this moment and evermore.

"You are home now," he whispered, hesitating only an instant before leaning in to kiss her mouth, full and eager, for the first time in their life together. It was a triumph of such intense ecstasy that no entwining promise, no ardent avowal, no other utterance of devotion would ever be necessary.

So, without a care in the world—not for the cold, for the filth, or for propriety—at long last, they held and held and held. . . .

BOOK TWO

The Life and Times
of Reb Perchik

I am that I am.
—*Exodus*

seventeen

The decision to have political prisoners work the mines was made out of both necessity and foolishness—for where better to discuss rogue politics with like-minded thinkers than deep within the cavernous infinity of Siberian darkness? This was katorga, the system of frozen work camps in the Russian Empire, which had settled into its shameless stride. Throngs of criminals branded with their crime were being flung across the Urals in chains to labor the land—generally for mining lead ore, salt, and silver, but also in foundries, as well as coal and mineral-processing factories. Many said the revolution began here.

This particularly brutal camp was among the most remote prison camps in European Russia, located in the Nerchinsk *okrug*, or district, of Transbaikalia, between the Shilka and Argun Rivers, near the border to Mongolia. It had been in operation since the 18th century, and since the establishment of the Nerchinsk Katorga Administration, it had been reserved for keeping political prisoners as far away from Europe as possible. These men—at least in the eyes of the law—were essentially dead.

Perchik lifted his face to the sun and wiped his

brow; his skin was sore and tight, hands cracked, lips flaked and bleeding, skin falling away—all from the salt in the mine's atmosphere. Salt in his hair, in the very tissues of his lungs, filling his nose with a stinging, dry agony. He exhaled and began again.

"Perchik!" came a raspy voice from down the shaft. "Do you have a sip, brother?"

Perchik did indeed. Liquid was at a premium here (and liquid that would not freeze was more valuable than gold). He rummaged through his knapsack and slid the regulation flask down the shaft, where a withering hand reached out from the darkness. "Thank you, brother," the voice said. Perchik took up his pick and began again.

Mining was harrowing. It was more than the jagged bite of the Siberian elements. More than the backbreaking physical labor performed in a shroud of darkness. No. It was a torture of the mind. A wretchedly lonely, mind-numbing, insanity-inducing task. And if you were very lucky, you could avoid what was cryptically called "the preservation" and escape from Nerchinsk alive. The leading cause of death was not freezing, malnutrition, exhaustion, or starvation—the murderer of Nerchinsk was dehydration. Assignment to the salt mines was, more often than not, a death sentence.

But all these burdens were lightened by the

presence of his wife. Hodel was assigned her own tasks with the other women throughout the day and remained with him in the lightly boarded barracks at night, its floors mostly permafrost throughout unending winters, full of plunging temperatures and howling blizzards. They shared a room with ten others, who allowed them the privacy of a drawn curtain in the corner of the room, where they fashioned a provisional home for themselves.

He had been in Nerchinsk for over two years now. Hodel had arrived sixteen months after him, a faded shadow of herself, yet steely and undaunted. The journey itself—for many it took as long as two years—was enough to kill a man; and it did, by the thousands. The transit prisons were racked with typhus, scurvy, smallpox, and syphilis.

Every day of the last eight months they had been together in this place. Perchik marveled at what Hodel had endured to be with him. He could not believe she had come at all.

He ran his tongue over his broken lips and groaned. The thought of what she had abandoned made him ache far worse than any corporeal abuse he could ever endure in the mines. *She is a pillar of strength,* he thought. *Well, if only my uncle could see me now.*

To say things had not gone according to plan would be putting it mildly.

There was never a moment in Reb Gershom's long life that ever indicated he was anything but an elderly man. His mouth was tight and void of color, and his hair had turned white long before old age. A learned man—who, despite his Jewishness, had attended university at the age of just sixteen—Gershom was always revered as tremendously intelligent, though somewhat overly serious.

Gershom's younger sister, Malkha, on the other hand, had run away from their Orthodox community at the age of twenty-five, after she and her husband had endured the loss of their second child in under three years. Shortly after her departure, her husband hanged himself in the back room of their general store. No one blamed him. He was distraught beyond reason, and her abandonment was a loss too great to bear. It was the greatest scandal the community had endured in decades.

More than any feeling of personal remorse, Gershom felt the situation reflected badly upon his name. He cursed his sister for blackening his reputation with scandal. *Blessed be to Him our parents are no longer alive,* he thought, *and that no children were involved.*

But Malkha—blissfully unaware of the scene she left behind her—joined secular society with pleasure. Her body, her mind, even her hair was free for the first time in her life. She cut off ties to her past, changed her name, and threw herself into the throngs of bohemian society with lust and passionate abandon. When she died giving birth to an illegitimate son, the infant was born to a woman without regret, for he had come into this world the child of a contented, liberated woman.

Gershom, for his part, did not mourn her departure. Yet he never anticipated that God's punishment for Malkha's sins would so profoundly impact him. His sentence came four years later, announced by a knock on his door.

A weedy-looking woman stood on his doorstep with a young boy.

"He came to us as an illegitimate infant with this around his neck," she said, presenting Gershom with a necklace that featured the Star of David. "*M. Tselen* is engraved on the back of it, sir—dead in childbirth.Authorities believe her to be your sister."

Gershom sniggered. He found it rather fitting that God should punish her wickedness with a suitably grisly premature death; he was pleased with the evidence of the Lord's sense of perpetual justice.

The woman explained that the vastly overcrowded Terestchenko orphanage would no longer look after Malkha's boy because the child had living relatives—namely, Gershom.

"That's why I'm here, sir," said the woman with a hint of impatience. As soon as Terestchenko had discovered Gershom's residence, they promptly sent the boy to Gershom's home, accompanied by a representative to inform him of his social responsibility.

"It is the godly thing to do," said the representative, pushing the boy toward his unfamiliar uncle.

"Do not speak to me of God!" raged Gershom. "What am I supposed to do with the boy?"

"That's not my concern, sir," said the representative, staring at Gershom with the pale gray pallor of an undertaker. "I'm not taking the boy with me. We simply cannot keep a child who has living relatives. If you don't look after him, you'll just have to cast him out onto the street altogether—and what would your Lord God think of that?"

Gershom shifted his eyes downward. He glared at the boy with deep disgust.

"He's a good boy, sir. Obedient, well-mannered, bright. He'll be a good aide to you! Certainly no bother."

"Well, if it is the will of God," conceded Gershom.

The representative smiled, then leaned down and spoke in the boy's ear. "You hear that?" she whispered. "You are not wanted here, boy. So watch yourself."

The boy kept his eyes on the floor and nodded obediently, clutching his cap.

Reluctantly, Gershom ushered the orphan into the house. "Come in then, boy."

Thus their life together began.

eighteen

Stale water, heavy, masculine sweat, raw fish, overboiled cabbage, and spoiled kasha—the stench of the dining hall was insidious and distinct. Here the prison's daily workers gathered for discussion and release, and cramped over familiarities.

Prisoners woke with the sun. In the haze of the dawn, they convened for breakfast, then reported to their designated posts. They worked twelve-hour days without reprieve, their gray countenances rimmed with ice, salt, and tears too frozen to fall.

At every hour of the day and night, Perchik and the other felons were under the constant surveillance of the overseer and the soldiers in charge. But even under these watchful eyes, Perchik had managed to gather a motley crew of exilic companions. They were all assigned to the same rotation, and, for better or worse, they were fated to share their days with one another.

The three and a half hundred convicts of Nerchinsk were almost entirely male. Alongside the violent, the brutish, and the common thieves, some men had been condemned to exile for a variety of baffling offenses: prizefighting, begging with false distress, vagrancy, and taking snuff (a crime often punished by ripping out the offender's septum), not to mention illicit tree-felling and fortune-telling. This river of unfortunates was purified by the political exiles: cultured dissidents, Polish revolutionaries, aging Decembrists, and aristocratic liberals with a disgust for the autocracy.

But it did not matter why they were there. The prisoners rarely knew the crimes of the men working beside them. There existed a natural balance within the prison's barriers in which each of the men were on miserably equal footing.

"There will always be a man with more than another," explained Perchik. "And not just financially, but more intelligence, more strength, even more beauty. This proves the existence of a universal law of unevenness. This is the law that stands in the way of our social equality, and it reveals itself most sharply in backward countries such as our own. Yet under the whip of necessity, our culture is compelled to make dramatic leaps. But how do we reach the cynics as well as the idealists? That is the practical question."

These political discussions were a daily occurrence, of course—though kept carefully beneath the noses of the guards.

"I do not disagree with that," said a bristling, bespectacled graduate student across the table.

"We must outsmart this inequality," Perchik continued. "Overcome it with a social pragmatism. Change now—but with stability. Change bit by bit. A state of perpetual revolution."

"Ah," groaned the companion across the table, "a Trotskyite. I should've known."

"A pragmatist." Perchik smiled.

"I don't understand how you can dismiss two-stage theory and call yourself a comrade. It is like this meat without salt—tasteless," the student replied.

This graduate student was Dmitri Pavlovich Petrovsky: thinker, musician, and premature curmudgeon. Dmitri had been born with twines of music lodged tight around his heart. Like rusted barbed wire, they clutched at him, and the harder he struggled, the deeper the barbs would cut. The wounds festered, encased in the pus of his dulled imagination.

In the time the men had known him, none had ever seen him laugh. Life was serious business for Dmitri Petrov, and being convicted for treachery was no laughing matter. A shy man of extraordinary height, it was precisely his shyness, seriousness, and towering physical measurement that made him, above all other qualities and skills, a truly exceptional cellist.

Dmitri Petrov hailed from the tenements of St. Petersburg, his parents leading their family of locally celebrated folk musicians. He held reverence for a different variety of music than his parents—classical (far too refined for the folk-based roots he grew up absorbing from his family). But coming from a family of folk musicians in a city as bright as Petersburg made no difference whatsoever to a boy so innately fraught by the simultaneous demands and admonitions of a world in which he felt he did not belong. Depression blanketed Dmitri from the time he could remember, though his family was quick to dismiss it all as family flair or histrionics.

"*Nyezhnaya* Mitya!" they had said all his life. "Tender Mitya!" They did not—they *could* not—know what to do with him. Nor did he know what to do with himself.

Dmitri's broad shoulders hunched over a lanky body as if to protect the heart that ached within. His face was beautiful and surrounded by a mop of dark, messy curls. Large expressive hands with long fingers were often curled into fists and plunged deep within his pockets, or else wringing, itching to be used to play his cello. His small but ferociously intelligent eyes, shielded by the spectacles he'd worn since childhood, held all the world at arm's length. He tagged along with his family, of course, to play in the city venues with them—folk songs soared and crowds cheered as his father led with accordion, his mother on balalaika, and his sisters on violins. He was grateful to his family for the instrument itself (handed down from his grandfather) and for the ability to play it. But his family, however musical, could not hear his music at all.

Dmitri had been deported to Nerchinsk for questionable editorial leadership of the university newspaper. Because of his decidedly anti-imperialist sentiments, he was expelled, interrogated, and upon his interview with the authorities, sentenced to eighteen months of disciplinary servitude.

The cello, remarkably, had made the journey with him. Despite his exhaustion, Dmitri continued to nimbly apply his fingers to the ragged chestnut hourglass at every opportunity—preferring to retreat into the instrument's company rather than engage with his fellow men. Education, politics, family, and Russia herself be damned—the cello was his first, his only, love.

"The problem is the degree of separation, the dramatic polarity of rights and equalities between those who have a lot and those who have nothing," Perchik continued. "It is the tenacity, the dogged, righteous nature of the working classes—not to mention their sheer numbers—that make the proletariat the only group capable of taking on the battle for democratic rights and following through to the most complete solutions. We must root and carve out exploitation, tyranny, and oppression like viruses."

"To manifest such ideals into action would

be nearly impossible," said Dmitri Petrov, his temper rising. This talk provoked him.

"I don't believe anything to be impossible," replied Perchik.

"Pah! Be careful, Reb Perchik—your idealism may be your downfall."

Perchik smiled. "What good will a violent revolution be if we are unable to maintain the principles for which we initially rebelled?" He caressed the curve of a spoon that lay beside his tray over and over again, methodically wearing a groove deeper into the utensil with the side of his thumb as he had done since he was a boy. "We are in the business of ideals. A man's soul wishes to aspire; it longs to grow. I believe all growth is plausible when we do it together, bit by bit."

Dmitri stared at him through the thickness of his spectacles, his gaze fierce. "Hogwash," he said.

"Oh, come along, Dmitri," Perchik said amiably. "It is only discourse. I mean no disagreement for the sake of it."

Dmitri nodded in apology. "Of course, Reb Perchik," he said. "Of course."

There was much about Perchik that Dmitri Petrov admired, even desired to embody. But Perchik's even disposition profoundly irritated Dmitri Petrov, for they were not qualities he possessed himself.

"I am a simple man, mind—a laborer, not

learned like the two of ye," said Anatoly Gromov, respectfully interrupting the tension. "And I reckon your dander is properly up about the mess around here, but what you speak of sounds so learned and fancy—it has nothing to do with me and mine, I'm sure."

Anatoly, a man of tremendous heft, was a native of Vladivostok, a far eastern land exotic to the men even from these parts. He insisted with a curious sweetness that most people in Vladivostok were good because of the harshness. He had a powdery complexion, strong hands, and a shock of coarse, poufy hair that swirled from the top of his head like steam from a pot. He had the familiar, straightforward, easy, cheerful temper of a common workingman, with eyes that echoed a sad smile.

"I'm not afeard to say it: perhaps I'm simple, though I fancy m'self thataway, and I do not understand the better-most part of the changes you suggest. And though I may be a criminal and sentenced here for good, I am a citizen of Russia, same as the two of you, and I ain't exactly interested in things changing so very much, and that is the truth for me, that is."

"Our system will only work if it can be applied and utilized by real people, like yourself, Anatoly." Perchik both meant and managed to say this without the slightest hint of condescension.

"You are all exasperating," another man bleated. This was Grigory Boleslav, known to the men as Grisha.

Puzzled, Perchik smiled and asked him, "Are you cross with your cabbage, Grisha?"

Grisha shot him a dark look. "I eat with intention," he said, cutting his cabbage savagely. He possessed a flare for the dramatic.

Youthful, delicately built, and with a creamy pale complexion and dark burning eyes, Grisha's whole countenance intimated a cunning temperament. But it was his softness that made his presence in such a place a great mystery to his companions.

Yet he was the one who noted the little changes in his companions. He remembered name days. He gave away his wedge of bread when the old men looked particularly despondent. Indeed, for every tempestuous drama he stirred, there would always come a gesture of great tenderness that balanced it. And it was precisely these gestures that were so keenly lacking among the company of three hundred plus laboring men.

"When you speak, it is in circles, and what you say is, yes, exasperating," Grisha said. "There you are."

"I am exasperating?" inquired Perchik, amused.

"Yes. Oh! And tedious."

"Goodness, Grisha!" chimed an old man with a mouth full of some overcooked root vegetable (its mushiness all the better for the man's failing teeth). "Do ease up!"

Here was the voice of petty thief Yevgeny Ashenko, the elderly bunkmate of Dmitri Petrov, condemned to penal servitude in Siberia after a series of disciplinary "wrist slaps." He was not, as it turned out, a very good thief.

Aging, chronically messy, and forgetful, Yevgeny was what one could only describe as dear. The men loved to laugh with him, for he was constantly full of good humor. They delighted in him even more because he was most likely the root of Dmitri Petrov's consistent ill temper—which the men also found most amusing.

However, for Dmitri Petrov himself (who bore the brunt of Yevgeny's bright ideas, nifty schemes, and endless idiotic enthusiasms), Yevgeny was, in Dmitri's estimation, nothing more than a completely useless imbecile. Yevgeny's popularity flummoxed Dmitri, which only irked him further.

Dmitri played Bach suites. He had been the editor of the university newspaper. Yevgeny had the intellect of a cornhusk. Dmitri read smuggled political pamphlets, the letters of Engels, and the poems of Pushkin. Yevgeny watched snow melt in his hands. And while Dmitri pondered social reform and existential meaning, Yevgeny pondered absolutely nothing.

During the days, Yevgeny would accompany

Dmitri everywhere, constantly sharing fleeting thoughts on just about anything. Once in a while Yevgeny would look as though he was about to say something terribly clever, and Dmitri would get very hopeful; then Yevgeny would merely impart things like: "You know, kasha is preferable to potato because it is chewy rather than mushy!"

It was sweet, but pathetic.

At night, Dmitri would stare at the ceiling and imagine ways to escape the company of his bunkmate—he dreamed of cafés, study halls, chamber music, and scores of people to really talk to. But he'd wake to a snoring Yevgeny: mouth agape, face pressed to his pillow, his fetid breath wafting right up into Dmitri's nostrils.

Dmitri would complain to Anatoly, "Yevgeny is a numbskull."

But Anatoly was of no use. He loved Yevgeny. They all did. Yevgeny was all sincerity and joyful merriment. Dmitri was a disagreeable curmudgeon.

Dmitri couldn't understand their devotion. Yevgeny had clearly been assigned to his bunk to destroy him; he could see it in his idiot eyes. The fact that Yevgeny was such a favorite was enough to give Dmitri an ulcer. The other men playfully scoffed him.

"You two!" Grigory howled. "Oh, you do amuse me! The way you carry on!"

Before Yevgeny came along, Dmitri might have been lonely, but at least things were quiet. After he came, Dmitri was still lonely. Only now his nerves were also frayed.

"Good God, everyone is in quite the peevish state today!" Grigory declared, snapping Perchik back into the present. "But I would not be a friend unless I said how it really was!"

"Now, now, Grisha," cooed Perchik, smiling.

"Well, what? It is always politics and ideals and policy with you boys! And whether we should revolt in one big go or every day in small bits. Don't you 'now, now' me! Now, now, indeed! Who in the world cares? I don't. If and when your magic revolution arrives, I shall still be breaking my back in this hole if I am around at all. I shall die from the cold if not from the tolls of hard work. But I am not at all concerned, for I shall more than likely die first from the boredom of listening to all of you." Boleslav stabbed his cabbage with finality, slammed down utensils that shrieked upon the tin tray, and stormed off.

They glanced after him as he huffed.

"An exasperating politician, what a shock," joked Perchik, breaking the silence. They all sniggered and shook their heads with varying degrees of exasperation, resignation, and amusement; Perchik had a gift for raising their spirits. They returned in due course to their trays. Perchik smiled and asked, "More kasha?"

"Salt, please," a forlorn-faced Yevgeny asked, not even looking up from his gruel.

Dmitri glared across the table. Sharing a bunk with Yevgeny was eating away at his soul.

Yevgeny was constantly trying to impress him. That morning Yevgeny had come right up to him before breakfast with a childlike glee slapped across his face, hands hidden playfully behind his back. He'd been shaking with excitement, eyebrows up and grinning ear to ear.

"Close your eyes."

"No."

"I have made you a gift. It is a surprise."

"Yevgeny, I haven't the time for this."

"Come along, Dmitri Petrov, please. . . . For an old man."

Dmitri had felt a migraine beginning. He groaned. Then capitulated. "Fine," he agreed, "but make it quick, old man—it is nearly mealtime, and people may see."

Yevgeny opened his hands wide. "Open!" he cried.

Dmitri had yelped. Yevgeny's hands were filled with dung.

"Do you like it?" he'd inquired proudly. "It is a little cello! I have fashioned it for you!" Disgust had been visible behind Dmitri's glasses. Yevgeny had just paused, face aglow. ". . . for you."

Dmitri, revolted by both the figurine and its

creator, had taken it up all the same and placed it in his pocket just to make the man go away.

"Oh!" Grigory had said, laughing. "How you two amuse me!" He was folded over himself. "One would never think Dmitri was the boy and Yevgeny the old man!" Grigory had grabbed his eyes, for they were tearing. "His humor and your hatred of it, Mitya. God, it is delightful!"

"How can you eat salt?" Dmitri asked now. "It is seeped into our pores; it flakes from our scalps; we discover it in the pockets of our coats, the crevices of ourselves; it sloughs off into our beds!" He shook his cap over Yevgeny's food.

"Bah!" Yevgeny cried. "Look here, Dmitri! Mind your business! And here when I gave you my extra half a slice!"

"You are a halfwit," Dmitri said. He was in another ornery temper.

"Come, Dmitri," Perchik said, ever the peacemaker. "Leave the man and his tasteless food alone."

The men shifted, exchanging looks, chewing through their amusement. For a moment all they could hear was the clanging of the spoons against the tin trays.

"The food tastes of nothing!" said Yevgeny, unable to let it alone.

"Better of nothing than of salt, surely?" berated Dmitri once again, his voice rising.

Yevgeny had no response.

"You are a bore," Dmitri said.

"You are," Yevgeny responded.

"You!"

The two returned with renewed zeal to their respective tin trays, leaving the rest of them bemused and silent once again.

Outside, a prison cart entered the camp, horses braying with discontent outside the windows. Long-coated soldiers—top to toe in black, sleek like panthers, and armed with rifles—dismounted. They moved to the back of the cart with sinuous grace, opened the padlocks, unfastened the bars, and released the door of the grate with frightening, machinelike efficiency. They grabbed the new prisoner and ripped him from the back of the cart. And as they deposited him into the bitter morning air, the world around him appeared somehow to suspend.

There was something about him.

He landed hard upon the frozen soil, hands and feet restrained. The haze cleared as his head rose to the sky, revealing what was merely a boy. The face itself possessed an expression that sent a hush upon the onlookers.

"Who is that?" asked Dmitri.

"Newly committed," Anatoly said. "Fresh from Omsk this very morning."

The boy shook his head, clearing a cluster of gleaming golden curls from his eyes; and as he steadied himself upon the solid ground, his gaze lifted and landed fleetingly, but firmly, on Perchik.

Perchik shuddered.

"Such a young man," murmured Yevgeny. "Just a boy."

The youth in chains had a quality no one could place.

"He goes by the name of Tenderov, I believe. Yes, that's it: Andrey Tenderov. I saw him before his processing."

"What did he do?" Dmitri whispered.

"I dunno," Anatoly replied, shaking his head. "Scarcely looks capable of anythin' other'n sincerity. His expression is almost joyful, aye?"

"Yes," they replied.

As the soldiers escorted Andrey Tenderov away, gray clouds gathered low, slowly smearing Tenderov to nothing, and all at once, it began to snow. Man or angel, they could not tell, but whatever it was, he had been just a boy.

nineteen

He had been just a boy.

It was a life of relative privilege under Gershom's care; his uncle was a respected and tremendously wealthy accountant with a thriving business and a set of uncompromising ethics. Gershom did perform his parental duties, no matter how costly or inconvenient, but without a scrap of affection, no matter how hard Perchik tried.

Gershom's occupation was in *arenda*—he designated the lease of money in the form of fixed assets (such as land, mills, inns, breweries, distilleries) or special rights (such as the collection of customs duties and taxes). Together he and Perchik inhabited a flat along the left bank in the Jewish pale of Kiev, where the great Kiev pogrom of 1881 was still in everyone's memory, resulting in a paranoid, insulated community. Gershom worshipped God, hard work, and the accounts—in that order—and Perchik in turn worshipped Gershom, longing for his affection above all else. By day, he accepted Gershom's menial tasks eagerly. At night, he would simply pray for some small crumb of love.

It became clear as the years churned onward:

there simply was nothing Perchik could *not* do. Any action, task, or talent came naturally, without consciousness or a scrap of pride. This both thrilled and threatened Gershom, for he knew he could never match what Perchik was already promising to become. It was as though, with every generation that passed, the families' attributes were being strained through a sieve, allowing nothing to pass through but absolute talent. Perchik: the very pith of an otherwise useless lineage.

The boy required schooling. But school was not where Perchik wished to be! He wept the night before he was first to attend the *beth hamidrash*, for Gershom's love was the center of his universe, and only at home could he ever hope to receive it. Yet within, there burned a soul teeming with greatness.

"Do we all recall the story, my children?" Rabbi Syme asked his class of schoolboys at the beth hamidrash. Rabbi Syme was younger and more open-minded than most religious leaders of his time, and possessed both a flare for the theatric and a deep love for the molding of young minds. "Famine, disease, plague, death, blight, and terrible destruction!" He belted, "Of course, my sons, this is not recent news; it happened three thousand years ago in Egypt. . . ."

Perchik had quickly discovered that being

gifted was isolating, so it was in the very farthest corner of the room that Perchik shifted in his seat—the tale of Exodus left him with a feeling of disquiet.

"I am speaking, of course, of Exodus," continued the rabbi at a murmur, "the second of the five books of the Torah. Exodus is the book that recounts to us how Moses led the Hebrews out of Egypt and through the wilderness to the mountain of God, called Sinai. There, Adonai, blessed be to Him, through Moses, gave the Hebrews their laws and entered into a covenant with them, by which he gave them the holy land of Canaan in return for their faithfulness."

Rabbi Syme glanced over at Perchik with curiosity.

"We all remember the tale of the biblical plagues of Egypt first detailed in the *Parshat Va'era*?" said the rabbi with vigor. "Try to imagine the plague of *tsefardeah*, or frogs. Frogs everywhere: in the homes, in the ovens, even in people's stomachs! The noise from their croaking was deafening. Envision it, my boys"—he spoke in a hush—"Pharaoh, the king of all Egypt: in his splendor he sits on a throne in royal garments surrounded by officers. He opens his mouth to speak, but they cannot hear his voice! It is drowned out by the croaking of the frogs in his stomach! Can you imagine anything more disgraceful than that, Zindell?" he exclaimed, looking at the butcher's son, who wore overly large spectacles that constantly fell down the bridge of his nose. He adjusted them now, awestruck.

"It must have been very humiliating," replied young Zindell, mouth agape.

Rabbi Syme pressed on.

"So: Pharaoh calls to Moses and asks him to pray to God to remove the frogs from his stomach and from Egypt. In exchange, Pharaoh promises to release the Jewish nation for the three days they have requested to worship their God. And what do you think happened next, my sons?"

"Moses agreed, but Pharaoh did not keep his end of the deal," answered the puffed-up Avi, the fourth in a line of sweaty sons of the tinsmith. "Isn't that true, Rabbi?" he added with a touch of self-congratulation.

"Yes, indeed, very good, Avi, but *why* did Pharaoh do this?"

The answer came from the far corner of the room: "Because God had hardened Pharaoh's heart." It was young Perchik, his brow furrowed, his gaze set. Perchik mostly hid his abilities to gain acceptance—he deliberately underachieved, purposely let the other boys win all the marbles, answer all the questions. He was a bore. He even bored himself. But Perchik knew a great deal about hard hearts.

168

"What was that, my boy?" It took Rabbi Syme a few lingering moments to realize that he was staring.

"God hardened Pharaoh's heart," Perchik repeated. He was wearing a groove into the parchment before him with the side of his thumb, as if his thumb could wipe away every confusion and nagging shame, every scrap of loneliness.

The rabbi continued to stare.

"Yes, boy," he replied, treading carefully. "Very good. Pharaoh had the human power of free will to *choose* the path of righteousness and instead chose selfishness." He opened himself to the rest of the students. "Thus our Lord hardened Pharaoh's heart, and as a result of this heartlessness the entire nation of Egypt was destroyed."

Rabbi Syme was fascinated. He had always noticed that there was something different about the boy; he possessed a quality—a light that surrounded him.

"Yes," said Perchik, gaze still set low, "*Shlomo HaMelech*, King Solomon, the wisest of all men, wrote in *Mishlei*, 'The heart of the king is in God's hands.' "

"Indeed," the rabbi concurred.

Then all at once Perchik's face grew very grave. His hand shook slightly over the groove he had now fully worn into the parchment.

"Pharaoh cannot just think about himself. His actions and decisions affect everyone. . . ."

Lord in heaven, thought Rabbi Syme. At once he straightened himself and addressed the rest of the class.

"Now, boys, is the lesson of Exodus still true today?"

"Yes."

"In what way?"

"These are times when the Jewish people are in great danger," Avi said. "It appears that our fate is in the hands of a few bad leaders."

Zindell added, "From Exodus, we know that our hearts are in God's hands. The Jewish people are really being influenced by Him."

"Right, boys, but God still desires something from the true service to Him that has saved the Jewish people time and time again: *tefillah,* or prayer; *tshuva,* or correcting our mistakes; strengthening our Torah learning; strengthening our mitzvah performance; and giving more tzedakah, or charity. Are we ready to give it our best, my sons? Let us do our part to help our people. God will surely take notice. Amen."

"Amen," chimed the boys in chorus.

"But, Rabbi," piped up young Perchik once again from the corner of the room, "I believe the Exodus from Egypt symbolizes something else as well."

"And what is that, my boy?"

"Imprisonment to freedom. The story reso-nates. It is true of any oppressed person," he said quietly. "And we learn from Exodus that the heart of a good man is not wrong. It is not unreliable or bad. The heart always knows the truth. There is nothing more important than living one's truth. The heart knows when it is thriving and when it is being trampled. . . ." The boy looked out the window.

"And since the heart knows this," said the rabbi directly to Perchik, "the question cannot be whether it is better to express or suppress the gifts that God has given. Rather, it can only be: Is it better to express or suppress life itself?"

Perchik did not blink as he spoke. "Yes."

It was this moment. The moment when Rabbi Syme was overwhelmed with a desire to preserve this tender prodigy. To save him.

"Human life is to be lived, my sons," said the rabbi to the whole group once more. "The Israelites are told to 'choose life.' They are promised a long and fruitful life if they abide by God's commandments. If the purpose of life is to live it, then the Exodus from Egypt is a journey from death into life—from a culture that focuses beyond this world to one that embraces it. And thus the theological question changes too, as we ask whether a God who loves life would ask

God's children to throw their gifts away in any kind of slavery. Do you see?"

The boys nodded uncertainly, like boats bobbing in the early-morning Dnieper River. Rabbi Syme fixed his eyes directly on Perchik and made his way slowly around the rectangular table of young men, who followed his movements with curiosity. The rabbi stopped before Perchik with a sense of the definite.

"What think you of that, Reb Perchik?"

Zindell and Avi locked eyes, traded furtive shrugs. The rest stared at Perchik and Rabbi Syme as they exchanged a look of understanding. Perchik had been too good and too bright before, but this moment rang out differently. It was communicated on the rabbi's face.

"I believe you are correct, Rabbi."

Later that week, Rabbi Syme went to visit Gershom.

He twisted his way through the crowded morning streets of the city—from the temple and the schoolhouse, past the town market, past the wigged and kerchiefed women, the beggars and the scholars too engrossed in talk to mind the road. It was a cold winter morning laced with a dense fog, and as he approached Gershom's imposing black door, he felt his throat close up with nerves. He did not know whether his hand shook more from cold or apprehension, but in spite of his trepidation, he knocked. For the boy's sake.

Gershom was startled when he heard the knock at the door. *This is not a working hour,* he thought, for no one ever came to call on him. That was just the way he liked it. Want required refusal, and refusal was his business— the one with which he had made his considerable fortune. Keeping others away was Gershom's pleasure; after all, just look where opening the door to an orphan had gotten him *ten years ago it was now,* he thought as he answered the door.

Gershom's face contorted to make out the form within the thick morning fog.

"Rabbi."

Gershom was suspicious of Rabbi Syme. This far too open-minded young rabbi was a smudge on the coat of his long-dead, far more traditional predecessor. "What an unexpected call." His face contorted further with visible displeasure. The rabbi's breath frosted as he stomped his feet upon the stoop and rubbed his hands together to warm them. "Do come in." Red-cheeked and face aglow, Rabbi Syme did just that.

Gershom pointed to a chair beside a pitiable fire. Afraid of being uninvited, the rabbi removed his coat and placed it on the back of the chair.

"Thank you, Reb Gershom. I am much obliged

for your audience," the rabbi said, settling himself down.

Gershom sat across from the rabbi and merely stared at him, expressionless.

"That is"—he stuttered slightly—"for taking the time to see me. I know you are quite busy. I will not be long."

"What is it I may do for you, Rabbi?" asked Gershom. The last word almost frothed from his colorless lips like a noxious taste.

Rabbi Syme gathered himself. His mind was blurred, as if the fog had followed him in and clouded his mind. Gershom unnerved him. But in the cloud of his anxiety flashed the young boy's face. He heard Perchik's voice and recalled the clarity and brilliance in the boy's eyes during the lesson of Exodus. The boy was remarkable, and Rabbi Syme would not leave until his uncle knew it.

He was once again coherent. Looking straight into the man's eyes, he leaned forward and declared his purpose: "It is about your nephew, Reb Gershom."

Gershom was eerily still.

"He is brilliant, sir, and requires special attention."

Gershom remained impassive.

Rabbi Syme pressed on. "At first, I believed he was unreachable," he said. "His aloofness made it almost impossible for him to communicate with the other boys or indeed with me. I now know better."

Gershom remained unnervingly steady in his gaze. "I don't believe I understand your point," he said tersely, adding almost as an afterthought: *"Rabbi."*

His words hung in the air for a moment.

The rabbi continued, "I believe Perchik needs educational opportunities that are tailored to his unique talents. He has the potential to be a great scholar. Indeed, I believe he could become whatever his imagination is capable of conceiving!" The rabbi could now see how small and quarantined a world the boy was growing up in. *No wonder he is so withdrawn,* he thought. "I wish to open the world for him."

He smiled broadly, laughing nervously as he observed the expression upon Gershom's face.

"His reasoning skills are, frankly, breathtaking. His insights astonishingly far beyond his years." Perhaps Perchik's uncle didn't quite yet understand. "The boy is a *wonder,* Reb Gershom." But there was still no reaction. "Truly . . ."

Rabbi Syme was suddenly aware of the awkward, inhospitable angle of the chair and the sound of Gershom's almost imperceptible breathing as he sat motionless before him.

"Perhaps we could arrange for him to be tutored

privately? Measures such as these can be the best thing that ever happened to a gifted child. If we make room for his progress, just *think* of the extent of his potential! It is truly so exciting. . . ."

But the young rabbi felt the heat leave the already frigid room as his words reached no audience whatsoever. Gershom thawed from his position only to glance severely at the floor.

At last he spoke. "Are you suggesting, Rabbi, that I do not know the best way to care for my own nephew? My community standing, my devotion to God, and my professional merit would suggest I am responsible, would it not?" he asked in earnest.

"Come, then," returned the rabbi brightly. "I meant no offense, Reb Gershom."

"Well, what else am I to be?" returned Gershom, his voice growing in harshness. "What is the boy to *you,* Rabbi? To me, he has proven no such giftedness. He is good for nothing but balancing books—and does not even do that particularly well, I might add." The elderly lender had taken it upon himself to ensnare his nephew in the ways of his profession—an honor Gershom considered so tremendous, he felt he had performed good deeds enough for a lifetime. "He is a boy so lacking in gratitude that I am bewildered. Year after year I find myself older and not a bit more prosperous, no thanks to him. Why should

I extend additional consideration when there is nothing to gain?"

Rabbi Syme was shocked. He had hardly expected a warm welcome, but even this was more frigid than he had anticipated. Did Gershom feel it was his God-given right as surrogate parent to insist that Perchik revere him? Was that why he made such demands of his nephew? Because he perceived the boy as a thankless minion? What had begun to dawn on Rabbi Syme was solidified by Gershom's next words.

"The boy is an afterthought, Rabbi—the product of a harlot's indulgence," said Gershom coldly. "Nothing more. He is leftover bread."

The rabbi stared, thoroughly horrified. "The boy is an afterthought, Reb Gershom? Surely you do not mean that. Surely not."

"I do."

The rabbi despaired for them both. *Lord in heaven,* he thought. *For all the demands placed upon this boy, it truly appears this man despises him.*

"Gifted!" Gershom suddenly scoffed. "What right has he to be gifted? What authority have you to tell me so? You are a younger man than I, Rabbi, and not a parent. I mean no disrespect for your rabbinical status, but beyond that, what sovereignty do you possess to lecture me so?"

"Please, Reb Gershom—" the rabbi pleaded.

"Rabbi," said Gershom, rising from his chair. "Teach in your own way, sir, and let me look after the boy in mine."

"Look after him?" Rabbi Syme said in misery. "It certainly seems to me that you do not look after him at all." He stood slowly from the chair and moved to take his coat. The meeting was over.

Once he had reached the door, Rabbi Syme turned around once more. "Brilliance, sir, is a gift from God," he said. "I have come to know your nephew to be a good boy: a remarkable, bright spark of humanity. It is an honor to teach him. And I know this to be certain: a mind such as his cannot be reined in. Good day."

Rabbi Syme left the house without another word.

Outside, he stalled as the boy came running up the street, arms full of the daily papers and a stockpile of fire kindling. The rabbi paused to bestow a look of compassion upon the boy, who emerged from the throngs of the street and still, cold as he was, greeted Rabbi Syme with a dip of his cap and a smile so full of sorrow and resilience, the rabbi could scarcely bear it. He returned it and dissolved into the mist of the morning.

"Good day, Uncle," said the boy as he entered from the cold.

"Let me hear another sound from you," said

Gershom, "and you shall lose your situation here and back to the orphanage with you."

With that, Gershom turned on his heel and stormed farther into the house, leaving young Perchik alone and mystified in the thickness of the cold and empty room.

One day, after class had been dismissed, the rabbi beckoned Perchik, who gathered his books and made his way to the rabbi's great wooden desk. Rabbi Syme grasped the tzitzit on his prayer shawl thoughtfully before setting his gaze upon his student.

"Perchik, my boy, your thoughts are extraordinarily advanced for a boy of your age," he said gently. "Indeed, your grasp of the trials of Exodus is so exquisite and all comprehending." Perchik's stillness neither refuted nor confirmed this fact, and as the rabbi's heart flooded with emotion, he could barely continue. Once he had gathered himself again, he locked eyes with Perchik. "Tell me, my son: Does your uncle have any idea what you are capable of?"

Perchik stared at the rabbi in shock. No one had ever seen, let alone named, his condition; that of his innate specialness, and of his subjugation to Gershom, like the Jews by the Pharaoh he understood so well. The pain of this condition, matched by the feeling of liberty at being understood, was a sensation no cleverness, not even his, could ever fully comprehend.

"No, sir," he replied, his voice so small, he was unsure he had spoken at all.

The rabbi's eyes glinted. "Perchik, I wanted to share something that you yourself reminded me of: freedom is dynamic. It is an active thing."

Perchik tilted his head, intrigued.

The rabbi continued. "On Shabbat, when we are commanded to rest instead of work, we are experiencing what, on the surface, seems to be the opposite of something else. But just as Shabbat is much more than the absence of toil, so too is the freedom of Exodus more than the absence of bondage."

The boy understood.

"Free a man of the constraints that limit and inhibit his development, and you have a free human being. Freedom is the natural state of man." He looked away from the boy for a moment and recalled his youth, his own search for self. "My boy," he imparted with a ferocious passion that shook them both by the throat, "there is nothing negative about our human potential—do you understand me? God Himself created you the way you are. Do not let anyone in this world convince you otherwise. And you are capable of anything, my boy. There is and shall always be a disparity among the gifts God has granted men, but we all deserve equal consideration. All men, no matter how low, how basic, or how tormented, deserve compassion, dignified brotherhood, and respect.

"But part of respecting all men is respecting ourselves. Recognizing that God has blessed you. By embracing these gifts, we live as God lives, with love for all He has created—with an open heart.

"Thus our sages have said: 'In every generation a person must see himself as if he has himself come out from *Mitzrayim*.' You, of course, know what Mitzrayim, this Hebrew word used for 'Egypt,' *means,* do you not?"

"Boundaries," the boy said quietly.

"It does indeed—and the effort to free ourselves is a perpetual one."

The rabbi removed his spectacles and looked deeply into the eyes of the boy. "I promise you, Perchik: you are a truly blessed child of our Lord. I promise you will find the strength to overcome the oppression of your circumstances. This fight is your purpose—the strength for it inherent within you. Like rocks of salt shaken in water, the turbulence soon asserts itself in perfect order. My boy, you are supported by the greatest parent of them all. As it is He who has endowed you with your gifts, you can be sure that He therefore believes in their power. And for the record, my boy, so do I."

Perchik grew very still. The foreignness of these caring words caused his eyes to sting with tears. He was filled with a gratitude he had never known.

"Do you recall the Father's response to another one of his most gifted sons?"

He did. The boy wept silently into the blackness of his coat and whispered: "I am that I am. . . ."

twenty

"You are inattentive, boy," Gershom said one morning in deepest winter when Perchik had mishandled a ledger.

It was not the first time Perchik had been scolded.

Perchik was now seventeen. He worked for his uncle full-time, having once again acquiesced to his uncle's demands despite every effort of Rabbi Syme. *What is it that ensnares me so?* he thought. *What tempts me to return to this dry well for nourishment again and again?* Perchik exhaled deeply—from a place of anguish. He possessed no language for it, but the promise of something—anything—resembling love and approval from Gershom was the intoxicating flame to Perchik's fixated moth; he was caught, crippled, and trapped for life. He could not help it.

"You think I bring you here to my business day after day to abuse it?"

"No, Uncle," Perchik muttered, his head bowed.

"What was that?" Gershom shouted.

Perchik jerked his head up and looked his uncle in the eye. "No, sir," Perchik said louder.

Ever since Gershom had pulled Perchik from

Rabbi Syme's shul, melancholy had blanketed the boy, as he struggled to survive living in the stark gap between his daily life and his abilities. And so he filled in that space with daydreaming. He invented a world for himself in which he thrived, and cultivated every last detail of it. He drew maps of this illusory place within the quarters of his mind—constructed its inhabitants, filled its streets with innovative buildings, the buildings with encouraging mentors, gifted peers, and a community of innovative thinkers. Perchik lived in this world; the world he expected to find. He thought of it while he copied the accounts into his uncle's large, imposing black book. The place where he could at last become himself.

The time Perchik spent in this imaginary world irritated Gershom to no end. "Have you another occupation to which you would rather see to?" he would demand when he saw his nephew's mind had wandered. "Perhaps you wish I had turned you away from my doorstep all those years ago?"

"No, sir," Perchik would reply, returning to the task at hand.

"Forgive me," Gershom continued. "I had supposed I was doing you a service by saving you from the streets. But perhaps you would rather dwell among unfortunates than among the accounts? It would be straightforward enough, to summon them to take you back. You are certain you do not desire me to do that?" He said it slowly, turning the question over, as if it were a coin that had left dirt upon his palm.

Perchik did not answer. He merely shook his head. He went silently about his business as he had all of his youth: performing the duties of an *arendar* in training.

Perchik's life with Gershom was painful and enclosed, and lived at a sonorous, stagnant pulse, like a toad in winter. His existence throbbed for something—something longed for and lingering beyond the horizon. By day Perchik obediently copied, counted, organized, and shuffled papers back and forth with frightening expertise. But at night, he read and wrote and dreamed. After he had devoured all the holy books on his uncle's shelves, he sought out literature, philosophy, history, engineering, mathematics, and poetry—his mind a sponge with limitless thirst fueled by a kind of formless urgency; an undirected aspiration toward a mythical, unnamed terminus. The tug of the world was too strong, the draw of the horizon too seductive to confine a young man such as he to the grid of this colorless life. It was the university that called to Perchik. It was there that he believed all his longings would be quenched. Great minds would converse in foreign tongues. Ideas would be developed. The truths of the wider world would be revealed. Only there could he truly envision himself as free.

He smothered these longings with work. He anesthetized with more work, but the ache cried out. Perhaps the cry was the voice of Gershom's God, ready to lift him out of the confined enclosure of this melancholy life. Perchik feared he might never know.

Soon, Perchik had all the tools and skills necessary for a life in the business—a life of accounts, ranks, and files, zeros, percentages, and endless numbers. Of stable comfort and unwavering security. But he possessed no knowledge of the wider world. No knowledge of love except what he could glean from his books. What he did possess were darts: tiny missiles of instinctive perception he would occasionally thrust toward Gershom's heart in hopes of achieving a reaction—one that might indicate any kind of feeling. But to his devastation, there was no heart. No feeling. Only numbers. And ideas you were not allowed to contradict, trickling out. He followed Gershom's orders, attended to his needs, laid the groundwork for a lifetime as an office drudge—all in the hopes that one day his uncle might approve of him. It was on this hope that he survived: *when one is starving, crumbs are food*.

"What is it that you write in those ledgers anyway, boy?" Gershom swooped down over his nephew, clasping the account book that sat upon his desk. The old man twisted his neck and peered into it, holding the pages close. Perchik noticed a strange expression on his uncle's face as he gazed deeply into his ledger.

Perchik's notes were scattered upon the pages—his scribbles covered the paper as if there had been an explosion of thoughts. Little drawings and sketches, flecks of collected musings—he tried his hand at poetry, physics, and mathematics the way children play with toys. Gershom stood above him, looking.

"Perchik, how many terms of abstract mathematics have you taken?"

"One term, sir."

"In whose hand is this calculation?"

"My own, sir."

Gershom's eyes flicked wildly. Perchik did not know that what his uncle stared at was a rough version of a partial differential equation.

"You copied it from a textbook, of course."

"No, sir."

"In heaven's name. Who showed you how to do this?"

"No one, Uncle," Perchik replied. "That is merely something I was in the middle of figuring out."

Gershom straightened and pursed his mouth. He studied the boy hard, eyes piercing behind his spectacles, seething in both awe and envy.

"How old are you now, boy?" he inquired, his tone suddenly slightly less harsh than normal.

Perchik was surprised at this sudden change and hesitated.

"Don't get smart with me!" Gershom said, resuming his normal tenor. "Answer me! What age are you? Sixteen? Seventeen? You think me impervious to the passage of years, because I am a man of numbers?"

"I am seventeen, Uncle."

"Seventeen. A nettlesome age, if your wretched mother is anything to judge by."

"Yes, sir."

"Nettlesome is right, boy."

"Perhaps, Uncle," Perchik began tentatively, "perhaps I might trouble your patience a bit more, for I wish to discuss with you, once again, a desire to seek further education."

"What is that, boy?" Gershom replied. "Your business is not with dreams, but with accounts."

"I understand, Uncle, but at university they could harness these very skills to your benefit! If I have taught myself this much without tutors, just think how much your enterprise could benefit with the guidance of a university education."

"Am I to understand you wish to deny yourself the opportunity to work in one of the most prominent businesses in our community?"

"N-no, Uncle," he stammered. "Not at all. I simply wish to learn more to benefit your business, to gain new insights that will increase your capital, securing your future. Perhaps even my own."

"Enough," Gershom snapped.

The boy had a point. Sensing an economic opportunity, Gershom removed his spectacles and sat down at his great desk to contemplate this proposition. After many silent moments, he spoke.

"Perchik, if I allow you to go to university, I shall do so as a future investment in my business, not in your individual future. Do you understand?"

Perchik nearly wept with happiness—he could scarcely believe it. He choked to control his voice in his state of elation. "I do, Uncle, I do."

"The finances of this education are to be paid off in the form of work here, yes?"

"Yes, Uncle, yes."

"A university education might indeed discipline you," Gershom continued. *Well, at least this way I can be rid of the boy,* he thought to himself, and punctuated this thought with a stab of his pen. "You will be indebted to me, Perchik. Indebted further. Is this indeed very clear to you?"

"It is, Uncle." Perchik rose from his chair, not knowing what to do with his body, warm with gladness. "I will not let you down."

"So, boy, so. The Kogan account. Recite to me from the second quarter, with the calculations complete; and heed—the income is irregular. I'll note the sequence here."

Perchik sat back down and smiled. For the first time in his life, there was nothing of substance to account for, and nothing more to wish.

twenty-one

The katorga system was not created as a form of punishment—not solely anyway. Economic crisis had rankled for centuries. Underpopulation in Siberia resulted in a failure to exploit the nation's natural resources. But a government directive initiated in 1754 ordered convicted criminals into the underdeveloped region in hopes that Russia's exiles would solve that problem. It was considered a spectacular success. No wonder it was so readily adopted by governmental successors. By 1906, there were over six thousand convicts serving sentences in Siberia.

But there were also forced settlers. These people were citizens plucked from their poverty in the West and relocated East with their wives, children, and sometimes extended families. These people were another kind of prisoner altogether—though not convicts laboring in chains, they were sentenced to exile nonetheless.

It was around the same time, in the early years of the 20th century, that the prison reforms spreading through Europe (in the previous century) were finally catching on in Russia. The daily abuses inflicted upon the mine workers remained inarguably brutal, but overall the katorga system was shedding some of its previous harshness as both regimes and policing relaxed.

Katorga consisted of two convict categories as defined by the 1845 penal code: a convict became a *probationer* when he first entered the camp. Probationers resided in the barracks while their families occupied separate domiciles nearby. But after a certain number of years, if probationers were well-behaved, they graduated to become *correctionals*. Correctionals could marry, fraternize, enjoy the occasional reprieve, and were eligible to have every ten months served count as a full year toward their sentences. Most continued to work the mines in Nerchinsk, though a small number served as domestic servants in officials' homes. Crucially, correctionals were permitted to live outside the prison barracks, allowed to lodge in the adjacent village with their families in the homes of settlers. The convict paid for bed and board, as well as for a soldier charged with the duty of policing them, but it was a small price to pay for this luxuriant freedom.

Four months after Hodel and Perchik's reunion in Nerchinsk, Perchik had been a probationer for a year and eight months and was up for reassessment. Perchik could not believe the mastery that he had come to gain over himself with the guards and officers, and due to a compliant interview (and what Perchik deemed to be a soft spot in The Gentleman's regard for his wife), Perchik and Hodel were afforded the liberty to live together out of the barracks—a benefit far greater than any improvement on their penal labors.

They thus moved into the home of Vladimir Volosnikov (a local, the unremarkable aging son of a forced settler) and his wife. They dwelt there with two other coupled felons in a large room divided by a screen adjacent to the main house. They hardly ever saw or interacted with the Volosnikovs, or indeed their fellow prisoners, making the Volosnikov home a very pleasant and indescribably welcome reprieve. Perchik and Hodel were able to leave the ordinary dwelling of the felons far behind them.

To think of all the emptiness that had been their lot ever since his sentence began, and to have it replaced by a shared daily existence—a center of peace and warmth and hospitality, not merely a place to sleep—was beyond articulation. There were days when he could not believe she was there beside him as he slept: to hold, to have as a marker of profound sanity and virtue.

Perchik stood at the river washing in the sun, the cold water brilliantly soothing upon the sun-scorched heat of his skin. It was Anatevka in 1905. His shirt clung to his body in long, damp patches down his back. He looked about to make certain no women were nearby and, sensing none, removed it and dunked it again and again into the cold water before wringing it out and placing the cool, damp shirt back upon his torso.

As he adjusted the collar and sleeves, Perchik thought of the days that had passed and were still passing him by. He thought of Gershom and the business, the accounts he could be tending to, the money that could afford him far more than this singular shirt he had been wearing for months. Money that could keep him safe, in a comfortable life; a life so numb he would likely not have the cognizance to enjoy it.

Besides, a part of him adored the splendor of *lack*. There was a glory to this state that thrilled him; the starving rumble of his guts reminded him of all the starving people he fought for, and his heart would surge with satisfaction, making him evermore poverty-proud. If only he could survive solely on that feeling. It gave him a keen, curious pleasure to wrestle with his need.

Then what of his ideals and all the work they required of him? *What of that?* he thought as he stared across the muddy riverbeds and morning landscape. The articles he could be writing and publishing, the speeches he could have been making in the cities, the fine people he could be educating; he thought of all the important things he, perhaps, should have been doing. Things, most likely, he would never be doing again.

He observed a pain rising in his sternum. Was

this his unused potential raging within him? He regarded it with a detached curiosity. *Here it is again,* he thought, wanting to see how long it would last this time. He observed his fight with it, like David and Goliath, the smallness of Perchik against the monster that was his guilt.

When this feeling manifested, he felt as he did in his uncle's office: that he had to think through a series of equations to find a complex solution, that he had to appease and compromise, all to drive a mental wedge between his highest self and the ache within.

But here in Anatevka such moments were rare. He liked it here. Tevye the dairyman and his family had made it feel like a kind of home—more welcoming than any home he had known before. They did not have much, but they had enough: faith, hearty food, their home, and one another. He thought of the first night he had arrived, how they had welcomed him, a perfect stranger from the road, into their home for the Sabbath. He thought of the humility of their Sabbath table, but the pride this family took in appreciating what they did have. He thought of Hodel's first witty retorts, and her eyes, which blazed with intellect.

All at once, she appeared.

Downriver, she emptied the large metal containers that her father used for collecting and distributing the milk. Perchik stopped. She had not seen him. He tucked himself behind the branches of a nearby tree and stood watching her. She submerged the containers into the river one by one, rinsing and scrubbing them clean before placing them back upon the shore. The work seemed arduous—a job for a strong and capable woman, and Hodel threw herself into the work thoroughly, not a scrap of energy withheld. She engaged in this simple task with all of herself. It thrilled him.

He waited. He watched. *Look up, look up,* he repeated silently. *Look up.* He willed her eyes toward him like an incantation. This longing filled him; it had been filling him for a while now, drop by drop. He was the vessel catching Hodel's strong wine; he threatened to overflow.

At last she raised her head and regarded him, as if she had felt him, heard him call to her. Her face told him that she expected him to be there, that she knew he had been staring all along. She did not turn away.

Perchik stood motionless, unable to grasp his faculties in her presence. *What is it about her?* he thought to himself, both enraged and intoxicated. Hodel's expression did not change, though her eyes flashed like lightning as if to say she understood fully the meaning of his gaze, that she challenged him to be the first to look away, to move toward her, to run in terror; her expression told him she would continue to challenge him to the end of days.

In the fire of her scrutiny, Perchik looked away. Defeated. Delighted. She smiled in victory, gathered her milk pails, and walked back toward the house. *Look back, look back, look back,* he thought. But she had won that round and would not look again.

The day Perchik first danced with Hodel, he bore witness to an act of profound virtue that altered him. In a flurry of feeling he moved away from her in the yard, only to be interrupted by a family announcement minutes later. Tevye left the house, called Tzeitel—his beloved eldest daughter—out from the barn, and announced to her that Lazar Wolf, the wealthy butcher, had asked for her hand in marriage. Perchik's insides churned; Lazar was a widower at least thirty years Tzeitel's senior whose only virtue (as far as Perchik could tell) was his tremendous wealth. Lazar had a large, lavish house, a servant, and a thriving business along the high street, but he was also crude and uneducated.

Golde was thrilled; she clucked and cooed like a mother hen.

"Fortune and honor be upon you, my Tzeitel," she said, kissing and kissing her. Golde took no notice of Tzeitel's despair, for her firstborn daughter, the pride and joy of their family, was going to be a bride and build a new family of her own, in luxury no less. But in the wake of their mother's departure, Tzeitel's horrified face begged her sisters for help.

"Mazel tov, Tzeitel," Chava and Hodel muttered in disbelief, unsure of what else could possibly be uttered.

"Please," he heard Tzeitel whisper desperately as her sisters backed away, "don't leave me here." But they left her nevertheless, not knowing what else to do; left her alone to beg their father for her happiness, left her to the safety of their house and perhaps to the fading remains of the childhood it represented.

Marriages arranged by a matchmaker were still common in these isolated shtetl towns. After all, young people had to get married; it was commanded by Genesis to "be fruitful and multiply." And so matchmaking was an art as ancient as marriage itself. Perchik had learned this in shul. The first biblical matchmaker was likely to be Eliezer, sent by Abraham to find a wife for his son Isaac. Eliezer returned with Rebecca, and they gave birth to the Jews (*Blessed be to them,* Perchik recited in his head instinctually).

But a great deal had altered since the days of Eliezer, at least in Perchik's estimation—young people still wanted to form couples, and parents still wanted the best for their children, but the matchmaker worked for the parents more than for the future bride or groom, and though this community might find that very ordinary indeed, Perchik knew that the world around them was changing. Besides, it was no secret that Tzeitel had far greater troubles than an arranged marriage to the wealthy, aged butcher. Tzeitel was very much in love.

However much they tried to hide it, however guarded they had become about their promise to each other, the tailor Motel Kamzoil adored Tevye's eldest daughter, and Tzeitel loved him in return. But Tzeitel was nearly nineteen, approaching the age for being married off, and time was running out. Motel would have done anything to win her hand in the customary manner, but he was poor, had no prospects. Thus they were left with only their secret pledge and a fervent prayer that God would bless them with the gift of each other.

The book of Numbers stated, "When a man makes a vow to the Lord or takes an oath to obligate himself by a pledge, he must not break his word but must do everything he said." Perchik knew the passage well.

How could their families disapprove of a thing so sweet, not to mention sanctioned by God? Tevye and Golde treated Motel Kamzoil almost as their own son—he and his widowed mother, Shaindel, found in them a very warm and welcoming home. If their parents only knew of the depth of their feelings, how could they feel anything but gladness?

Perchik picked up his rucksack and stormed out of the yard, disgusted. Forced parental will combined with the priority of money? It all reeked of Gershom. He was disappointed in his new friend Tevye and stalked down the road toward town.

Suddenly, belting past him up the path came Motel Kamzoil. He was running at a frightening speed, lungs screeching, without time to even acknowledge Perchik as he passed, and at this, Perchik turned on his heel and followed him back to the yard.

Every so often, miracles happen here on earth— miracles that are not at all of God's making. These are the glories belonging to mankind itself. They incubate within, like a long-dormant seed, gestating in the innermost recesses of a soul. A man must marshal every scrap of courage for the sake of this burgeoning phenomenon, and he must do so in the face of absolute, darkened uncertainty. But if one can confront the waiting and the fear, one will have earned the greatest human reward achievable in this life. The time will come to flourish. One must stretch one's confines until the miracle expands, emerging at last in a great flash of light, so that all that was once dull and gray is now colorful. On this day, that miracle happened.

"Reb Tevye, I might be poor, I might be nothing, but I am devoted to Tzeitel, and even the poor have a right to happiness."

He had said too much—but it was that or say nothing. Motel Kamzoil did more than stand up to the only authority who truly could permit or prevent his life's happiness. He had become a man before their eyes. It was far greater a thing than self-actualization (which is no small thing). Motel grew that day—not so much for himself, but in order to deserve her. He earned Tzeitel. He burst through his threshold, fought for her, and won. It was the greatest act of heroism Perchik had ever seen.

It was not until that moment that Perchik realized he wanted Hodel in a way he had never wanted anything before. He too would have to earn and fight for Hodel. But as quickly as he realized it, he despaired, for he knew he did not deserve her.

It was good that Perchik had felt that way so long ago, as here in Nerchinsk their marriage was truly tested. But they had made a home for themselves as best they could, adorned with that most priceless of décor: love.

"This is lovely, my darling," Perchik said as he observed a table thrown together from sheets over a crate, with a centerpiece of found branches at its heart. Perchik admired the lovingly arranged decorations, the carefully prepared teas, and best of all, the welcoming of neighbors into their ramshackle home and the offering of what hospitalities they had to share.

"Tzeitel always said, 'A lovely tablecloth and a handsome centerpiece go such a long way.' I will never forget that. She said it before scolding me for some form of household negligence or another." She shook her head at the recollection, laughed, and kissed him.

Their large room attached to the Volosnikovs' house was filled with the loving gestures that transform a run-down dwelling into a home.

There was a knock upon the door.

"Perchik?" called the voice of Dmitri Petrov. "I have brought the papers."

Dmitri Petrov was over often—one could quite easily assume he lived there himself, an extension of their happy home. He would come and join them after hours for tea, discussions, and, most likely, for the company of thinkers, though more than anything he was there to escape Yevgeny.

In their company, one could see the rare sight of Dmitri Petrov at ease: the quiet smile, the occasional chortle of laughter, and even, after perhaps one sip of vodka too many, the odd murmur of singing that so surprised them all.

"Come in, come in!" Perchik opened the side door that the prisoners used.

"Good evening, Perchik," Dmitri said as he entered. "Hodel," he added, nodding in the general direction of her kerchiefed head. He turned back to Perchik and handed him the papers. "There is news from the city."

"Excellent!" Perchik took up the papers and shut the door fast. "This is excellent." He wrapped his arm around his wife as he showed her the papers. "There is news from the city," he said to her.

"I heard him," she droned, then kissed the soft skin peeling beside his eye and brushed the flakes away as best she could. She looked over to their guest. "Come, Dmitri, let me look at you." Still cloaked in his work attire, Dmitri edged closer to her but stayed at a distance. "You look pale and have far too many worries on your face."

"I have not been sleeping," he replied. "It is that damn Yevgeny. He snores like a wolfhound!" Perchik and Hodel laughed, and even Dmitri cracked a smile; the couple made him feel so infectiously pleasant.

"Make yourself at home," said Perchik. Dmitri stood still a moment before removing his coat and hat. Perchik smiled at this, his hand grazing Hodel's waist as he made his way to a tattered chair, his other hand clutching the papers, and Hodel adjusted the thick woolen headscarf that had come loose at the base of her neck.

The makeshift teapot, which had been fashioned from a tin cup, started to rattle.

"Tea's ready!" she announced, and she neatly poured tea into two cups and hot water into a third, for she never did care for tea. She placed the cups on a tray that had been pilfered from the dining hall and brought the tray over to the sheet-covered crate that served as their kitchen table. "Bread!" She jolted, remembering, and as she stood, the scarf containing her hair came unfastened.

Soft, wavy tresses poured out in rippling lines—they cascaded from her head, spilling an ocean of color so deep a brown, one became lost in its infinity. It begged for one's eyes to close.

"Oops!" she cried, gathering the locks together.

Dmitri carefully lifted the scarf from the floor and extended it to Hodel, adjusting his glasses as he stood.

"You dropped this," he said.

"Oh, thank you." She smiled at Dmitri, her throat letting out a little laugh. "Nothing can hold in these locks!"

She twisted her hair into a ropelike knot at the base of her neck, and then, with a single graceful gesture, she breezily placed the scarf atop the coif to secure it all in tidy bundle. Then, careful not to spill his tea, she sat firmly down upon her husband's lap.

twenty-two

Perchik woke with a jolt from his slumber.
Sitting upright, he looked about, taking in the strange-smelling bed. Where was he? Ah, yes. University. His head was thick and pounding—each thud of his heart a thunderous hammer's blow at the base of his brain. He sank, folded over, skin sweating out the stink of yesterday's liquor. His hands gripped the sides of his skull. *Stop the beating*, his thoughts wailed.

It was then he noticed a woman asleep beside him. The dark-haired stranger was breathing hard, yellow teeth bared in her gaping mouth, brown scum lining the crevices of her oily fingers. The stench of her was palpable in his throat. He shuddered. Took in the sight of her. He groaned. *No one is appealing the morning after,* he thought. *This nauseating creature is no exception.* He covered his face in almost comedic shame. *What an idiot.* Had he met her in the tavern? Had he paid for her in town? He remembered nothing. Only whirling flashes: color. Music. The first fetid bite of her mouth on his. *God, women all looked and spoke and smelled alike. . . .*

He was nineteen years old. This was a an average morning.

He stared across his dismal little room—gloomy and airless, with the blazing premature light of late spring strewn as haphazardly across the space, detritus visible on every possible surface. Unlaundered clothing, piles of untouched lesson books, scraps of uneaten food in various stages of spoilage, countless bottles, soiled linens, and in the farthest corner, stacks and stacks of aging, unopened letters from a certain Rabbi Syme.

Though Perchik had been pulled from Rabbi Syme's tutelage long ago, he had remained a strong presence in the young man's life through their correspondence. But Perchik could no longer stand being believed in—belief was heavy; it was burning sunlight in his eyes. There was a time when Perchik had been grateful for the rabbi's consistent, deep investment in him. That time was over. They had long since lost touch. Perchik could no longer bear it.

University was not the dreamworld he had imagined. The crash of this fantasy—one he had created from a primitive place of survival—destroyed him. He felt at times as if it were a death fight between his ideals and the truth of the world. The people here were no less disappointing, no less competitive, duplicitous, judgmental, or small-minded. It was only their vocabularies and the landscape that differed. Someone always had to be better than another. Someone always had to have more. It seemed to Perchik that those who were least deserving of accolades were always the ones fighting for and receiving them. It made him sick. Coming from an upbringing where everything had been counted, he longed for a world in which acquisitions bore no weight. He knew now that such a world did not exist. The world belonged to his uncle and every man like him.

He was now committed to stupefying himself into oblivion. What else mattered? What was the point of modesty? It was absurd. Offensive. *The world is sad,* he thought to himself, glancing once more at the awful stranger beside him in the bed. He pressed the palms of his hands against his eyes and held his breath, allowing the pressure to build behind them for a moment before he released a full exhalation.

Perchik was not worse than other men. It was true that he drank himself stupid and sometimes paid for access to the bodies of women—all done with the funds of his uncle's patronage. Yes, these actions would most definitely incur the wrath of his uncle and their conservative community. *But so what? So what?* he thought. He preferred it. Offense was neither here nor there. Perchik knew that what disgusted Gershom most about his nephew was what disgusted him about all brilliant men: the innate knowledge of their brilliance—endemic to brilliance itself. *Fuck brilliance,* Perchik thought, clutching his head harder still. This so-called gift had kept Perchik from everything he had ever desired in his life.

He winced. The woman shifted beneath the fetid sheets. He clutched his face and groaned again.

An idiot. That is certain.

twenty-three

Perchik gazed upon his wife from across the room.

Hodel's assignments often varied according to the wants of the camp. She would attend the hospital ward one day and work the kitchens the next, as many of the wives did. She would cook in vast quantities, clean endlessly. She swept, organized rations, and attempted to maintain as reasonable a level of sanitation as possible, often to no avail.

But just now Perchik caught a flash of the girl he had first encountered. He smiled to himself. How they had kept their guards up! Never had Perchik felt so strongly for a woman, and it had frightened him. He had never met a living soul like her.

So many men had encountered Tevye's second-eldest and been intimidated by her passions, by the strength of her will and shrewdness of her mind. She clearly expected him to be the same. Hodel was proud and vain, often contrary; but despite her limited knowledge of the world, there burned a flame within her, a kind of universal wisdom. He was captivated. In her presence he felt free to not simply recant and debate the academics of his ideals, but to open up his heart and release his overwhelming passion for them. He had been a teacher to her little sisters, but truly he learned from *her*. Perchik had known women, oh yes, but here was another kind of creature altogether. She would ask illuminating questions, challenge him with a fire that would ignite him. It was intoxicating. It was real.

Once he felt what it meant to love as he loved Hodel, he was incapable of anything else. Oh, the milkman's stubborn daughter had caught this radical student so. Hodel made him feel, even at the height of their arguments, almost indescribably *understood*. When Hodel threw her eyes upon the world, she saw what he saw, and he, in turn, shared her visions too. It was not political. It was human.

Their intimacy felt familiar from the very first moment. They would wake in each other's arms and, despite their bleak surroundings, they were happy and warm. They spoke of a future filled with fairness, prosperity, and fruit trees. They touched each other's hands, enfolded in each other's company. They would pore over the newspapers and wonder what their friends were doing now. *We shall change the world,* they vowed, *and we shall do it together*. There were no games, no proud veneers, no wonderings or hesitations. They were clear.

His love for her was a reverence, not a worship. It was a joy received from her very existence.

"You taste sweet," he whispered that night as he came up for air after making love to her. They were buried beneath a collection of woolen blankets in the dead of the night, silver moonlight reflecting off the thawing river and falling through the threadbare curtains.

He didn't cling to, clutch, or embrace her; he held her. Her long, radiant hair—returned now from its shorn days—surrounded them in a perfumed blanket. He caught its fragrance and was breathless.

"You smell sweet, too," he said.

"I don't believe we have eaten anything sweet in years," she said.

"I have." He grinned, burying himself in her again.

They were in this, together, for a long time to come.

twenty-four

In the course of his daily inspection, The Gentleman would occasionally make an appearance at the mouth of each mine. With a silent satisfaction he would watch Perchik and his fellow miners hard at work, then clasp his hands behind his back, nod, and smile. Today, he adjusted a dilapidated sign that read work or die in several languages before nodding to the overseer as he departed, indicating that the men may now rest.

Perchik seated himself upon a heap of barren rubble outside the mine alongside Anatoly. Anatoly spoke the least of all their company but was good-humored on the whole. As they caught their breath and cleaned their faces, Perchik observed that Anatoly was well made, a jolly giant quite splendid to see. He would hold the suggestion of what had once been a soft belly contemplatively as he drank from his flask after supper. Or indeed, after breakfast. Or as he listened to Perchik read aloud in the evenings, or as he chuckled at the continued antics of Yevgeny and Dmitri Petrov.

He and Perchik sat, wrapped thickly in regulation overcoats, their faces ruddy from exertion and cold, *ushanka* hats secured atop their heads in a way that made Anatoly's hair wisp out at the sides and shake indiscernibly in the breeze.

"You drink, friend?" Anatoly asked, sipping his flask.

"I don't." Perchik replied.

"Not even for inspiration? For your great speeches and that?"

"No."

"For making merry?"

"No." Perchik smiled broadly. "Not for a long while. Not anymore."

It was the light that made the People's Tavern unique. It was 1902 and Perchik was lecturing at the tavern. It was not the sticky wooden floors or the faded pillars supporting the sunken structure. Not the sounds of carousing academic arguments and soft murmurs of local women, nor the music of a makeshift Jewish band (complete with accordion). It was not the hot moisture of clean tankards, nor even the specific musk of collegiate desire. It was the light. The flickering haunt of the oil lamps along the sturdy walls illuminated the faces of the bar's inhabitants with a buttery glow. One was never certain whether it was the atmosphere or the liquor that intoxicated the guests.

"Hark, fellow drunkards of Kievan depravity!" Perchik shouted. He was drunk. "You students of perpetual indolence! Listen to my words from the fog of your oblivion!" he bellowed from atop a table in the center of the bar. This was the scene every Saturday evening at the People's Tavern, after the rush of academia had been dispelled for the week.

Perchik's disillusionment had taken hold and begun to rot. Here, where he had expected other great minds to reside and thrive, cheats hovered like a murder of crows. Here was snobbery and counterfeit—boredom, *just about*s and *good enough*s. *Perhaps the university is too small,* he thought. *Perhaps the world itself will be the answer.*

But no. When he roamed into the city, things were worse. He was in the constant company of those who lacked culture both morally and intellectually. He was more disgusted than ever before, for the reality of the world was yet another in a long line of disappointments. He turned away to take another swig from a tall glass.

He was twenty-one years old. The young boy had blossomed into manhood. Education had given him new weapons. This was their release—a weekly speech at the People's Tavern. He paused. Dozens of eyes were fixed upon him, expectant. He licked his lips and spoke again, his voice swollen with combativeness.

"Now that we are all so educated," he said,

addressing the crowd, "we should probably acquire some kind of knowledge of ideals." He sang the words through a glittering smile, and the room shone brighter. He lifted his arms high and the people cheered, lifting their drink-adorned hands along with him as if on cue. The crowds at the People's Tavern knew Perchik to be a charismatic speaker; they expected nothing less than entertainment and always hoped for inspiration. It had become a weekly custom. But something was off tonight, and the crowd could sense it. Perchik's well-established radiance had been tarnished by something foul from deep within.

"Let's speak of social responsibilities." He leaned toward the crowd and they responded in kind. "I think all those fortunes we have been promised are in fact for the benefit of the poor, the underprivileged, or indeed, the unloved."

Perchik no longer attended classes. He skipped lectures, declined the study groups and lab-oratories—yet he effortlessly passed the final exams. The boredom annihilated him. His only pleasures now lay in the lairs of Kiev's dark underbelly, the campus Bundists, and the Socialist society—they shared his burning sense of injustice.

"But what is it all *for*, ladies and gentlemen? What are we here to do about the corruption of the tsars, the viceroys, the employers, and the priests? The rich, the desperate, the searching, the corruption of every authority in the universe?" The crowd roared with a bellowing recognition. "What are we to do but endure?" He took a moment to command their attention, communing with everybody in the building.

"We must never surrender our ideals to the limitations others have placed upon life. Suffering is necessary, and those who don't know how to suffer shall not endure our political shift from the crushing oppression of imperialism to the sweet release of Socialist freedom! Those who cannot suffer shall not endure any hardship. People who face obstacles and overcome them are those people whose dreams come true.

"God . . ." Perchik paused, and at his silence, the crowd shifted. "Our heavenly Father. Such glorious promises. Such unimaginable gifts." A hysterical intensity grew in his voice. "A wise old friend once told me that there is a disparity among the gifts God has granted men, but that all men, no matter how low, basic, or tormented, deserve dignity, brotherhood, and respect. . . ." Perchik pressed his thumb into the side of his leg, thoughtfully. "Today I learned that my wise friend died." He looked at the floor and tried to control his voice. "His name was Rabbi David Syme. He was my teacher and my friend. I should have been better to him. He saw the very best in people; he had hope; he had vision. I should have written back." Perchik smiled sorrowfully, not realizing that he smiled at his own agony. "But God really is the most meticulous of all the deities; no wonder we all bow down to him." Quite suddenly, his voice turned black. The air was thick and hot, and the room was stunned with pity. "His command of suffering is so elegant, no? Really, now. What man could pit himself against so skin-boiling a Lord and come out intact? No human, I swear it! 'But of the tree of the knowledge of good and evil, thou shalt not eat of it: for in the day that thou eatest thereof thou shalt surely die.' " He screwed up his eyes and kept them fixed to the floor. "We are already dead, Father. Didn't you know? You killed us long ago. We men who have devoted our lives to you, who have bled and cried and compromised the deepest longings in our hearts, who have fought holy wars in your name! *There is no quarreling with genius like yours!*" Perchik got down on his knees—a monk in the temple of the tavern.

But even while he spoke, the memory reverberated in his head: *I am that I am. I am that I am. I am that I am.*

Stillness had fallen over the room. Faces fell. Hot and stinging tears fell from Perchik's eyes, and he brushed them away. He tried to master control of his voice as he continued, "There are times when the only reasonable thing we can do is bear out our troubles until a better day. Believe me: the vision of our destiny does not reside with the doom prophets. There shall be times when we feel defeated. There will be days when all one can see is the gap between the ideal and the reality. But that is something we shall face." Alone, Perchik swayed there. This was not a pulpit. "We must . . ." This was just a sticky table of a tin-pot tavern. "One has to laugh. I know I do. I believe I have a right to laughter—and, oh, how laughter heals me."

I am that I am.
I am that I am.
The phrase rang in his head like an incantatory curse and he froze.

Each face within the crowd, each glassy-eyed, sweltering face, stared at him. People squirmed. They glanced tentatively at the ground. At one another. Some started to move away, until most had crawled out of the tavern altogether.

There was one man who did not move. One man whose eyes did not blink or shift in their sockets. The anchored presence. The malevolent scrutiny. Perchik locked eyes with this person in the crowd. Even through Perchik's drunken, tear-drenched gaze, the person was unmistakable.

Staring up at him from the crowd was a still and seething Gershom.

In Nerchinsk, Anatoly was tucking the rest of the flask away. "Never in my life have I met a Russian who didn't drink," he said.

"Oh, I did." Perchik chuckled. "But no longer."

"I drink all day." Anatoly laughed his easy laugh and offered Perchik the flask. Perchik opened it, downed a dram, and sighed as Anatoly spoke again.

"Russia is cold," Anatoly said with an almost comedic look that swiftly turned very grave.

Perchik looked out across the flatland beyond the river. "Yes."

Before long, the men were sitting in a silent reverie together. No one was better at peaceful silence than Anatoly. It occurred to Perchik that he did not know how long his friend had resided in Nerchinsk.

"Have you been long in these works?" he asked.

"Five years and three months," Anatoly responded, quietly removing his ushanka hat. He rested his head upon a hand burrowed deep into the nest of his hair, as if the hand controlled the unruly thoughts within the brain contained there, before reaching for the flask again. Perchik did not need to ask the reason. It was easy to forget in day-to-day dealings that the prisoners of Nerchinsk were, more often than not, violent criminals. Eventually, Perchik became blind to the crimes of his closest friends. At a certain point the crimes no longer defined them—the person would emerge from below, as with a foreign accent that eventually melts into the wholeness of who the person is.

Perchik nodded. "And for how long are you sentenced?"

"For life."

This was the way it was.

Soon after, they went to work again and did not stop until nightfall, without another word about it.

twenty-five

Perchik had polished the table himself.

The massive slab of marble, black as ink with flecks of the deepest green, reflected not only the prosperity of its owner but also the grave, important faces of a dozen Kievan businessmen gathered in the colossal main room of Reb Gershom's counting house, a simmering expectancy in the air.

His attention to the details of this moment was meticulous: the cups were set in order, the water drawn and poured into a lacquered jug. He had arranged the hulking dark wood chairs, dusted the mantels, and laid out the documents in an orderly alignment.

The moment had arrived. It had been months in the making, and nearly a year since he had been removed from the university.

The community of businessmen highly approved of the scheme. Kiev was growing, and a merger of the five most prominent Kievan accountancy practices would make the resulting company the strongest in the region, rendering the heads wealthy beyond imagination, and possibly earning Perchik the respect and freedom he had desired for a lifetime.

Each businessman voiced his pleasure at this

arrangement throughout the village. There were even such times when the more exuberant among them would clamor to shake Perchik's hand in the high street. "Here he is—the young mastermind!" And Perchik was cheered.

Throughout this process, Gershom would disclose nothing of his feelings toward the boy's inarguably grand idea and went about displaying every agreeable behavior he could possibly muster.

Perchik's thoughts were primarily distracted by the endless filing, menial fire-stoking, and other such overwhelming petty tasks Gershom continued to have him perform.

But now was the moment: the vision of a new future lay clear before him, flourishing with possibility like the sails of the ships along the Dnieper River. He stood motionless behind the closed door, and only the furrow forged by his thumb along the spine of his ledger gave away his unsteady anticipation.

He anchored himself, like the ships in the harbor, shook his head to clear it, opened the door, and stepped before the city's most important men—toward his new life, his acceptance, his freedom.

"Gentlemen, we all know why we are gathered here. . . ." He felt his voice ring out.

For years, Perchik's conscience had flickered like a faulty flint, his debaucheries conveying his raging, passionate uselessness. Racked with guilt, and moved by this both literal and spiritual confrontation, Perchik was eager to impress and prove himself to his uncle. Using everything he possessed and everything he had acquired, Perchik set about to become the best possible assistant his uncle could hope for.

But Gershom never forgot Perchik's indiscretions. Despite the temperance of their outward relationship in the wake of his removal from the university, Gershom had been waiting for the boy to slip up. Perchik's shame-drenched return to the business was just the act of pathetic knee-crawling Gershom craved after a lifetime lost on child-rearing.

Perchik's current state delighted Gershom. What good were those "remarkable gifts" now? What good was genius to a common bondsman? Gershom was owed far more than gratitude; he had earned Perchik's eternal subjugation. *Truly,* he thought to himself as he ordered the boy about, *there is nothing better in this life than finally being repaid.*

"We shall start the signatures with you, Reb Haskel, seeing as you are the bank owner," Gershom said, and the papers, ink, and pen were passed to Reb Haskel.

From there, the signatures were collected quietly, the scratching of the pens accompanied by skylarks singing high above them, and the light from the feeble windows strewed the great marble table with dark shadows of clouds and trees.

Next was Reb Gavrel, owner of a smaller accountancy firm. "You must be so proud, Reb Gershom," he said. "It is a great thing indeed to have so bright and diligent a young man by your side."

Perchik beamed.

Gershom scoffed.

Reb Elzik, the money lender, said, "Clearly everything he has done he has done for us all—this scheme shall secure our futures into infinity. The businesses we have all spent our lifetimes maintaining and building shall merge and thrive!"

Yes, thought Perchik, *and that not-so-selfless nephew will at last be able to return to the university, complete his studies, and then escape this life without the worry of Gershom's financial well-being and future. When this merger is complete, I can finally be free.*

Next Gershom nodded to the bookkeeper. "And you, Reb Isser?" The man signed.

Perchik's heart swelled. This was his chance to make his uncle see he was not a waste, he was not a threat, and he was not useless. Everything Perchik had struggled with—all he had worked so hard to overcome—the greatness Rabbi Syme had seen and fought for would be revealed today.

Gershom's approval—which was only Gershom's approval and not another's—had the power to massacre all else.

At long last, the papers fell in front of Perchik, who passed them proudly to his uncle. Gershom slowly picked up the pen. He held it in his hand for a charged moment. He could, in his mind, see himself writing out the signature as he had done a million commonplace times. A signature was a mundane thing. A scribble, a scrawl, a dash upon the parchment. Perchik's heart raced as he looked at Gershom with heated anticipation. Gershom gripped the pen hard, then, with a deliberate and heavy motion, he placed it down atop the papers. Perchik somehow had already known it.

"Uncle?"

Gershom's brow rose, and his eyes, black with hate, looked upward to the anxious and proud young man who stood above him. The eyes themselves were blacker than the ink of the still-wet signatures, blacker than death and flecked with an unmistakable green, identical, in fact, to the marble that lay below Gershom's trembling hands, reflecting the faces of half a dozen dumbfounded men.

There was no time for dread.

"What have you done?" asked Gershom.

"Uncle, I—"

"Stop. No. How could you, boy? How could you?"

The men around the table shifted uncomfortably in their seats.

"I do not want this. I never did," Gershom said in anguish. "This business is the culmination of all I am. It is my life, my legacy. And now you auction it off like scraps of fallow land to the highest bidders? You break the spine of my life's work as if it were my own spine. You cannot sell my life, boy; you cannot erase me."

The realization of what he'd done dawned slowly upon Perchik. *But the scheme was foolproof, the numbers faultless.*

"Well, boy, clearly there is nothing that can stop the mind of Perchik. . . ." And with that, Gershom left the great marble table, the men, and his nephew altogether.

Perchik, in turn, stood upright. "Gentlemen . . ." he said, nodding, and took as stately a leave as he could.

His head rang. *Clang, clang, clang.* What had he done?

Clang, clang, clang went the evening bell.

"Are you all right, brother?" asked Dmitri Petrov to a faraway Perchik as they packed up their tools and headed back for the day.

"I am," Perchik reassured him.

They joined the line of workers being checked and then escorted back to barracks, and as the men wiped their brows and brushed the salt and dust from their jackets, trousers, and the cracks of their skin, Perchik felt a shudder shoot from his belly to his brain. Then, as quickly as it had come, it disappeared into the blackness of the mines.

twenty-six

Perchik ran across the city. Face streaked with tears, heart pounding, the insidious *clang* still echoing in his skull, a lonesome varmint near blind with creature-need. Perchik ran until his chest stung. Until the raw night air crushed down upon him, constricting every nerve and tissue in his wrenching heart. The muscles in his legs burned with such ferocity. Exceeded fatigue— passed into the realms of liquidation. He did not care where the train was headed, only that it headed away.

Maybe Belarus. Belarus would be beautiful, he thought, *or perhaps the thrill of a big city?*

Trains ran hourly. He didn't care. He cared for nothing. Not anymore. He boarded a freight car and collapsed.

As he shoved the door closed with the last remaining vigor in his body, the train gained speed. It was in this moment that the starkness of his circumstances fully struck him. Whatever remaining dregs of strength he possessed were gone. He was now alone aboard a train whose destination was unknown. Utterly exhausted, he fell into a deep sleep.

When he awoke nearly half a day later, he was in Moscow. He disembarked from the train and stumbled into a nearby pub in the swarming city. The bar had a familiar stink of stale liquor—all bars such as these smell just the same, though this bar was permeated with a wretched, putrid odor of a particular sort of misery. All of it was oddly comforting.

Red patterned paper peeled from the walls as if protesting its presence there, committing a kind of wallpaper suicide in hope of finding a better fate. He knew the feeling.

Perchik felt the sticky residue of the pub beneath his boots and noted the prostitutes lingering in the corner, circling desperate men like ravenous vultures.

He drank.

"Another," he said to the bartender unceremoniously.

He drank to his shattered life. He was free from it now. But he did not feel it. His uncle had plunged him even further into wretchedness. Whereas he'd before been neglected in his uncle's house, now he was entirely on his own.

What a useless character I am, he thought as he burned himself with a drink so vile, it felt as though God himself were gripping his throat.

"Another," he barked, as the steely bartender eyed him.

He was lost.

Oh, to carve Gershom out of the world like a verruca.

Restlessness and despair, far more than any liquor, were the slow poisons he knew all too well. *Hello, friend,* he thought as he began a very purposeful disintegration into the oblivion of glass after glass. *Hello. You have never turned me away. . . .*

twenty-seven

H e had never turned me away," Grigory Boleslav said one day, quite out of the blue. "But one day, he did, and I killed him. I killed him, for I knew he was unfaithful."

Perchik froze.

Daily interchange with the men was inevitable, and Perchik appeared to possess a kind of shamanistic wherewithal, a proclivity to elicit these stories.

"What was that, Grisha?"

Grigory sucked hard upon a cigarette as he spoke. "He was behaving suspiciously," he said. "We always had to show discretion, but he had suddenly become aloof. He did not want to meet as frequently; he was cold. I began to suffer horribly from the suppositions in my mind!" *Clearly,* thought Perchik, *the wound still festered.* "One night I followed him. I watched as he snuck into a flat in the Vladimirsky region of Petersburg. I did not need to see anything further—I knew what lay within."

Perchik often heard from his companions the accounts of their lives, but in this moment he was struck by complete alarm.

"I cajoled him into the idea of an excursion in the countryside! He hesitated at first, as if he knew. But eventually he consented, on the condition that he might bring a female companion along. That of course did not suit my plans in the slightest, but I had to endure it, for I sensed he was suspicious. We started out, all three of us. I was armed with a revolver. . . ."

Perchik's gaze was locked upon Grigory.

"I walked beside my lover, cool as anything. I held his hand. I spoke softly. The woman sulked several feet behind us as we made our way through the trees."

"Where did you acquire the gun?" asked Perchik, trying to keep any sound of shock or form of judgment from his tone.

"I stole it," he replied matter-of-factly, his inky eyes betraying a hint of sentiment at the recollection. "I worked at a dress shop in the city that was often burgled. The owner purchased the revolver for security. That owner was always so terribly suspicious of me." He sucked harder on his cigarette at this thought, irked. Then, releasing the smoke, he sighed. "Well, I suppose rightfully so. . . ." He shook his head, continuing, "Anyway. We walked on. I began to shake slightly, for although I was on the brink of killing him, the sincerity of his face was sweetening me." Fat tears began to silently roll down Grisha's cheeks. "He was never so fair or so loving as he was that day."

Perchik saw many shapes of misfortune far

worse than his own. Perchik himself had at some point escaped the state he witnessed now in Grigory Boleslav: this very lowest state of spiritual suffering, the final state of shame.

"At last we stopped in a field. Placing my arm dotingly around his shoulder, I pointed out something in the distance, which made him look away. I kissed and kissed his neck, the softness behind his ear, as if to say goodbye. Then, in an instant, I brandished the pistol in both my hands, pointing it straight into his body. He began to inch backward, arms in front of him pleading. Then, without thought, I pulled the trigger. But my hand was shaking with nerves, and I only wounded him, grazing him across the shoulder."

He is still such a young man, thought Perchik as he listened.

"The female companion ran screaming toward him. Bleeding and stunned, he clutched his seeping shoulder and threw himself upon his knees before me, weeping, 'Grishushka! My love! Forgive me!' in a tone of voice so heartrending, it made me tremble. 'Forgive me, my darling! Forgive me, please! I *love* her!' And suddenly, it was all very clear indeed. My love loved her. He betrayed me, and they had to die for it. They had to."

It is an indescribable torture to know that a menacing watch is being kept upon one's every movement—Grisha had lived a lifetime with it, the unrelenting eye. But nothing could be worse than the eyes that are set upon you in the final gazes of those whose lives you have taken. Perchik need not guess at such a torture, for it was all there on Grisha's face, engraved like a tenebrous watermark.

Grisha continued, his voice more delicate now, "When you are in pain, how little you contemplate the pain of others. I answered his plea for mercy by plunging the weapon directly into his heart and releasing the gun into it. I watched his eyes go blank before he fell down, stiff and dead." Perchik could see the eyes of Grisha's lover were burning into him—forever burning and pointed, like two hot needles.

"Then I caught the horrified grimace of his lady-friend. She tried to run. I felt my hand rise quite uncontrollably, and I shot her through the stomach when she attempted escape."

Perchik could see Grigory Boleslav set his quiet, feverish glare back upon those two persecuting eyes, defiant in the simple act of recounting his story.

"Then I did a most unthinkable thing," he said. "I aimed the gun toward my lover's face and fired into it, obliterating him beyond all description." Grisha grew very pale, his expression perfectly still. "Hatred. Loathing. Hatred it was, really— how thoroughly it guided me. The pain of his betrayal mutilated me. I had to mutilate him too." He stopped then, but he was not weeping. His voice was clear and free. "You see, comrade, I thought an act of violence would ease my suffering. Somehow, though I cannot explain it at all, it was not enough to simply *kill* him. I had to disfigure him as well."

"But you murdered the man you loved—"

"The face . . ." Boleslav recalled, voice barely audible now. "That beautiful face. I liquidated it." He was staring, catatonic. "It was in his face that the love for her lay. Yes, I suspect that was probably it."

After a few moments Perchik cut into the silence.

"What did you do then, my friend?"

"Well. I turned on the sight, walked slowly away, went straight to the authorities, and gave myself up. Now here I am for life."

"But does your conscience not gnaw at you?"

"I don't believe I shall ever forget it. But as for conscience? No. I was quite right in killing them both."

Perchik was baffled. "So you feel no crime has been committed?"

"I blasted them out of the world. *Pfft*. Like exploded stars gone in an instant, without a trace, without a thought, into the blackness and silence of the universe. Poetic, eh? And how good it feels, really. They are dead while I labor here for life. That is fairness. That is justice. I need not justify a single action. He took away my peace, she took away my love and my dignity, and so I took away their lives. Where is the crime?"

His question was sincere, as if he was looking to Perchik for a genuine answer. Grigory Boleslav inhaled deeply, the tears from his eyes dried upon his face in sharp white streaks, his nose frosted at the edges. Perchik stared hard into him— false righteousness of deed and thought was not unrepresented among these men he considered to be his friends. All the same, he could not help but feel for him.

"Oppression. Misunderstanding," Grisha continued, stubbing out the nubbin of his cigarette. "They *do* things to you. They fill you with a pressure that boils over. Perhaps that is why I—" He stopped abruptly. "Perhaps that is it." His throat was tight. "I feel much better, you know!" he declared, sighing, his shoulders loosening. "I feel stronger and better having told it. Thank you." Grigory Boleslav looked away again and thought another moment. He gazed upon the horizon, the ground, and his hands, and at last his look landed on Perchik as he spoke with candor.

"When you have won, Reb Perchik, do not forget Grigory Boleslav and the others like him. I shall certainly rot away in here, but the vast numbers of others . . ." His voice trailed away. "Do remember me."

Grigory Boleslav looked once more into the

distance. At the rising Siberian sun. At the painful piercing of its light as it cut into the wet blackness of his eyes—as black and infinite as the mines they sat before.

twenty-eight

The cello sang from the corner. Dmitri's hands had been aching to play; he had been waiting several weeks for his fingers to heal after the long winter had ravaged them. Now, in the flushes of Siberian spring, the men sat idly in Hodel and Perchik's open front room within the Volosnikov house as they were wont to do most Sundays. Grigory Boleslav was smoking in one corner while Anatoly and Yevgeny played cards in another. Andrey Tenderov lay prostrate in the center of the room, legs sprawled blithely, thumbing through a pile of both novels and pamphlets, thoughtlessly adding his own hummed melodies to Dmitri's concert.

"Oh, Mitya, do play the Bach suites—number three, please," Yevgeny asked. "It is my very favorite. Oh, say you will."

"Yevgeny," sighed Dmitri Petrov. "I cannot do the sarabande. My thumb is still healing."

"The second, then. Even just the prelude. Come! No one does mournful cello better!"

"Yevgeny, I am almost as weary of the Bach as I am of you," Dmitri said. "Now be still, stop nagging, and don't let Anatoly beat you with a pair of fives yet again."

Anatoly smiled broadly at this—he loved to win.

"I wouldn't know a prelude or an allemande if it jumped up and bit my arse, but I like the sound of Sarabande—is she spoken for?" joked Tenderov, not even looking up from his books, still sprawled upon the ground, his hair gleaming even in the ambient light. The men chuckled approval.

Yevgeny was unfazed. "Please," he pleaded, eyes batting, smiling.

Dmitri sighed again. "Oh, very well," he said, agreeing only to silence the nagging, though the sincere light in Yevgeny's face was, admittedly, charming. "But the second—and only the first movement."

They all cheered at the predictable squabbles of the mismatched bunkmates. And then, at last, Dmitri began to play.

There are times when we witness a creature being essentially *itself*—it happens when we watch beavers build their dams, when birds launch into the heights of the open skies, or as mothers feed their young. In this we witness a kind of glory, not with our senses but with something else entirely: the essential parts in us respond to it, our nerves tremble, and we are ignited with a kind of knowing. So it was when Dmitri Petrov played his cello. There was no visible shift in them. They soaked in long strains and mournful chords as they continued to sit and read and stew and smoke. But the shift was there, real and present, the cellist crying out to the essential with these inessential men.

Andrey Tenderov took a flask from his coat pocket and drank. He passed the flask around before wiping his mouth and exhaling with pleasure.

"What is this?" Boleslav asked, impressed.

"Wine!" Andrey exclaimed. "Beautiful wine!"

"Where in the hell do you get all your liquor?" Grisha asked of Andrey, thoroughly vexed.

From the very first moment the carriage doors opened, delivering him to this place, Andrey Tenderov was forever sneaking. He snuck into the kitchens at night to gather scraps of food to share with the others. He'd shuffle workers away to lead them in song during working hours. He strolled to and fro on the officers' grounds (often even walking directly into the residences of The Gentleman and his compatriots), then emerge with swagger, as if he owned the camp! All of this, only to be caught moments later and sentenced to some punitive task or another. Andrey Tenderov was charismatic and likable, with limitless spirit. No one could understand how he could be like that in such a place as this. He also always appeared to have a spare shot of vodka, a slice of bread, or a pinch of tobacco, no matter how downtrodden he became.

"Yevgeny here showed me a storehouse on the eastern front where they put it all in great crates. Then he taught to me break in, he did. You see, Dmitri? The man is good for something!" And Andrey laughed, shining his golden smile upon the room, then took another swig of wine from the flask. "Now," he continued, "do you know apparently Tolstoy and his wife, Sophia, had a rather tumultuous marriage? Yes, it says here that the onset of their union possessed extraordinary passion, followed by a steady decline in contentment alongside his growing faith."

"Fascinating," droned Grigory Boleslav, ever acerbic.

"That's what it says," said Tenderov, shrugging. "Mysterious." He looked at the paper a moment longer before asking, "What think you of marriage, Reb Perchik?"

"I?" asked Perchik, looking up from his writing. "Why do you ask me?"

Tenderov smiled. "For you are the only one among us here who is in the presence of his wife!" He flashed his broad teeth in delight. "Think of it—Anatoly, alone in Ekaterinburg, was it?"

"Vladivostok, actually," said Anatoly, shuffling his cards.

"There you are. And Yevgeny? Have you ever had a love?"

Yevgeny thought for a moment, then said

241

uncertainly, "I loved my mother. And we had a dog once we called Malenkey Petya—I loved that dog no question."

They all paused, taking that in.

"And darling Dmitri over there," interjected Grigory Boleslav, gesturing from the opposite corner. "The confirmed, crotchety young bachelor who, despite this, has all sorts of fancy ideals about love—can't you tell? Who would want to marry *him?*" Grigory Boleslav smirked as he sucked his dwindling cigarette.

"Well, what about you?" hollered Dmitri over the Bach. "Nothing more than a—"

"A bachelor! A bachelor myself!" he shouted back, punctuating the word with a flick of his cigarette stub.

"Oh, is *that* what they are calling it nowadays?"

"Now, now, men—settle!" said Andrey Tenderov in a pacifying tone. "Regardless. Reb Perchik, Hodel is the only wife . . . well, any of us know, and you are the only one to whom she is truly married. So: What think you of marriage?"

"The word, comrade?" Perchik asked coyly.

"The notion, comrade! The thing of it. Come now! Tell us."

He thought for a moment, rubbing his thumb into the arm of his chair.

Veren ferherret—Yiddish for "to get married." Perchik recalled once asking Tzeitel and Tzeitel's husband, Motel, for the secret to a good marriage.

"The most important words in a marriage," Tzeitel said, "are: *you are probably right*."

At that Perchik had laughed. He then turned to Motel and inquired, "Reb Motel?"

Motel shrugged and said, "She's probably right."

In the company of men, his thoughts traveled first to marriage's adversities. He thought of Hodel's fire, her obstinate will, her temper. But in light of such a connection, these details seemed to serve as merely a backdrop for a wealth of shimmering virtues: her implicit, almost clairvoyant understanding, the calm of their silences, the buzz of their discussions. The way his thumb fit perfectly in the palm of her hand.

Indeed, all in all, marriage was wonderful— because he was married to *her*.

"You know," he said with a smile, "truly, I do believe there is not a thing about it I detest."

The men laughed together, complete with kissing noises and shaking of their heads. "Oh God!" shouted Boleslav from across the room. "Please save us from the presence of the lovesick—my teeth are rotting in their sockets!"

With that, almost as if she had known, Hodel entered from the cold of the afternoon, sunlight and frost streaming in with her.

"Hello, men!" she greeted, shivering, then kissed her husband while removing her cloak and shawl.

"We were just speaking of you, my dear," Perchik confessed, reaching for her hand and smiling softly.

"Oh? Did someone get hungry or spill something again?" she said, her eyes laughing, ears simultaneously pricking to Dmitri's playing. "Dmitri, I thought you were weary of that piece," she said over her shoulder, making her way to the stove.

At this, Grisha retorted, "Yes, quite right, Perchik, a very pleasant business this marriage seems. We are inarguably missing out. Just think, indeed, if it weren't for marriage, men would go through life thinking they had no faults at all."

Perchik looked on as even Dmitri surrendered a smile, shaking his head in reluctant delight, and he saw Hodel catch Dmitri's eye and nod before she walked back across the room to sit atop Perchik's waiting lap. *If he come in by himself, he shall go out by himself,* he thought, quoting the Good Book to himself. *"If he were married, then his wife shall go out with him." The Good Book is a good book,* he thought, *and this is my wife. . . .*

He scarcely noticed Dmitri's cello playing. Perchik gazed upon her: her look was impassioned. She leaned over and kissed him, eyes filled with yearning, mouth full of tenderness—she could not hear the music at all.

"A flush!" cried Yevgeny suddenly. "A flush of

244

diamonds! I cannot believe it! You see
you see how your Bach suite inspires! It has
me clever for the briefest of moments, enou
to trample even Anatoly! Thank you, thank
you, Mitya; thank you, my worthy opponent
Anatoly; thank you, one and all!" With that, the
Bach came to its end as the group cheered and
applauded, Yevgeny already giving little bows to
the many corners of the room, forever basking in
the smallest of victories.

twenty-nine

A s he returned from the mines and stood in the entrance of the Volosnikov house, Perchik caught a glimpse of Hodel washing herself in a basin. Her beautiful hair was unraveled and flecked with the thawed light of the wasteland he knew would always be imprinted upon his mind as their first home. He bathed too—in the autumnal light of this hazy evening—and realized he had asked Hodel to be his wife nearly four years ago. . . .

Light, he thought, *has a funny way of imprinting itself upon our memories*. He was suddenly stung with regret. How quickly things had changed.

From Gershom to Rabbi Syme, from university to squalor. From an evening with a stranger in a faraway bar and back again. Back to university—and paying his own way, on his own terms. Learning more—more than one ever could from any book or school or teacher. Becoming a man. Becoming a leader. Then taking to the road—to reach and teach the people of this vast and glorious land. A road that would eventually lead him to her.

For all his talk, for all his rhetoric, his dreams and visions for the future of the People were minute in comparison to his dreams and visions of a future for her. He loved her and all that she was—more than he had ever loved anything, and his commitment was more than a promise to honor her throughout his life: it was a commitment to opening his heart. He vowed to give her not all that he had, but all he knew she deserved.

Her love was palpable in the still of the bitter nights—he would enfold her while they talked, and she would lean deeply into him, resting in the circle of his arms as they made plans and dreamed. After a day in the mines, he would come to her for a few moments of sanity. To listen. To have his life held in her discerning mind. To hold hers. To provide some semblance of helpful commentary, and to bask in a contentment that felt like the hand of the divine upon his chest.

He gazed at her as she rose from the basin. She gathered her hair up into a knot, and as she wrapped a sheet around herself, a lock of hair fell across her face and along the curve of a naked arm. He entered and saw her body respond to his presence. Glancing toward him, her expression fully open, her frame suggested knowing tranquility—as if her innate attitude were that of sheer luminosity.

Half dressed, hair unleashing with each deliberate step, she moved toward him. He brushed the hair from her face, hands grazing her carefully, with great attention, as if she were breakable. Then he held her face between his hands—beholding her. She smiled, and his heart leapt so suddenly that all he could do was raise her forehead to his lips, pressing them upon her as if endowing her with all he possessed.

She placed her cheek against his, and emotion rose within him—swollen, bursting, like waves of an inner ocean. It was this surge of feeling that moved him to kiss her face with a covetous thirst, as if drinking in her very essence. The salt of Nerchinsk may have been slowly preserving him, but it purified him too. He was falling, dissolving into her. He relinquished himself to the ebbing pull of her tide.

"Hodel," he whispered into her neck, "Hodel, I love you." He held her with his crumbling fingers and inhaled deeply the scent of her hair. She did not need to reply. The devotion in her embrace said it for her. She kissed his mouth, tasted the salt, and smiled.

"King David," she said, wrapping herself around his knotted bones, reviving him like a cool wash of water.

"King David?" Perchik replied.

"Yes. From scripture. The salt covenant. Every time we kiss, I think of it. Papa always said salt signified permanence, fidelity. A symbol of unchanging, incorruptible purity." She grinned and kissed his eyes.

" 'Should you not know that the Lord God gave

the dominion over Israel to David forever, to him and his sons, by a covenant of salt?' " Perchik quoted. "From Chronicles."

Hodel nodded.

"Every kiss is a salt covenant?" he asked, smiling.

Suddenly, she grew very serious. "For us. Yes. The unbreakable promise."

He was overcome—all his life he had been waiting for the woman before him and had never even known it. This woman, who was a reflection of all he cherished. It was with her sense of life that he had fallen in love. Her way of seeing the world as reflected in her tiniest gestures, her distinct, irreplaceable *self*. He adored her. It was the greatest reward of his life.

It was this love that existed at the core of all his holiest thoughts. *Love is not, in any way, a sacrifice,* he thought. *It is the transmission of life.*

Yes, he thought, *yes.*

He clung to her for a lingering moment—his equal, his partner in life. Then he lifted her up and took her to bed.

The heart, you see, is a muscle; if you make no use of it, it atrophies.

Everything Perchik would do from here on was about love.

Perchik had always been driven by other forces, as when he stumbled into Moscow a few months before he met Hodel. So bitter was the wind outside that all inhabitants of the bar felt its sting as it whipped the ragged glass panes in the walls of the basement locale. The skins of the prostitutes were pimpled with chill; their still, predatory gaze only faintly unsettled. In an abrupt swirl of wind, a diminutive man entered. Shivering, he made his way to the bar—a cough from the depths of his lungs rang out as he moved toward the stool beside Perchik. The man sighed, eyes watering, and hands with curiously ink-stained fingers began clearing the cough-induced tears away from beneath the wire rims of his round spectacles. As he gained composure he brushed snow sharply off his long black coat, which hung loosely over his suit.

Perchik lifted his eyes. Light streamed down through the windows from the bustling street above, casting a kind of celestial glow behind the man as he settled. Flakes of snow were melting in the heat of the basement bar and reflecting the dingy gaslights affixed to the walls, glittering like stars all around them.

Without knowing why, Perchik signaled to the barkeep to bring two. When the drinks arrived he raised his in inquiry. "What brings you here tonight, comrade?"

"Comrade?" the stranger stated with recognition. "All the young people in the cities are using that word nowadays!" He laughed, nestling down farther into his long coat. "Ah, thank you for the drink, comrade." He smiled. Perchik lifted his glass to the stranger and nodded before downing its contents in a single quaff.

"Love," the man answered, chortling brightly.

"Love?"

"What brings me here tonight? Love. For every reason that is good and bad, love always seems to bring me to the bar!" He threw his head back and laughed, then smoothed his beard and adjusted the frames on his face. "I love this city; I love a woman in this city. What about you, comrade? What do you love?"

"The vodka, of course," Perchik lied.

What a waste, he thought, slamming his glass down. *I love nothing. I am nothing.* He shook his head sharply, and requested another drink. "Tell me about your love."

The man looked suddenly childlike. His gaze shifted from his ink-stained hands to the dancing lamps along the peeling walls.

"Well, I am no great lover, my friend. I have come to Moscow with a love letter of sorts, hoping I will see its potential realized."

"A girl!"

"No—a young woman."

"I see!"

"A real woman of such culture and refinement. She speaks several languages, plays piano. I have, thus far, loved her only through letters—which

251

is how I know she is also a wonderful writer. Wonderful. Yes, I have loved her through these letters . . . and in my mind of course." His eyes glimmered.

"I see," replied Perchik, though he did not.

"I did not love her at first, you know; it took time. It took time to see that it was indeed this thing called love I was feeling. The feeling was foreign to me, but it was delicious and grand once I stumbled upon it and once I pulled myself together. So now, two years later, I cannot help myself! Better late than never, eh, comrade?" He laughed. "Would you believe I used to be a confirmed bachelor?"

"Ah, my friend." Perchik chuckled wryly, eyeing the vultures in the corner. "I'm afraid I know all too well about that."

"Indeed—as any good young man should. All I know is that I far preferred dalliances to any kind of meaningful intimacy. I did not like the irritation and discomfort of imperfect matches. I wanted a woman who was somewhat like the moon. I would miss her when she was away and appreciate her when she returned, but I did not want her around all the time!"

The man's hearty laughter made way for a return of his terrible cough. He produced a handkerchief from within his breast pocket; it was large, soiled, and seemingly employed for this exact circumstance. Recovering, he wiped the corners of his mouth, crumpled the linen messily, and begged apology. "Forgive me, my friend," he said, and then sipped his vodka, cleared his throat, sniffed sharply, and steadied himself before he went on, his voice now re-anchored. "I've had many professions in my life. Many friends, roles, jobs, obligations. But one role I never expected to play was the romantic lead. I've searched all my life for meaningful work. But I have found that love—for a cause, for an art, for another living soul, at times just for the sake of it—is purpose enough. It is more than enough. I'm so pleased to have discovered that at long last.

"I will find this woman and ask her to love me, and if she will, I hope we will share a life filled with the love of our work, our home, our causes, and each other. And then one day . . . that will be that." The man fingered the crumpled linen in between his hands thoughtfully. "The heart, you see, is a muscle; if you make no use of it, it atrophies. And I would know," he finished, smiling broadly. "I'm a doctor."

The man was so earnest, Perchik could not help but smile. He hailed the bartender to bring two more glasses.

"Thank you," said the man, running the tip of his finger over the top of his glass. "And you, my friend? You never *really* answered my question."

Perchik winced. The man had displayed such admirable candor that Perchik felt obliged to be honest in some small way. But the thought of such honesty repulsed him.

"I suppose," Perchik started, haltingly. "Well, I suppose I am a businessman." He winced again faintly; so much feeling had already been numbed by the drink, but still it stung. "I was at university. Studying God knows what. . . ." He glanced over at the man, whose gaze was so keen, Perchik could feel it in his nerves. "In truth, I barely attended classes. I admit, I was mad. I was reckless. I tried to find meaning in the lessons—some form of kinship with other bright people. But it wasn't there. I don't even know how to describe the circumstance, my friend, but it's safe to say I never advanced much. My professors joked that I would be stuck there forever, blessing me with the title of 'perpetual student.' They were not inaccurate, I suppose. I was always studying—but for what? I did not know then. I don't know now. I do not, it would appear, know much at all. So much schooling and yet I don't know anything." With that, he finished the dregs of his drink and then slammed the glass down. "So, to your question: I have come to Moscow for what? To carve out my *purpose?* To shape and define my aspirations? I have many thoughts, comrade. Some have called them gifts. But to me, they seem to be curses. And dreams, yes, I have those too—many of them. But as of yet, no actions, no calling . . .”

He drifted away on the stream of that thought, then after a moment, he spoke again quietly. “The truth is, I have been forsaken.”

There it was. Out loud at long last.

“I had to get away,” he continued. He welled up with feeling, which he choked back harshly. “There. I said it. The truth, that is.”

The man nodded, adjusting his glasses. He understood.

They sat in silence for a while, and when the man finally spoke, it was almost at a whisper.

“I have—” he started. “I have recently acquired a new property. A beautiful plot of land on the outskirts of Yalta. I have taken up agriculture and horticulture, tended an orchard and ponds and planted many trees. But I have been ill, my friend,” he said, indicating the handkerchief now inside his breast pocket. “Yes. I, the doctor, have been ill, and it is immensely interesting what happens when the doctor becomes the patient.” He paused, then chuckled. “It is funny. I do not tend to speak so openly about my feelings. You certainly have a way about you.”

“I am glad you think so, sir,” Perchik said.

The stranger continued, “Anyway, after all those years devoted to stalling death, it is the business of living life to which I now commit myself. Life—the most fundamental business of all. I suppose, in a way, that makes me a businessman myself!" He nudged the young man lightly with his elbow. "You understand?"

Perchik nodded. The man was delightful.

"I love Russia. I love her vast, stark body. Her ferocity. Her warmth. I wish to share this love with her and with all she looks after. I look at my trees, at the ponds and the plants, and dream of what they will be in five hundred years. Soon I will plant more; I shall keep dogs and tame cranes and, most of all, receive guests. Guests like yourself, comrade. For life must be shared. My friend—the perpetual student—you are welcome anytime."

"I would like that, sir," said Perchik. "Very much."

The man coughed once again, this time less violently, but he still produced the hanky and covered his mouth before taking its corners and wiping his eyes underneath his spectacles.

"I only fear there will not be enough time to appreciate it. After all, life does not begin an hour from now." The stranger stopped there, folding the handkerchief back into his breast pocket.

Fear, thought Perchik. *Fear. There is no more time for it.* How much time he had wasted with his paralyzing hesitations?

"Oh!" Perchik cried out suddenly. "Do not fear!" He found himself speaking loudly, as if the voice was not his own but came from a deeper

256

place within him, possessing a far more emphatic tenor. He gripped the man's shoulder with a passionate sincerity and looked him right in the eye.

"Soon this great and beautiful motherland will belong to us all," Perchik told him. "Just as you have said—the beauties and glories of our spectacular motherland can and shall be shared in fairness with all men regardless of their import, their wealth, their status, or their social value. Someday—and soon I hope—we will see that every man has value, every man has purpose, and no one man shall tower over another with judgment or spite. There will be no money to poison us. No love withheld. Only that which is shared and free-flowing. One day quite soon— just think of it! We shall all value our land as you value your plot; we shall all share in your garden of life. Can you imagine it? I can, my friend; I see it and believe in it with all of me. Soon there will be hope. Soon all Russia will be our orchard."

The man stared at Perchik for a moment. Then, blinking, he fumbled within his jacket and pulled out a small black book. He began to scribble.

"What are you doing?" asked Perchik.

"All . . . Russia . . . is . . . our . . . orchard," the man said as he wrote. "That is a nice turn of phrase, my friend—a good line!"

"Thank you," said Perchik, astonished.

"You should give speeches, my friend," the

man said. "Or perhaps teach. Go back to that university of yours. Use that lovely mind. But do not forget the heart! You speak with command, wisdom, and tremendous passion. Perhaps there is something to tend your purpose there. Believe me," he said, his eyes glinting, "I would know." He finished his scribbling and returned the small pencil to the center of the worn black book and the book to the folds of his long coat. "Inspiration is everywhere, my friend! I like to write such things down, you see. Ah! I am inspired tonight! That is hope, my friend. That is progress indeed. You have given me a great gift. A great gift. And I thank you."

The stranger dropped his gaze and drew a circle around the rim of his vodka glass with a stained finger, creating a barely audible ringing. Perchik felt as if the man were conjuring a spell, drawing some kind of enchantment from a well of wisdom lurking deep within the darkness of his long black coat.

The lights of the bar flickered slightly as the man turned to Perchik, his formerly diminutive figure somehow appearing much larger now. When the man spoke again, there was a power in his voice Perchik hadn't heard before.

"You are a young man, my friend. And, I sense, a good one. You speak with command, wisdom, and tremendous passion," he said. "I do not know much, my friend. But I do not believe we are given gifts we are not prepared to realize. A way exists, if the longing is in earnest." He stood and buttoned his coat. "I must go. I thank you, comrade."

Perchik nodded, unable to speak.

The stranger raised his glass to Perchik. "*Na zdorovie.*" He drank the last of it, took a long look at Reb Perchik, then left and was swallowed up by the darkness and mist of the night and the wind and the un-known city.

"Congratulations, Reb Perchik," said The Gentleman. "We feel you are absolved."

The Gentleman was seated behind a wide desk. Across the room was a Mongol girl with a heart-shaped face.

"Your conduct has been without fault," The Gentleman said, his words clipped with mannered, perfect enunciation. He nodded to the girl, who crossed the room with a document ready for signature. "Thank you, Irina," he said, and she sat beside The Gentleman, ink pen in hand. It was clear, seeing them next to each other, that this must be his daughter.

"We have decided you have labored long enough." His mouth was as tight as his voice.

"It is the accounting house for you."

The posts in the accounting office of the processing factory were especially desirable to those who had any form of education, and the prisoners who occupied these positions were envied. But all were alike in the eyes of the law, and at the flippant whim of an officer one might be "removed to other functions" at any moment.

It was an unnaturally early hour. Perchik, thanks to the ingenuity of his wife, was as well-groomed and tidy as any prisoner could be. He stood before The Gentleman, bowing his head to show respect before replying, "No, thank you, sir." He stated it calmly. "I would not care for the reassignment. At least not in accounts."

The Gentleman eyed him blankly. "Is that so?"

"Yes, sir. Perhaps the general office. But not accounts. I would quite prefer to labor, sir."

The Gentleman blinked. "Very well." He arranged the papers before him and handed them back to Irina, who silently prepared them for redrafting. "Make ready the next reassignment case," he called to the overseer at the back of the room, who instantly went out and escorted a young man inside.

"Tenderov, Andrey," announced the overseer.

The golden-haired youth held his head up and caught Irina's gaze; she returned his stare and did not flinch. He moved toward her, as if she had left a scented trail, then after a moment, he flashed a smile so broad, so clean and white and blinding, it made Perchik's insides palpitate.

"Here we go . . ." Tenderov whispered as the

overseer shoved him forward, bellowing "Off with you!" to Perchik as he passed.

"Oh, and Reb Perchik," The Gentleman called after him. "Before you go. Do send my regards to your lovely wife."

Perchik looked back unblinkingly for a moment. Then he simply nodded and turned to go, returning to the mines once more.

BOOK THREE

Mine

If he come in by himself,
he shall go out by himself:
if he were married,
then his wife shall go out with him.
—*Exodus*

thirty

H odel looked out across the vast gray land of Nerchinsk.

Where she had come from, Siberia was synonymous with wasteland, an eternal winter of colorless turbulence. But for all its violence, Hodel knew Nerchinsk to be a land of great memory, a land that reached back centuries.

That day, as Hodel gazed at Nerchinsk, its great recollections all unfolded before her: in the ever-watchful hills laced with precious metals, in the dignity of its native beasts. It revealed its mystery in the first slip of the moon blessing the land with its soft glow, and in the worn roads that had held the feet of many a journeyman.

Her eyes feasted on the wild beauty of Siberia's landscape. Every day, it looked different.

The sky, once heavy as eyelids fighting sleep, was now a luminescent blue. Where once there had been only threads of smoke fading into night, now clouds came belching up from chimneys in great billows. The barrack sheds and village shacks, once only smudges of blackened wood, now displayed shocks of color—window shutters, painted doors, and makeshift murals. The old silence was now punctuated by sounds of picks and carts and heavy hammers, cows and chickens, and, above it all, the wailing whistle of the ever-growing railway.

The eastern winds that once wafted smells from deepest Asia now blew minerals from the ever-expanding mines: the sour sickness of sulfur, the sharpness of silver, and the harshly cleansing scorch of salt that burned the nostrils as you searched to define it further.

Hodel's yesterdays, todays, and tomorrows might fall away, yet her memories did not exist in time, but in her soul, and their riches nourished her, revealed a limitless depth within.

Memory, she thought, *is a sacred place. It is the place where the past is gathered—an inner synagogue where we make meaning of our existence.*

She had been here nearly three years.

Nerchinsk had changed. But so had she. *How wonderful,* she thought, *that as our bodies age and weaken, our souls get richer, deeper, stronger.*

All of it had altered. Or perhaps it hadn't. Perhaps it was merely their perception that had changed. They had been rubbed down; they lay worn and raw like scraps of glass washed up upon the shores by the frigid waters of the Nercha. Hodel could see what could never have been seen before: that Nerchinsk indeed held good men, and dark ones, and those so torn apart by madness that they scarcely knew themselves. Time leached the impurities from the companions until all that remained was a pearl.

Days passed and grew to weeks; weeks grew to months, which succeeded each other, one after the next, and swiftly grew to years. They were nearer to ash, to dust, to eternity than they had ever been before.

But, still, they had endured. Thus far.

"Bludgeon him!" cried a guard.

Hodel, Perchik, and the others watched from a distance. All of them clumped like bits of clay crudely molded together, motionless, watching. Hodel, nestled in between the men, looked on. Everything in her prickled.

The Gentleman stood above two guards as they beat Andrey Tenderov. But Tenderov refused to bow. So upright he stood! Like a tree rooted to the frozen soil. The Gentleman shook his head at the scene, as if his position pained him, then nodded to the guards and returned up the road to his office.

Tenderov was often getting in scraps like this— always in chains, always being pummeled by a guard or two for one thing or another. They would take him into officer's custody, make him tend the furnace, or send him into isolation.

"Hit him! Do it now!" the first guard cried again

"I'm trying—oh Christ, he's getting away!" shouted the second guard.

Andrey Tenderov began to sing. It was something he often did as they worked around the camp, the ballads emitting from him so sweet and the tone so golden and woeful that one could not listen without a warmth of feeling. But now, as he sang and ran from the guards, it did not seem possible for such a sweet song to come from a criminal—he seemed a part of some sort of macabre street play.

Andrey Tenderov sang as he dodged and ran sportive circles around the guards—his hands roped together but clapping, his golden hair wild, his face alight with an impish exuberance.

Ah vy, seni, moi seni
Seni novye moi,
Seni novye, klenovye,
Reshotchatye!

Kak i mne po vam, po senichkam,
Ne hazhivati,
Mne mila druga za ruchen'ku
Ne vazhivati!

The guards were incensed. "You there! Come back!"

But Tenderov only sang louder.

"What is that song?" Hodel whispered.

" 'Ah Vy, Seni, Moi Seni'—it is a traditional Russian folk song," answered Grigory Boleslav.

"What is it about?"

"It tells a simple little story of a girl in love with a young brewer named Vanya, but the girl's strict father forbids them from seeing each other."

"It's very sad."

"It's *Russian*."

"True."

Grisha shrugged and chuckled with Hodel in his dark way.

The guards were roaring now. "Don't mess with me, you fool!" the first guard threatened. "We are professionals, boy. My great-grandfather bludgeoned the Decembrists!"

"What's he done this time?" Hodel asked Perchik, who was deep in thought. "Perchik . . . ?" she asked, touching his chest, but he made no reply.

"Russia has been exiling people for needless crimes since the eighteenth century," Dmitri said abruptly. "It happens all the time. How else do you think the tsar could build such roads, fortresses, factories, ships—not to mention Petersburg itself?"

"Oh, it's appalling," Grisha sneered.

"That's Peter the so-called Great for you," said Dmitri.

"Would that make him simply 'Peter'?" asked Yevgeny. Dmitri stared at the old man in revulsion. Yevgeny continued, "Well anyway, that is *government* for you! Just like family: part habit, part fear, part wishing to God we had a different one!" Yevgeny beamed as the men roared with laughter, Anatoly patting Yevgeny squarely on the back in approval.

"You know," Dmitri said, "some communities band together and elect certain social outcasts to be sent eastward. Sometimes simply for being irritating." *Not at all unlike what I am certain happened to you,* he thought.

"Well, I think Tenderov is very agreeable," Yevgeny said.

"You would."

"And terribly kind to me. Always there with an extra slice or sip or pinch for an old man." Yevgeny reached into his pocket and revealed a small pot of chewing tobacco, then put a bit into the pouch of his cheek beside his worn-down molars.

"Where on earth did you get that?" asked Dmitri Petrov.

"Oh." Yevgeny tittered. "I stole it from The Gentleman."

"The Gentleman himself?"

"Yes. Lifted right from his pocket. A good score, eh?"

Dmitri sighed, shaking his fists in front of him before folding them over his chest again.

The guards stood together now, both breathless

from the chase, as Andrey Tenderov made a break for the forest.

"Well, shit," the first guard said, resigned.

"Shouldn't we go after 'im?"

"Nah, the forest will quash him if we do not."

"But with all the talk of uprisings . . ."

"Forget that. I am out of breath!"

"But—!"

"Forget it, I said!"

"Right, then. Anyway, we'll just bludgeon him later when he returns for food."

Hodel placed her head upon Perchik's chest. She could feel the loud, deliberate thudding of each beat of his heart. She held him closer.

"Incredible," said Grisha, staring at Tenderov in the distance.

"Aye," Anatoly agreed.

"He is. He is goddamn incredible."

"Oh aye."

"He's a wonder," said Yevgeny.

"He's an idiot," said Dmitri.

"He's a hero!" Yevgeny replied.

"An absolute hero," Grisha added, almost giggling with pleasure. "Even his name has a brio to it: *Tenderov* . . . God, it's like a musk."

Anatoly reached into his coat pocket and withdrew a large flask, unscrewed the top, took a sip, and with his gigantic hand offered it to Perchik. "For you, friend—you had'n said much. Awful quiet."

"No, thank you, Anatoly. I am not in a drinking mood," Perchik replied. He looked sober indeed. Something had changed.

With the arrival of a letter and nearly two hours spent decoding it, Hodel noted that Perchik appeared more vital than he had in weeks. A light had returned to his eyes, though skin flaked from his face. *At last,* she thought, *to see him cheered by his purpose.*

"Hodel!" he had cried, standing and running toward her, laughing. "Oh, at last! At last!" He had taken her in his arms and lifted her clear off the ground—spun her around and kissed her hard despite being winded.

"What is it, Perchik?" She had smiled, laughing too. "News?"

"The only news, my darling! Hodel, will you go fetch Dmitri and tell him to meet me?"

"Where?"

"He will know where."

He had kissed her again, and she had felt his eyes upon her as she went. She'd lingered in the doorway and observed him at his desk. Alone with only his mind (and whatever promise lay within that letter), she had watched him revel in this great moment of human endeavor. It had electrified a kind of poetry from within him that promised dormant men would soon be roused to action. They were to be the curators of the century.

It was 1909. How the world would come alive—real and pulsing and transparent.

The men turned and made their way back to the barracks.

All except Perchik, who—Hodel observed from a few yards away—stared outward at the scene beyond and, arms wrapped fiercely around himself, merely shuddered.

thirty-one

Hodel awoke beside him—he was calling her away from the dream. Her breath caught as she rose from slumber to his touch; her female softness pressed against his density.

"Perchik?" she said in a hush, bracing herself against both the distinction of his muscles and the unuttered substance of her own desire. "How do you know how to hold a woman?"

"I never truly held a woman until I held you," he said, slight shame in his reply, as they both knew he had held so many. Oh God. How she loved him. He swelled instinctively toward her. His hands, though rough with labor, were still gentle and almost reverent as they grazed her body. "But my arms were formed to hold you, Hodel." He clutched at her. "Yes," he said, clasping her tight within the nearly terrifying grip of their desire. "Everything else felt like pretending. . . ."

He was Jerusalem, and she a holy pilgrim.

"Hodel, stop!" Tzeitel was cross with her. "Stop it!"

This was Anatevka in 1904. Tzeitel's wedding day.

Days before the wedding, all Tzeitel could do

was fervently pray—for her future husband, and for the new life they hoped to build together. She prayed for loving kindness, for faithfulness and devotion, for good health, for provision, and for any children God in His grace might grant them.

Tzeitel's new home above Motel's tailor shop was mostly bare (though Motel's mother, Shaindel, had gone to great lengths to prepare it for their growing family). Motel and Tzeitel were to live upstairs, Shaindel below, on level with the tailor shop; and though there was still much work to be done (including the impending arrival of the sewing machine that would, blessed be to Him, change their fortunes, as well as the lives of everyone in the village), Tzeitel was looking forward to every moment of the building of this new beginning with the man she had loved her whole life. This union was, indeed, a miracle.

Tzeitel sat, surrounded by sisters. She was watching the day unfold at long last.

Her mother marched endlessly in and out of the room (attending to thousands of tiny tasks). Chava brushed (and re-brushed) Tzeitel's hair, then arranged it delicately on either side of her head. The little ones were attending to her shoes, her nails, her undergarments. Everyone squabbled.

"It is your wedding day!" Hodel cried, pinching the waist of the wedding dress.

Hodel was testing Tzeitel's patience (again),

trying to convince her to better display her figure.

"The dress is sitting on my figure, Hodel, not squeezing it!"

"Please!" Hodel threw her head back. "You are swimming in that dress and all the village will be there looking at you!"

"Hodel, a bride's vanity is just a sad display of her submission to worldly temptations. When her wedding dress is too tight, there is no room for holy thought. And no room to breathe."

"I am sorry, Tzeitel; I only—"

"That said," Tzeitel continued, "I don't know a single bride who wouldn't want to look her best for the sake of her husband." Tzeitel's voice changed to a timbre Hodel had never heard before. There was a tenderness emitting from her that startled them all. "Oh," Tzeitel whispered so quietly, Hodel didn't know if she was meant to hear. "I do so want Motel to see me as he has never seen me before."

At this, Shprintze began to weep.

"Come now, Shprintze, there now," Tzeitel said to her younger sister. "There is no need to weep. This is the most special day in a woman's life!"

Even on her wedding day, Tzeitel was still leading them. Hodel could not help but think what each of the others would be like on their own wedding days. Chava would enjoy the pampering and attention, until of course she became frustrated with her hair. Bielke would mollify the others, making certain everyone else was all right. Shprintze would be on a knife-edge, her mood fluctuating from high to low, laughing and then weeping. And Hodel? In the silence of her own mind, she knew she would be a vain monster (before her mother and Tzeitel both put her in her place again, that is). She smiled at the thoughts of all of them in white dresses with rings on their right index fingers. Of each stepping under the marriage canopy, circling her husband seven times, sipping the wine, making vows. And, of course, of the wives they all promised to become.

But in her heart, Hodel knew that none of them would ever display so thoroughly graceful a dignity, or so great a strength, as Tzeitel did today. Suddenly, it struck her: they were all losing Tzeitel, their leader, forever. Their family would never be the same.

They all loved Motel. In many ways he was already a brother—as much a part of their upbringing as any of them. Hodel felt deeply for him; they all did. But none so much as Tzeitel.

It had been a remarkable thing to behold— watching Tzeitel and Motel as they grew together. At first, they had been childhood playmates. Tzeitel would make Motel play house in the barn, pretending all the animals were their children. They built forts, made mud pies, and sometimes splashed in the stream behind their house. No matter the game, their roles were always the same: Tzeitel was the strong one, Motel always keen and attentive behind her. If Tzeitel was the certainty, Motel was the hope. If Tzeitel the pragmatism, Motel the dreams. For as long as anyone could recall, they brought out the best in each other.

But as they grew, Tzeitel became more reserved—she was well aware of the restrictions their community placed upon their relationship; she recognized the roles they were supposed to fulfill, even if Motel didn't fully comprehend them. Playtime was over, and their childhood companionship had to end. And yet, as Tzeitel returned to her family and Motel apprenticed at his father's shop, Motel found a new way to connect. A brilliantly talented tailor whose gifts far exceeded his father's, he displayed his talents in beautiful gifts for Tzeitel—at first little quilts and pillows, and eventually aprons, waistcoats, and headscarves for the Sabbath. It was how he showed his love before they were allowed to express it.

Hodel had never known or observed anything like what existed between Motel and Tzeitel—it exceeded the devotion she understood toward her family or for God. This was something altogether different. Something simultaneously earthly and holy.

Tzeitel never shared any of this with her family;

her sisters merely observed it for themselves. If Hodel had Chava, and Shprintze had Bielke, within their family unit, Tzeitel had no one at all. No one, that was, but Motel. Motel had been her "person" for as long as anyone could remember. But love matches were not made in their community; people had not married for affection for as long as anyone could recall. Love grew out of marriage; it did not instigate it. And no matter how lovely or capable, the eldest daughter of a milkman—a girl with no dowry or family background—was in no position to be selective, particularly if her selection was a poor, almost comically feeble tailor.

On this day, Hodel finally understood: for Tzeitel, life without Motel would have been a death.

What a miracle that Motel and Tzeitel would soon become the Kamzoils—the unit that, in some manner, they had always been. Theirs would be a humble life, but a life not worth living without the other. Their dreams were finally coming true.

Hodel's mind shifted in her skull. She wondered if she would ever feel for another what Tzeitel felt for Motel. She wondered if she was even capable of such feeling. She wondered if she would ever stand beneath a canopy with someone she more than admired, but loved. Suddenly, her heart filled for her sister—it filled ruby red and overflowing like a cup of Sabbath wine—in a deep way she had never known before.

"So," Hodel said, placing a hand on Tzeitel's shoulder and gazing upon all of her sisters, "let us make this a truly beautiful day. May we rejoice in pure thoughts and the endless love we feel toward God and our new brother, Motel. May we support Tzeitel as she dedicates herself to her husband. And may we be as faithful and helpful for her today as she will no doubt be to Motel for both of their lifetimes."

Tzeitel's face was glowing. "Thank you, Hodelleh," she said, placing her own hand upon Hodel's, still resting on her shoulder.

" 'And He shall love you and bless you and multiply you, and blessed will be the fruit of your womb and the fruit of your earth,' " Shprintze recited. "Amen."

"Amen," they all said together.

Then Motel and Tzeitel were married— moments before their town was annihilated by hate, by the pogrom the town constable and all his soldiers called a "demonstration." Before all the destruction and enmity to come. Before Perchik stood up for their family and threw himself at the vicious strangers who had burned their barns, broken the windows of Anatevka's high street, destroyed every last wedding gift, and ultimately gripped Bielke by the hair. Before the smoke, which barely masked the putrescent stench of hatred as it filled their village and every village throughout the Pale.

Motel and Tzeitel's wedding was only the beginning.

There was a young woman about Hodel's age working at the camp whose face Hodel recognized. Hodel did not know her, but she saw her every day.

Her name was Irina, and she possessed a composition of features Hodel had never seen before in all her life, had never known to be possible! Her face was shaped like a heart and clothed in a light headscarf—not as Hodel would have worn it, but wrapped beneath her chin in the babushka style of a Russian grandmother. So unusual was this mix (of what some whispered to be both Cossack and Mongol races), at times Hodel could not help but stare—her tawny skin tone and small, flat nose; the height of her cheeks, the prominence and beauty of her bones. Irina—none other than The Gentleman's own daughter.

She was small, her body relentless in its productivity, her manner so reserved, she seldom spoke in anyone's presence. Perhaps it was due to The Gentleman's overprotectiveness that she remained so silent. He kept her close, unvisited, forbidding anyone to speak to her—not only the prisoners, but fellow sentries, guards, and keepers, and soon she had managed to learn a life of silence so effective, she scarcely seemed bothered. Irina would leave her residence in the morning with her head lifted proudly, repelling any man who ventured near her. She'd dart straight from her home at The Gentleman's house to the office and back again, avoiding the taunts of the camp. Life was kept from Irina by an invisible paternal boundary.

But of course, that boundary made nearly every breathing man that stalked the grounds desire her all the more. Irina's was the plight of all unclaimed women in the camp—no matter how untouchable, she was an ever-vulnerable walking target. The majority of women present were not convicts at all, but were the dobrovol'nye. Hodel first heard the term back at her sentencing in Omsk—dobrovol'nye, the voluntary wives. Those that chose. Like her.

Marriage afforded Hodel status—something women such as Irina (no matter how vigilant the watch of her father) did not possess. Unmarried or "unspoken for" females were as exposed and as vulnerable as lambs, and known as "free girls."

Free girls? Hodel thought the first time she heard the term. *Was there even such a thing?*

One day, while scouring the kitchen, Hodel overheard two guards speaking of Irina. Their voices wafted through the tiny window as they polished and re-laced their boots, the smoke of cigarettes floating up with their voices.

"She can't hold out forever, can she?" spoke the first. "Sooner or later *someone* 'as to get her."

"What's the use, mate? What with 'Daddy's girl' written all over her?" replied the second.

"Ah, her skirt—it's precious, after all."

"Precious, indeed."

Like practically everything, women were always in short supply in the Nerchinsk katorga and subsequently were bound to an elaborate underground bureaucracy, which determined a woman's role within the myriad of camp gangs.

"You know, it is not just the skirt, of course."

"No?" The guard sat there, a stroke of genuine wonder in his voice.

"It is the girls themselves! Very useful. Great advantages to being female. Fuck 'em."

"Indeed!"

Free girls were treated like collectibles, trading cards of the flesh. A camp "prostitute" was not like a whore in the outside world—she was bought for a price, then ostensibly belonged to the purchaser until she was traded, lost, or inherited, or her master was transferred to a different camp or otherwise disposed of. Upon such circumstances the girl would then simply submit to a new master. Men could possess only one girl at a time, so they took it very seriously. And the very conversation Hodel was overhearing served as proof that camp officials did not protect the women: they enabled their exploitation.

"Someone's gonna nab her, mate!" cackled the first guard. "Some lucky bloke'll drag 'er out by one leg from the house 'e's always 'iding 'er in and take 'er over a cart behind the kitchen."

"Well, I can't hardly blame 'im," said the second. "It's a need, mate."

Free girls here existed only to satisfy. Such men learned this disdain from the womb.

"I wish it weren't a need, mate," the second guard continued. "I wish I had no need to scratch the itch. But I can't help it."

"Well, scratch what itches—that's what I always say. Hey, you listenin'?" the first guard said, hitting the second square in his chest.

"Yes! I am, yes!" the second guard replied, fending off the other with reciprocal blows to the back of the head.

"What's the matter?" the first guard said, laughing and continuing the beating. "You deaf?"

"Oi! Stop it!"

"Why you 'itting yourself?"

"Hey! Fuck off, please! And stop gettin' all flowery—the girls eat the very same runny soup."

Well. That was true as anything.

Age, infirmity, and disfigurement—those were a free girl's only protections, and even then there were no guarantees. The excessively old or excessively ugly free girls were of good fortune;

they were protected from these fates. Competition for the beauties led to feuds that went far beyond the odd brawl; some grudges between men lasted years, even so long as to be passed from one generation to the next. Eventually every woman ended up in one protective arrangement or another—it was in her best interest to seek it out.

But not Irina. The Gentleman did not see her as the world did, as the woman she was fast becoming. Irina was no free girl and never would be. Irina was the child he still wished her to be— and she would stay that way forever.

A strange place to bring up a daughter. . . .

"No, truly—the girls are far better at lookin' after themselves. Plus they don't need much food, so they don't get the bloody scurvy."

There were unspoken rules too. There were no polygamous relationships, no prostitution rings, no groups of lovers. Female criminals could not be paired with "good men"—only the other way around. And though homosexuality in the men was forbidden, the homosexual women were always left alone. (Some of the men couldn't have crossed those girls even if they wanted to.) This was their silent social code.

"And they get all friendly among themselves— they 'elp one another. Brush each other's hair. Lord, it is lovely!"

There were also a handful of arrangements simply referred to as "camp marriages," insinuating that the marriage was conditional to camp life. These relationships were more loyal (and more permanent) than a criminal "owning" a prostitute like a pack of cigarettes, but it was not sentimental. Marriage was serious, critical business. One man was brutally beaten for having relations with another convict's wife. Whether a legal marriage had simply transferred geographically or had taken place within the camp, it did not matter—a marriage was a marriage, and it was sacred.

thirty-two

Hodel returned that night to find Perchik slumped in his chair, head buried in one hand, a telegram in the other. She gazed down upon his hands and saw the peeling skin and never-healing cracks—the roughness he claimed he never wanted to touch his wife with—and the milky white spots that had recently appeared on the beds of his fingernails. Perchik coughed and ran his fingers through thinning hair.

He was ill. They knew it. The petrification was starting to take him. He would fight to the last. He coughed again; it felt as if his chest were filled with dirty air. Was this the residue of mining life finally filling him? Or just the bitter cold gripping him by the sternum? Or perhaps it was what he feared most: the presence of God appearing from the clouds, as He did to his ancient ancestors. But to punish him for all he had and had not done, God did not materialize before Perchik; he was strangling him from within. Could it be? He hacked once more and gasped for breath.

"Perchik," she said, "what is the matter?"

Perchik remained motionless, unable to rise to her question, and so she took the telegram from his hand, read it, and knew for certain: Gershom was dead. His estate and entire amassed fortune had been left solely to his nephew, Perchik. It awaited him in Kiev.

Perchik never thought about the Lord in the waking hours back in Kiev. In those early days of 1903, the Lord reminded him too much of Gershom. Gershom's God was merciless and uncompromising, dictatorial and cruel; not at all the benevolent teacher, the Father Rabbi Syme had depicted Him to be.

But dreams have a funny way of escorting one into the rich, darkened territories that a conscious mind has no desire to traverse in the light. A passing remark, a comment; dreams are an encumbrance upon one's ingenuity to outsmart the kernels of truth. Invisible in the day, these truths appear at night like heavy-packed horses— blood beating hard through the veins about their necks, cargo on back, straining along the viscid, muddy fields of subconscious as one slumbers.

"Uncle."

Perchik surrendered himself. For should he struggle, the muddy banks would only draw him deeper in.

"Uncle . . ." It was merely a whisper.

It was, of course, the scene he never spoke of. Never thought upon.

At first Perchik beheld the scene from afar, an audience member rather than a player. Gershom withheld a silent sob. His shoulders heaved, his face tormented, a hand upon the edge of a gilded chair supporting a body turned toward the wall. He was recovering from devastation.

"*Uncle . . .*" Perchik said again. This time the voice was not witnessed but, indeed, his own.

He was in the scene now—reliving it as one only can in a nightmare, the heat of his distress palpable as if happening in real time.

This was the scene.

The one that occurred moments after Gershom had rejected Perchik's merger.

The one with *that word*.

Standing on the opposite side of the desk from his contorted uncle, he felt each endless layer of inexplicably heavy clothing—drenched and cold with perspiration—weigh upon him, heavy with a lifetime of washed-out expectations.

"*Uncle . . .*"

The air was thick. Neither man was able to process truth adequately, so they stayed still in their respective positions.

"Perchik," his uncle finally began, ready like a coiled snake, "your *potential*. It's poverty. . . ." Gershom remained facing the wall, body held upright with a shocking strength of sheer will.

"Uncle, *please*. Please, I beg you—"

"Silence!" Gershom swiveled quickly, eyes ablaze. "You disgust me with your pandering repentance, boy." Gershom coughed viciously, as if to clear away the mucus from his mind.

An umbilical cord of desperation tied Perchik to this old man. The moment rang out—a moment of supreme choice. Would Perchik cut the cord, or hang himself with it?

When he had recovered, Gershom narrowed his eyes and spoke again, voice malevolent.

"I will not be taken advantage of. I will not stomach the humiliation of an ungrateful reprobate to whom I have the extraordinary misfortune of being related by blood. My sister filled me with identical rage. She blackened my name with identical infamy. But your vileness infects me as if it were my own. I will no longer endure it." Gershom shrank even further into himself, becoming somehow more venomous and concentrated with every utterance. "What appalling vanity."

The world blurred and turned with a sickening speed—and at once Gershom began to laugh.

"Really, you are so unclean and disappointing, all I can do is laugh," he said, a disturbing sting in his feeble voice. "It is not a lack of empathy! I am entitled. Everything I have sacrificed! I deserve your devotion. Do you not see that you are an extension of my hard-won self?"

Perchik willed him to explain; to apologize for a lifetime of withheld love. Love as counted, measured, and locked away, like every coin in every one of his wretched accounts.

I have worked solidly for you all the years of my life. A lifetime of indentured servitude in which I was denied every kindness, every opportunity for growth, learning, and affection; all to serve your grandiose image of your own worth.

"How you hate me, Uncle."

"Yes, boy, it is true."

Perchik cried out, his face swollen, eyes bloody with disbelief.

"Please," Gershom continued, shaking his head. "You are tethered to me, boy. Try to deny it. Try to be courageous enough to face the world on your own. Without the excuse of Gershom. It is lonely out there without your excuses."

A revolting grin emerged on Gershom's face.

"My boy. What an imbecile you are. For all your genius, you have no sense. Let Uncle Gershom teach you something once and for all: We do not come into the world full of love, my boy; we come in with an insatiable hunger for it. There's a difference. . . ." He sniggered to himself. "Oh, is there a difference. You poured your wealth into a venture unworthy of investment."

Gershom's words reached in, ripped Perchik's sanity from its root, and watched as it squirmed in the cold light of truth, beneath the hateful fingers of the extractor.

Of every test I have ever been presented with in all my life—every problem, puzzle, or complex theory—I have never been presented with anything I could not solve. I have never not *been able to see my way to the answer.*

When Perchik spoke again, it was quiet. "Damn you," he said, his insides churning with misery. "Damn you and your numbers, your beloved accounts. You emotional miser. You have left my soul in poverty!"

"It's odd," said Gershom, breathing more freely now, sitting down on the chair that had previously been supporting him. "I have lost the will to castigate."

Suddenly, Gershom's previously contorted face fell. He blinked hard as if to clear the fog of knowledge, but it was already gnawing away at his mind: it was Gershom's heart that had been broken, not his pride. If it had been pride, how easily he might have turned the boy away once and for all. How simple a matter it would have been.

At last, the old man, seemingly older, said quietly, "That is the gaping hole in my perfection, boy. That is your entrance in. And how you loot—I tell you, boy, there is nothing I detest more in this world than a thief."

Gershom thought another moment, and then said, "Will you not sit with me?"

Perchik did not sit. He could not, in fact, move at all.

For the first time in Perchik's life, he could see that his uncle, in his twisted manner, cared for him. He outstretched a hand to Perchik—the old man's stony face bore no resemblance to the near desperation in his withered reach, and Perchik flinched in horror.

"Do not dare to shudder from me, boy!"

"Did I shudder?" said Perchik, choking down hysteria.

"I do not wish to love things, Perchik." Gershom turned his gaze toward the window, speaking as if only to himself. "I fractured that long ago. But despite every instinct in me, I have loved you. More than money—can you believe that? More than God Himself. God, who taught me to create you in my image! I loved you, you worthless miscreant; I loved you to despair! Not the kind of feeling one would harbor for a child, no. Nor even for a dog. But that of an artist for his greatest work of art. It crept up upon me. Slowly. In amounts so slight and negligible, they were impossible to calculate."

The prison of this duplicitous truth closed in around Perchik.

"You were my dream . . . and that dream I must now abandon. So sit beside me, and take my hand. Do it now. For I must now forsake you; my *son* . . ."

Perchik cried out and left Gershom forever.

Hodel folded the telegram and placed it on the desk. It was Nerchinsk in 1909.

"Perchik," she said, kneeling before him and placing her hands upon his lap. "What would you say to each other now? After everything?"

"My uncle would only ask whether I made money or not," Perchik replied, eyes fixed on the telegram. "That is all he'd want to know."

"Come now, I'm serious."

"So am I," Perchik said, indicating the slip of paper. "According to this, Gershom looked for me for months. But I am certain that is all he would want to know if I ever returned."

Perchik closed his eyes, not wanting to snap at her but unable to utter everything within him in a single explanation; the pulsing shadows of all that had occurred between him and his uncle, the only family he had ever known.

"When I first met you," he said, "what I had done—far more than attempting to teach or proselytize or even simply survive—what I was truly doing was nothing greater than running away from home . . ." He blinked heavily. Her heart roared for him. ". . . like a common, petulant child. I disappeared into the night on a train that carried cargo freight."

She beheld her husband and scarcely recognized him—so contorted was his person. Not even exile burdened him more greatly than the memory of his uncle and all that had and, perhaps more crucially, had not passed between them. He stood and moved toward the desk, his shoulders encumbered with pondering. He turned over papers (as he often did to protect Hodel from the knowledge of his work), detesting every rush of feeling surging through him.

"Money conjured up a fog around my uncle. It can do that. Gershom applied himself so"—his voice caught, the words stuck within his throat—"so passionately, I suppose, to the acquisition of money that he forgot me." Perchik took his eyes from the telegram and looked away. "If the thought of me ever burst through that fog, then another thought crept right in behind it—that I was merely an imposition."

Perchik shrugged his shoulders, this single gesture silently alluding to understanding, forgiveness, a feeble stab at impassivity. Above all, it told her things were better this way.

"And now," he said, "I plot the extinction of private property, and Gershom leaves me his entire fortune. Funny, that—neither one of us out of spite . . ."

Hodel's own heart broke at that. *Goodness,* she thought, *acceptance is so vast a thing.* She believed his peace, yet she saw at the same time how he quietly wore a groove in his desk with his thumb. True peace would be a long time coming.

thirty-three

In open air, in rain and snow, in icy temperatures through the endless cold months of Siberia, long and gloomy were the days and endless was the work. When she first arrived, Hodel had been ordered to haul logs, draw water, or hew wood for fagots and stack them uniform as soldiers. And if the logs were not hearty, the water not clear enough, the fagots not placed sufficiently in tight, symmetrical piles, she was ordered, in a tone colder than the temperatures she worked in, to do it all again. Hodel worked, slogged, and waited. (Waiting was another hell of a convict—one with many depths.) Recently, however, Hodel had been working many a late night in The Gentleman's office.

One day, as Hodel knelt scrubbing mold from the lavatory basins, The Gentleman approached her from behind holding a pamphlet.

"Hello, Hodel," he said in his distinctive, quiet voice. "The guards say that your Russian has become quite impressive."

Hodel saw language as a puzzle—her instincts always led her to the next piece as it locked into place.

"I have always had a talent for it, sir."

"And you do not merely speak, but read and write. Is that so?"

Hodel nodded. "I do not think my husband would have it any other way."

The Gentleman stepped closer and handed her the pamphlet. "Would you care to demonstrate?"

Hodel worked while moths, beetles, snow, and wind all beat against the November-colored windows. The hours were loath to pass as she transcribed, but she was so comfortable here in comparison to the physical labor, she didn't dare complain. Besides, The Gentleman always provided her with a fire and (though modest in appearance) a cushioned chair. Yet, even as she finished and put away each paper, The Gentleman always had something else for her to get done, just one more task in need of completion.

She shared the office work with Irina, of course, The Gentleman's daughter. Irina sat beside The Gentleman's desk at a squat little table of her own, her posture upright as she wrote endlessly upon page after page of import and export, entry and discharge documents, in handwriting as precise as religion. A scrap of black hair swept across Irina's forehead, resting like a leaf. Her brows framed almond eyes so piercing a blue, they betrayed in every way the blood connection to her father.

Oh, judicious blood, thought Hodel, *to select so striking a quality . . .*

One night, Hodel was summoned to The Gentleman's office after hours. She made her way across the grazing land, past the village fences, toward the barracks, and down to the central office. It was a grim place—nothing more than a wooden cabin of heavy post and pillar built with plenty of triangulation to take the winter winds— where The Gentleman worked late into the night. The structure was raised, with nearly four feet of crawl space below it (to allow for ground settling), and the building stood nestled into the bosom of the forest.

The night was as dark as tar, and quiet. Hodel thought she could hear her heart beating beneath her shawl as she rounded the corner to the cabin when all at once she stopped dead.

She heard the heavy fall of unfamiliar feet behind her on the path. She glanced over her shoulder and caught the sight of an imposing man coming toward the office hut. Before she could speak sense to herself, she bolted and hid beside the entrance to the office, hugging the trees at the side of the building.

She could not see his face, for the night was moonless and the figure's head and face were fully covered by an ushanka. He did not seem to be a prisoner; there was too imperious an assurance in his stride as he marched toward the office, wrapped up against the cold. As he came closer, Hodel crouched farther into the shadows, moving into the crawl space below the building. She didn't dare to breathe as he walked up the steps, knocked upon the door, and turned the handle to make his way inside without even waiting for a response. She listened from her perch at the side of the building, irked that she could not see in the window!

"Nerchinsk is *magnificent*," she heard a man say from the shadows of the room. His voice was incredibly distinct—lavish, reeking of the highest breeding. "Eastern Siberia is going to save Russia from extinction. It is becoming one of the best mineral production contributors in the world— as you ought to know if you examined my reports."

"I have," replied The Gentleman.

Hodel thought she had encountered everyone in The Gentleman's circle, so she stood there puzzled, listening even harder. She heard clinking glasses followed by the customary ceremonies of shared vodka.

The unfamiliar voice continued. "How is your work coming along on our target?"

"Slowly," The Gentleman said, his words tight. "Though I can't imagine I've gathered any information you yourself have not yet observed."

"You know how I think on excuses, sir."

"I am attempting a side approach."

"Yes," the Voice said, "I have noticed."

Oh, what Hodel would have given for a glimpse

at their faces, their eyes! She adjusted herself in the spirit of her inquiry and, in doing so, made a terrible rustling in the space beneath the cabin. She cursed herself and held her breath.

"What was that?" the Voice exclaimed, sounding alert.

"Nothing," The Gentleman assured him. "There are creatures that lurk in the crawl space below the cabin. Likely just a rat."

"I see," said the Voice, though he did not sound convinced.

Hodel released her breath, chest thundering.

"Perhaps I am an antiquated man," said the Voice, now walking about the room, "but it certainly seems to be a world full of hostile ungratefuls nowadays. Or perhaps it is just the rancor of a frustrated God."

Brutal coarseness is so often concealed in good breeding. Hodel could actually feel The Gentleman start to wither beneath the glower of the Voice's covered criticism.

"I think without men like you, sir, Russia is to collapse," the Voice continued. "Do you no longer love Russia?"

"Of course not. On the contrary—I am endeavoring to *save* her," The Gentleman said.

"Ah!" the Voice exclaimed. "How arduous a task! Mother Russia, thou art indeed a beloved lady!" He chuckled heartily, and Hodel heard him settle his body down once more. "We cannot always keep a dog subservient, my friend. When he refuses to obey the whip, we must trick him into a muzzle. That is your employment. That is why you are here."

"I am trying, sir," The Gentleman insisted, betraying the slightest hint of a faltering man, "but the system—"

"There is a flaw in your system," the Voice said, icier than before. "The point is simple. Our friend has become markedly more reserved, and reservation is a quality I've never trusted. He also bears a glow of self-satisfaction. Terrible thing, smugness."

"Agreed."

"And not a bit weaker, it appears."

"What do you propose, sir?"

"Get it done," the Voice said suddenly. "You fail at your own peril."

With that, the man strode to the door and let it slam behind him. Once outside, he gathered his coat closer around him, the high collar covering any trace of his identity. He stood there a moment, and Hodel watched as he withdrew a flask from his pocket, unscrewed it, and emptied the contents into the snow.

"Tastes of a stain," he muttered to himself before twisting the cap back on and lumbering off into the night.

Hodel's blood was pounding, body sweltering despite the bite of the air. She inched forward, still clinging to the wooden beams of the building, looking hard into the dark that had swallowed him.

From within the room, Hodel was surprised to suddenly hear another voice.

"Father?" Irina asked. "May I go?"

"Of course, my doll, my *kukolka moya.*"

Hodel heard The Gentleman move to the window just above her head and she froze, tense even in her womb. But at once he turned and called to his daughter before she could depart.

"Irinushka?" The Gentleman said.

Hodel heard no response.

"Irina," The Gentleman said softly. "From the Greek for peace. That is what you give me, my darling."

Hodel heard Irina take leave of the room and then, before Hodel could think to retreat farther beneath the building, Irina rounded the corner. Startled face to startled face, the two women froze, like animals caught in a trap.

What was curious was that Irina looked guilty. Her breath heaved in billowing clouds of nervous air. But what had *she* to hide?

A sharp hiss came from the cluster of trees behind the hut. Irina gasped and turned sharply, imploring, "Shhh!" She extended her hands as if to keep the hiss at bay.

Then from the wood emerged—to Hodel's great astonishment—Andrey Tenderov. His skin was glowing, his curling hair practically cherubic in the feeble light.

Irina turned wildly back to Hodel. "You won't tell, will you?" Irina pleaded, her blue eyes shaking.

"*Please,* Hodel," Tenderov whispered from the wooded umbra. "I love her."

Hodel looked at them and felt a pang within her breast. She turned to Irina without smiling and extended her hand with the flourish of a bargain. Irina nodded silently, taking Hodel's hand in gratitude. Then she dashed toward Tenderov, and the two clasped hands before dashing away, swathed by a night now as dark as blood. She watched them go. She would stay silent because she understood.

Hodel gathered herself, climbed the steps of the cabin, and knocked twice (as she had been instructed since her first day in the office), then the door opened. There was The Gentleman.

"Ah, Hodel, come in, come in." He was noticeably off his center. "I am sorry you have made the extra journey tonight, for Irina has just finished the very pages I called upon you to complete. I hope you understand."

"Of course, sir," she said. Her eyes searched the room for any hints of the mysterious man.

"For your troubles, I would like to give you this," he said, doddering to the back room where he kept his teas and sweet things. He returned a moment later with a small brown bag. "I know how well your husband enjoys tea."

Hodel was caught off guard. "Thank you, sir," she said. "He does indeed—and tea is so hard to come by."

"I want you to be comfortable. We are family here, Hodel. Family."

"Yes, sir."

The candles flickered as she made a little gracious curtsy to him, throwing shadows upon the walls. These walls had heard so much in just one night.

"Good night, Hodel," he said as he moved back toward his desk and took his seat. "I look forward to the pleasure of seeing you again in the morning. Perhaps I might have the pleasure of escorting you from the Volosnikovs' again?"

She nodded. "Good night, sir."

thirty-four

"G ood evening," Dmitri Petrov said from the doorway, the shadows from the clear night stark upon his cheeks.

"Good evening, Dmitri," Hodel replied.

But he did not move.

So she added, "Are you well?"

"I am," he said, then paused again, as if waiting for her to indicate how he should proceed in conversation. She raised her eyebrows and smiled, and he shook himself abruptly and asked, "And you?"

"I am well," she said more brightly, amused by his blunders in the face of femininity.

"Good."

"Well, good."

There was another pause, this time even longer. At last, Hodel spoke. "Would you like to come in?"

"I would," said Dmitri Petrov, charging through the threshold with relief.

Their awkward dance in the doorway was surprising, given that Dmitri Petrov was in her home every day, sometimes for hours at a time. Yet she knew so little of his life, so few facts of his upbringing, tastes, proclivities, and cares.

She knew only what she could observe. What she could see, most clearly, was that Dmitri Petrov was a man of contradictions.

He appeared to be a man who, at every opportunity, attempted to regard life as indifferently as possible. She often heard him extol the virtues of this philosophy. "Not having to engage with petty feelings unless one chooses to?" he would say. "How liberating!" This was his starting point— as if someone (or something) had taught him he must not to be bogged down by care. He viewed his indifference as a shield against an adversarial world.

If only any of that were true. All his protestations indicated that perhaps Dmitri Petrov cared *too* much. He loathed, then cared, then loathed himself for caring. The very reserve he valued so highly burned a hole in him with ferocity. She watched him fidget as he waited for Perchik alone in her presence. Full of respect but lacking in all social graces, he paced the floors of their home, collar raised, injured hands (which ached to play the cello) in fists within his pockets, red-eyed from a seeming sadness.

When Perchik entered from the back of the house, Hodel observed immediate relief in the drop of Dmitri's shoulders, and straightaway the men began discussing in an urgent, impassioned shorthand only two possible subjects: the state of the country or Yevgeny.

Dmitri had not yet removed his coat and seemed content to pace across the room. "At least a vulture waits until you are dead to eat you alive!" he declared.

"Mitya, why don't you take off your coat and sit down?" Hodel entreated. "I'll make some tea." She remembered The Gentleman's fancy tea and removed it from her satchel as Dmitri finally sat down, coat still on.

The fact was this: all the People's plans had been deterred; the party leaders had scattered to various exiles.

"Back in the cities, you know the Bolsheviks and Mensheviks and all the splinter parties of the movement hate one another!" cried Dmitri Petrov.

"Yes, but in light of the new Duma—"

"I'm sorry—what is the Duma?" asked Hodel.

"The State Duma, darling. In theory it is a legislative assembly in place to advise and enforce some change with the tsar," Perchik replied.

"Surely it has some effect?"

"No, just the problem. It is conservative and largely useless under the autocracy. Nothing but agricultural talk that helps us not a bit thus far. But the new Duma is being convened in St. Petersburg, and various proletariat leaders are hoping to unite the party."

"But the whole country is still in upheaval and

the newspapers are in a frenzy!" said Dmitri, unconvinced. "Ah, well," he sighed. "One man's publicity is another man's propaganda."

Perchik laughed.

"What are you laughing at?"

"The way your glass truly is half-empty," Perchik said, smiling.

"I hate when you laugh me off as if I were some sort of stormy youth," Dmitri Petrov huffed.

"You are a stormy youth."

This caused Dmitri's inner storm to rumble even louder. "I am no such thing!"

Perchik laughed again. Dmitri still had not taken off his coat.

"I cannot for the life of me understand—" Dmitri began.

"How impatience can turn even geniuses into fools?" Perchik finished for him. *Where on earth did these leaders go?* he thought to himself. The scatter was all anyone could speak of these days.

"But the *People*," Dmitri insisted, practically choking from the strength of his pent-up passion, "and their rights—"

"All people have the right to foolishness," Perchik replied. "Some just abuse the privilege."

Perchik smiled, but his signature steadiness seemed less natural these days, more studied. Even when sitting, he was not still. A restlessness mirrored his ever-moving mind. Yet he was not thrown off his purpose, only off his serenity.

All Hodel could determine from Perchik's whisperings was that their leader had resumed his exile and was now touring Europe, practically nowhere to be found.

"The Stormy Youth broods, but the remaining half a glass shall evaporate by the morning," Perchik said.

"Well, the Revolutionary Zealot thinks the glass is completely full, even when it isn't!"

There was the difference between these friends: if Perchik was truth wrapped in human feelings, then Dmitri was truth stuffed to bursting with them.

"I fear man himself has become our greatest hazard," Dmitri muttered.

"And our only hope," Perchik said with a chaste smile.

Hodel could feel her heart shift in her chest; it ached for both of them.

"Anyway," Perchik said. "Arguing about glasses being half-empty or half-full misses the point."

"Which is what exactly?"

"That the bartender cheated you."

Perchik laughed. When the time came, he would be ready, prepared to go to battle with the hammers of his words, nailed upon the walls of the sky. He knew that these developments called for poise. For patience. He hoped only to make that clear to Dmitri as well.

" 'The gift of patience is patience,' " he said. "That's St. Augustine."

Hodel smiled, hoping to understand. Too often, she felt that she did not.

Perchik had told her to be quiet, to "behave," and above all, to trust no one. "Particularly those who appear innocent," he had said, adamant that she know as little as possible. "It is infinitely safer this way." He had been insistent. When she had said she wanted to be a part of it, he had held her face between his ragged hands and told her, "This work is not the most important thing in my life—you are." And he had kissed her. Hard. Clutching her close to him as their mouths parted. They would, all of them, persevere.

So Hodel contented herself to overhearing what she could of Perchik's conversations with his compatriots. But this one with Dmitri had now come to an end.

Dmitri stood, moved toward the window, and gazed out upon the camp, hands clasped behind his back.

He could not look at them.

"It is late," he said, clutching at the pockets of his still-buttoned coat. "I should go." He made his way to the door, and as he opened it, he noted workers at the border of the settlement. "Look," he said. "It would appear they are erecting some kind of fence."

• • •

Within days, it became clear: the fence was indeed a reality. Hodel, Perchik, and Dmitri stood at a distance, staring. Grisha, Anatoly, and Andrey soon joined them in a near perfect line.

"What *is* it?" asked Andrey Tenderov.

"Clearly it is a fence," said Dmitri Petrov.

"I know," said Andrey, wrapping his arms tight around himself in the cold. "But what *is* it? Why is it there?"

"Well, to keep things in, of course," Dmitri said.

"And to keep things out," Grigory Boleslav said.

The wind stabbed with a new kind of utterly forbidding cold. It reduced the prisoners to a constant nervous irritability that broke out over every trifle. No one could think or work or sleep.

"Oh, that's nothing," Grisha continued. "You should have seen the fence they put up around the factory where I worked in Petersburg. It was an abomination."

"No one asked for your life story, Grisha," Dmitri snapped.

"Oh, sit on your cello bow," Grisha shot back.

"Well, I don't think I would enjoy that as much as *you*."

"Piss off."

"Ah, 'piss off'—the retort of the inarticulate!"

Hodel could no longer take it. "Both of you be quiet!" she barked. "It is too cold."

Just then, Yevgeny approached with a broad smile, holding a dog nearly half his size.

"Hello!" Yevgeny cried in sheer delight. "Look! Look!"

"What on earth is that?" Dmitri Petrov asked.

"It's a dog!" Yevgeny lifted the dog toward them.

"I know it is a d—" Dmitri Petrov caught himself and pulled back his tone of frustration. Hodel had recently teased him about having a temper. He was endeavoring to be better, though he insisted that he did not have a temper; it was merely that Yevgeny had an effect on him. He closed his eyes, took a breath, and said calmly, "Where did you get the dog?"

"He crawled under the fence over there!" Yevgeny exclaimed, gesturing with his shoulder.

There it was, clear as anything: if you looked hard enough, you could see the dog had indeed burrowed a tunnel under the fence through the frost. The plainness of the action pleased Hodel. She looked back at Yevgeny, beaming. "Well done, little one!" she said, wrapping her hands around the dog's snow-covered face, scratching behind his ears.

"Isn't it marvelous, Hodel?" said Yevgeny. "Look at him—he's got nothing! No owner, no food. But he is free! Look at him! Take it in!"

With that, he placed the dog on the ground and watched as the creature took off, racing away and coming back, then repeating the pattern in an attempt to get Yevgeny to chase him.

"The rains fall, but he doesn't mind; he bathes in his freedom!" Yevgeny picked up a stick from the ground and ran toward the dog, then tossed the stick for him to fetch. Yevgeny turned back to them, his smile somehow warming the entire day.

"What shall you call him, Yevgeny?" asked Perchik.

"Dmitri!"

Dmitri Petrov scoffed angrily as Grisha doubled over in hysterics.

"Yes! In honor of you, Mitya! Now we shall have Dmitri the dog and Dmitri the person. Isn't it lovely?"

Dmitri Petrov looked to Hodel and Perchik for assistance in the matter, but they both just shook their heads and smiled, the entire proceeding deeply amusing to them both. Perchik extended an arm and patted his friend on the shoulder. He was met with a stony stare.

"I am leaving," Dmitri said. He folded his arms angrily and headed toward the barracks. They watched him go, muttering to himself, kicking the ground as he walked. Perhaps it was best.

Hodel turned to Perchik and they shared a laugh. Honest cheerfulness—the kind not manufactured or played at—was hard to see these days, but here it was. Perchik's thinning face produced a smile so spirited that Hodel's heart heaved. He pulled her toward him and kissed the side of her head, overcome with the joy of it all.

"Just wait until I show Anatoly," cried Yevgeny. "He so loves dogs!"

They all watched as the dog returned to his tunnel and slid to the other side of the new, imposing fence, then back again, his every atom free of care, his only interest merriment.

"Well, I'm going back," Grigory Boleslav said. "Watching creatures have that much fun in internment just depresses me."

They all turned to go, and in the distance Hodel noticed The Gentleman, noticing her.

She turned back to Yevgeny. He watched as the dog dug his way to the other side for the final time, under the fence and out of sight, as if he sensed the play was done.

"Look at that," Yevgeny said, suddenly reverential. "The dog does not know borders. We should learn from him."

thirty-five

The evenings could be brutally boring in the filthy barrack structures.

With what little they had, the men put into the *maidan*, an institution combining a black market and a gambling den, along with the kinds of games that could only be found in bachelors' barracks. Were it not for these games, their songs, and the stealthily acquired drink aplenty, all sanity would have been lost.

The men wore their work rags around the clock, but prisoners were known to gamble away or sell even their work rags for cigarettes. Or sex. Or vodka. Tonight, like all the others, was just such an evening. The men staked out their corners of the room. Their quarters were in a state of overcrowded, arrant disrepair—dark, encrusted with a coating of muddy ice, all caved-in lamely, as if against a crutch.

They were assembled as usual in what was beginning to feel like their assigned places: Tenderov lay reclined upon his bunk reading a slim, beaten volume of poetry, occasionally picking up his hand and making a play at the card game Grigory and Anatoly were both taking more seriously (but had trouble keeping track of due to Yevgeny's constant comings and goings with the dog). In the farthest corner, away from all the men and merriment, Dmitri Petrov sat upon a chair playing his cello; his flowing motions brought hushed vibrations to the room that floated above the cacophony of men. His eyes were closed, his forehead tense, but every other part of him seemed at ease in a way he never was in the life beyond his music.

Dmitri Petrov finished his song, opened his eyes, and looked at the men. They were crouched, playing cards on the ground.

"What happened to the card table?" he asked.

"We burned it." replied Yevgeny.

"Burned it?" repeated Dmitri.

"Yes."

"Why?" The heat of Dmitri's temper was rising.

"Well, fire is very hot," said Yevgeny, "and it was very cold."

"It is always cold."

"Well, look, we had a bit of a discussion about it and then we—"

"Burned it."

"Yes."

"For firewood."

"That's what I said, yes."

Dmitri Petrov considered this in disgust.

"If it is any consolation," chimed in Grigory, "it burned very well."

"Oh, well then!"

"Indeed, Mitya!" Yevgeny said cheerfully to his

bunkmate. "Quite bright! All those great games and laughs we shared were *in* the wood!"

"Yes," Grigory said with a smirk. "It went up in an instant and burned so brilliantly, as if it had been doused in alcohol."

"Woof!" Yevgeny laughed but could see that Dmitri was distressed, so he moved closer to console him. "Look, it's all right, Dmitri Petrov. We simply play on the floor now."

"Good God, what is the point of anything anymore?" Dmitri slammed his bow down and stood, clutching his head. It was precisely the overreaction of a thinking man whose mind has been kept idle in a prison camp.

"Dmitri, it is only a table!"

"Only a table? It was all we had!" Dmitri cried. "What will you all burn next? Our beds? The roof? My own cello—shall you use it for scraps as I sleep?"

"Calm down, Dmitri," Grigory barked. "Get ahold of yourself! Hysteria does not become you."

That was how it was when Hodel entered that night.

"Good evening, men," she greeted, a little breathless. Locking eyes with Dmitri Petrov, her face conveyed all the probing curiosity of her thoughts. "Mitya, Perchik says to meet him."

"Meet him? At this hour?"

She nodded. "Yes."

"Very well." Dmitri placed his cello on its side and grabbed his coat. "Not a one of you is to touch or stroke or even think of burning that cello—not out of any desperation. If a man even looks at it sideways, I will burn *him!*" He stared them down and stormed out with the look of a tiger about to shred his prey.

"Touchy," muttered Grigory Boleslav, eyebrows raised.

"*Basta!*" declared Anatoly, clapping. "I win!"

Grigory and Tenderov handed over their trinkets, three cigarettes, a little vile of liquor, a pair of fingerless gloves.

"Well, I'm off for some air," Andrey Tenderov declared, folding his book and rising. "Losing makes the air stuffy." He smiled, grabbed his coat, and left as Anatoly counted his winnings.

Dmitri stood reading the decoded pages as Perchik retched upon the rocks near their meeting point.

"Do you see?" Perchik asked, wiping his mouth as he rose for air.

"I do," replied Dmitri, rigid.

Perchik retched again, trying hard to muffle the sound through dry lips and thick saliva. The last few weeks had brought a successively more withered Perchik; his guts ached, and he returned from the belly of the mines with an ever-growing thirst.

"Are you all right, comrade?"

"I am, I am, read on, please," Perchik said. His tone was clipped, tense, and so unlike his usual self that Dmitri jolted in response.

Dmitri looked at the unbound pages in his hands. The title was a bit blurred, as if from an ancient printing press, but clear nevertheless: *Materialism and Empirio-Criticism.* And, at the bottom, a signature: *Vladimir Lenin, 1909.*

"I scarcely know what to say," Dmitri muttered. "It is certain?"

"Most certain," said Perchik. He lowered his voice even further, to the slightest hint of a whisper. "Dmitri, this is not only an ideological unifier. It lays the foundation for real life. This publication will eradicate all philosophic doubts about the practical course of revolution—it will make our theories a reality. More crucially, it is proof that he is alive and in Europe just as I suspected! Our friends would not have dared to contact us so brazenly if it were not so." Perchik's eyes were wild, gears turning in his head.

"Who are these *friends* you speak of, comrade?" Dmitri asked. "Why be so secretive?"

"I cannot say."

"No!" Dmitri said. "You can say and you shall. You wanted me involved—well, I'm involved. We are friends, Perchik. We're practically brothers out here in this godforsaken place! I collect and deliver your post, do all that you say, and I don't even know who the messages are from? I deserve better. Tell me."

"It isn't safe."

"What? Less safe than already being in internment, doing physical labor in easternmost Siberia?"

"Fine, fine." Perchik sighed and looked around them. "The messages are from Leonid."

"Trotsky?"

"Shh!"

Dmitri rasped in an angry whisper. "All right, comrade, you had me taken. I thought you were a dreamer. I had no idea you were this involved. I am out—I cannot help you further. I am a *musician;* I am a graduate student and terrible editor of a university newspaper. I have not the stomach for actual politics!"

"Dmitri. That is not true. You are a good man. A brave one."

"Nonsense. I am not capable of this kind of courage!"

Perchik took Dmitri by the shoulders and looked through the lenses of his glasses, square into his eyes.

"It would not be courage, comrade, if you were not afraid."

Dmitri hesitated, nodding. "What of your 'friend' himself—is he not threatened by—"

"Leonid Trotsky is a *theorist,* and we all know

320

it!" interrupted Perchik. "Lenin is powerful. A *doer*—and we must do. Quickly."

Dmitri shoved the papers into Perchik's chest. "Fine."

"We must get out of here," said Perchik.

"You think?" Dmitri rasped in exasperation—as if needing to get out of Nerchinsk was news.

"I am serious. We must escape this place, Dmitri."

"Escape?" Dmitri cried, only to be grabbed by his collar and shushed by Perchik. Dmitri now spoke in anger below his breath. "We are weak and starving—and oh, that's right, *imprisoned*—five thousand kilometers from Petersburg. How are we to escape now?"

"We must find a way to distract the guards and officers. Create some kind of grand diversion—a disturbance so epic, it will occupy them for just enough time for us to flee."

"Us?" Dmitri grabbed his eyes hard behind his spectacles. "Who exactly is 'us'?"

But Perchik did not answer that. He grew very grave as he spoke. "The People matter, Dmitri Petrov. *We* matter. Though we whisper here in hiding, there are thousands weaker still, whose voices cannot be heard at all. We must speak for them. Work for them. Believe for them." Perchik grabbed Dmitri by the shoulders and shook him so hard, his glasses jumped. "We have developed a talent for enduring calamity. The great calamity has yet to arrive, and when it does, think how prepared we shall be."

Not a soul alive had ever been capable of soothing Dmitri Petrov, let alone rallying him. He nodded. "All right," he sighed. "What now?"

"I will develop a plan with our allies—"

"How?"

"Never mind that! Listen, Dmitri. When they question you—and they will—you must profess that you know nothing. Can you swear that to me?"

Dmitri had never seen Perchik like this before. He gripped his head and took a long breath, his mind tied up in bleeding knots. He could not contemplate failing Perchik.

"I swear."

"It will be brutal—"

"Enough! I said I swear!" Dmitri turned away. Perchik placed a hand upon his shoulder.

From down the road, Anatoly called to them. "Hark, boys, what's all that noise up there about? Come then, it's freezin'. Whatever yer gabbin' about can wait. I got a glass 'er two o' liquor with yer names upon 'em! It's my winnings from the maidan."

Dmitri could not meet Perchik's gaze. "All right, then, Anatoly," he called, and moved to leave, but Perchik grabbed his arm.

"Bruises will heal, Dmitri Petrov," Perchik whispered. "The world might not."

thirty-six

Perchik lay slumped over his work, fast asleep. Remnants of tea sat in the bottom of his glass, papers sprawled and candles snuffed out. Somehow the objects captured the current essence of Perchik himself. Day after day, the men descended down coffin-like staircases into the bowels of the earth, the only light from flaming lamps and the mouths of the mines above their heads. The fact that he had his wits about him was more a miracle than a blessing.

She gazed upon him now—overworked, worn. It was late, and as was usual for the last few months, Perchik had returned from the mines only to spend the remainder of his waking hours poring over his papers. It was becoming more and more difficult to deny that he was physically withering. His nose bled constantly, his extremities were always cold, the skin all over his body had lost elasticity. He was growing progressively more lethargic, and sometimes, at night, he would riot against the cramping in his extremities—his limbs wriggling as worms might fight a hook.

But still, she gazed upon him and stared, breathless for a moment. What was it about Perchik as he lay curled at his desk, enveloped in the mining shirt of coarse, tarnished linen and fraying trousers? What moved her so as she saw him sleeping there, his visions sprawled before him, laid out like a map of all the universe? Drawings, diagrams, and plans, everything he aspired to build, invent, or create, set before him in neatly coded piles.

Her nightdress had fallen open slightly, and she gathered it around herself as she looked over the weighty volumes, candles that had extinguished down to nubbins, and endless sheets of scribbled, coded papers. She was careful not to startle him. Perchik's left hand was outstretched, having fallen almost elegantly atop his notebook like a small sculpture, as if he had collapsed into this slumber in the middle of a thought. The fingers were still holding his pencil, the side of his palm blackened with lead as it always was from the hours of writing from left to right in Russian—he always preferred to write in Hebrew for that very reason, and she smiled to herself at these details that made up their marriage.

Her eyes moved toward the hand, and she could not help but peek at the smudged scrawl below it. It was a coded telegram from the West, which Perchik had decoded lightly below the type. It simply read: *Empirio-criticism*. Below that, in his own hand, Perchik had made a note: *The People are important.*

That was all it said. She could hear the steady

beat of his heart, the quiet purr of his breathing, and she was at once torn apart with tenderness, unable to keep from pressing her ear to his back to listen.

He sat up suddenly, at once alert. "What is it?"

"Darling, you must come to bed," Hodel said. She carefully marked and folded his notebooks.

He glanced out the window into the inky blackness. "What is the hour?" he asked.

"I don't know. But you must rest. Besides," she smiled coyly, "I am freezing all alone in there." She extended her hand to him, and he placed his lead-smudged hand in her own. She kissed him as she helped him rise. He clutched her for a moment, but then, with a sense of defeat, he moved away.

"I can't."

This was another recent, more devastating development, though Hodel wasn't sure if it was a symptom of his health, a result of stress, or something greater.

"It is all right, my love," she soothed.

But it wasn't. Not for him.

"This letter. I must finish it," he said, turning back to the table. "It is important."

"Tomorrow, Perchik. It can wait."

He followed his wife to bed.

In the middle of the night, it awoke them: a wretched scream. And then another—the kind from the guts, a cataclysm of horror. Commotion outside mounted as Hodel rushed to the door to witness the scene.

Irina stood outside her father's house—feet bare, hair unraveled in a whip of anguish, the frosted earth staining the sheet that half covered her body. Her feral eyes looked at the glowing mouth of her father's door. The Gentleman exploded from the house as she inched backward through the mire. With one swipe of efficient malice, he gripped her by the hair, lifting her up like a kicking rabbit beneath the fist of a furious farmer. He smacked her hard across the jaw, his stoic face betraying a pain so great, a disappointment so profound, that the icy blue of his eyes practically burned within the rims of his spectacles.

"Oi!" the guards bellowed from within. "Oi! Here's the scum, sir. Here's the foul defiler!"

The guards emerged, grappling against the thrashing offender, who heaved in fury. Andrey Tenderov—incandescent in his nakedness—was thrown upon the ground.

This time, he did not sing.

"Father, no!" Irina screeched.

The Gentleman howled, "He has murdered my daughter to me—do you not see?" He shook Irina by the hair and slapped her face. "I will throw you in the box for this, Tenderov! The box, do you hear me? Though you deserve far worse!"

"Good God, Perchik, what is the box?" Hodel asked, her voice quiet with fear.

"The box," Perchik said, "is a type of living coffin. A packing case adorned on all sides with broken glass, rusty nails, and any other sharp blade, spike, or spare fragment. The box is almost entirely dark; some report a little facial window where officers and guards can look in on a prisoner, feed him bits of food perhaps. It is constructed in such a way that one can only stand, and even then is pressed tightly against the sharp walls. It is a torture."

"How can they do that?" Hodel asked, aghast.

"They can do anything, Hodel," Perchik said, taking her hand. Their group watched as The Gentleman rained blows upon Irina in his fury. "They can, and will, do anything at all. Surely you have realized that by now."

"No!" Tenderov charged forward demonically, the guards barely containing him. "Do not lay a hand on her! *Not a finger!*"

"Stop this clamor of heroism, Tenderov," The Gentleman said, releasing his grip on his daughter. He locked eyes with Tenderov and smoldered. "It is too late."

Not once before this moment had Hodel witnessed fear in Tenderov's eyes. But as the lovers clawed for each other, ripped apart by the guards in the mud-soaked squalor of the night, there it lay.

"Father, *please*." Irina's voice was dark and low, then she wept as the guards dragged her lover away.

Hodel stood at the door. She was unable to tear her eyes from the prints upon the mud. They were like lacerations of memory, motionless and weeping in the moonlight.

thirty-seven

Hodel used to find The Gentleman's office quite peaceful in its near silence—the imposing regulation clock with its harsh utilitarian angles, audibly ticking as if it echoed the sonorous heartbeats of the hutch's inhabitants. But tonight, as she and Irina worked side by side, the quiet unnerved her. Everything was stillness but for the etching of the fountain pens, the gentle thud of books as they were stacked. A flutter of papers, a drawer closed, a breath. Tonight, the din felt constant. The air was taut with it. Only the drained color in Irina's face indicated the fretting of her mind; every other gesture maintained her customary efficiency.

"Irina," The Gentleman said at long last. "The Irkutsk export files, please."

"Yes, sir," she replied, as if she were speaking to a stranger, and left the room.

Hodel watched the scene as if she were watching it from very far away. She observed The Gentleman in all his flawless machinations: the compulsive starch of his shirts, the shining shirt buttons, the blinding polish of his boots. Nothing on his person betrayed the violence from the night before.

"Hodel," The Gentleman said. "My ink is low.

Do please fetch a replacement and be quick about it."

"Of course, sir."

Hodel left the room and entered the large cupboard of office supplies in the back of the office hut. As she reached for an inkwell, Irina stepped into the cupboard with her, shoving a stack of bound-up letters into Hodel's hands.

"I do not work for or with my husband," Hodel whispered. "I know nothing of his work nor of his—"

"Those letters are not for him," Irina interrupted. "Those are letters that have been kept from *you*. I thought it was time you had them."

Hodel gazed down at what looked to be dozens of letters. She searched them for hints of the language, handwriting, or original location, but rough journeys over great distances and the ravages of time had worn much of the envelopes away.

"They are from your family, Hodel. Your oldest sister, I believe." Hodel looked from the bundle in her hands to Irina. "A few of them are open."

"How did you come upon these?" Hodel asked.

"You wrote and sent letters to your family from the jail in Omsk, yes?"

"I did."

"To whom did you give those letters to post?"

"Well . . ." Hodel hesitated. "A certain jailer, if I recall. He was a criminal himself. A Pole who had lost his family in the war of independence."

"Well," replied Irina, "how extraordinary. He posted your letters, and after discovering your assignment, he forwarded all their correspondence here."

"But why have I not received them until now, and in such secrecy?"

"Officers often intercept personal post—sometimes for protection, other times for punishment, but more often than not, because they simply forget." Irina shrugged. "On occasion I rummage through the lost and found, as well as the storeroom in the post office. I found these a while back. I saw they were addressed to you, and so I set them aside. I didn't know quite what to do with them—one never knows how another feels about their family, especially when they are interned."

Hodel looked down at the stack of letters and noted that the last one was in Tzeitel's hand, dated well over two years ago, postmarked from Warsaw. "Thank you," Hodel whispered, and tucked them deep within her coat.

They heard the door click, and as it locked The Gentleman subsequently knocked upon it twice.

"What is going on?" Hodel asked.

"Father's superior is here," Irina replied. "That is the signal to remain within until he has left the main office."

"Who is he?" Hodel asked. Such a thing had never occurred before.

"I have never seen his face," Irina replied. "He is just a voice—that is how most people know him."

So that was who Hodel had encountered that night she first discovered Irina and Andrey's tryst in the forest. The voices were muddled, the visit clearly tense; before long, there was another double knock upon the door, and Irina made a movement to leave the storeroom.

"Wait!" Hodel cried. "Please wait."

Irina turned and stared intently, her turbid eyes clearing to reveal their iciness for a blinking moment, and it occurred to Hodel that she had never really heard her speak—not really. The two women stood there in silence, recognizing each other. Hodel gazed into the luminous blue of Irina's eyes and suddenly felt clean in her presence. How odd that Russia was tearing itself to shreds with murder and torture, work camps, political unrest, and God knew what else, and here they stood: two women who loved their men with a ferocity no picturesque words could give shape to. *But I know her,* Hodel thought. *I know her through and through.* Yet something plagued Hodel's mind—like sand within the soft folds of her brain.

Here, in this scene of swamped humanity, they understood each other perfectly. Hodel shuddered. Irina's fate might be her own.

Irina's eyes clouded over; she nodded to Hodel and left without another word.

"Thank you, Hodel, that will be all for tonight," The Gentleman said as he put his pen away and tapped his paperwork into a pile.

It was odd to look upon The Gentleman now that they had all witnessed what lay so silently within. His mind, in its unnaturally quiet contemplation, seemed to reject the possibility of an independent daughter. He had exposed his weakness: his wild love for his child and his unexamined suffering was so surprisingly human, it humbled him in Hodel's eyes. If wanting is the overarching quality of existence, then there is no existence more terrible than that of the unloved. Suffering: it cannot be shared. And for this she pitied him.

"Would you care for a spot of drink?" he asked, quite out of nowhere. "I do think it is bad luck to drink alone." She noted that tonight, his corpulence did not look like an attribute of status, but more like a shield. "Did you care for your father, Hodel?"

Hodel almost could not answer; her throat was thick. "Very much," she said at last.

There was a certain expression that would reveal itself on her father's face whenever he felt a surge of deep paternal feeling. It was an expression of utter adoration. For all Tevye's bluster and grumbling on about how worn-down he felt by the women in his life, oh, how he loved his girls. There was a certain crinkling at the corners of his eyes, an unforgettable spark that would ignite whenever any one of them filled his heart. She remembered his laugh—big, bellowing, true. His smell—of milk and horses and work. Above all, she remembered the broad expanse of his arms tight around her the very last time they embraced on the frigid train platform in Anatevka, both knowing (though they did not utter it) that they might never see each other again. Until that morning, Hodel had not yet discovered who she truly was. Tevye learned who his daughter was that day on the train platform. He met her as she met herself, then just as quickly, they lost each other forever. A part of her would be on that platform with him for eternity.

"That is the most important thing, you know: family." He spoke with his back turned, filling two glasses before swiveling to face her. "Shall we drink to that, then?"

She felt the liquid scald her as it went down—so white a heat, no wonder the men adored it. *This is unbelievably strong liquor,* she thought as her head swarmed with sparkling lights. She blinked hard against it. *Too strong,* she thought, before trying to apologize but losing her balance for a moment, accidentally leaning against him with her hip.

As he caught her from falling over, his eyes locked on hers. They both stood very still, and she felt a chill run down her skin, for she knew he could feel Irina's packet of letters concealed within her jacket.

Had her mind been clearer, had her faculties been less roily with drink, she would have spoken, explained, rallied some excuse or story. But, as quickly as it had occurred, The Gentleman's expression thawed; he helped Hodel to her steadiness and muttered, "Perhaps too strong a drink for a lady." He smiled softly. "It is a very strong liquor, indeed. Best get yourself home. Here," he said, handing her a parcel, "take another package of that tea your husband so enjoys, with my apologies."

She gathered herself and nodded obligingly.

"Thank you, sir," she said, her mind murky. "Good night, then."

"Sleep well, Hodel."

Hodel stumbled homeward, barely able to see clearly through the murk of liquor.

She awoke hours later in a stupor; her head swam and her eyes throbbed, as if stung by bees. Her limbs were heavy, tingling. Thoughts rose within her slowly. She recalled her halting balance; she remembered falling into bed with her clothes on. She felt about herself. *Still dressed,* she thought, *and sweltering*. She clutched at her ears. Her head throbbed. *What has happened?*

She reached across the bed for Perchik's imprint and stretched out in hopes of touching his meager heat against her own. Then, piercing her consciousness like lightning was the coldness of his absence: *Where is he?*

It was in this moment that she knew the full force of Nerchinsk's distinctive iniquity. Before now she had glimpsed only at the surface—the unspeaking mouths of the mines, which, though silent, screamed. Small and potent was the devastation at first: a spark in a slowly billowing flame.

The room spun wildly. She clutched at the wall.

Perchik was gone.

thirty-eight

Nights, of course, had always been dark, but darkness was different for Hodel now. In Perchik's absence she traveled all of its corners and infinities, and knew darkness to be a kingdom with no bottom and no end. Her nights were still but never silent—she could feel Perchik's heart beating in time with her own from across the world, and that was how she knew with certainty he was alive. When she slept, it was to dream of Perchik, but as slumber wrapped her in its billows, a distant but familiar scene opened before her. A wave of warmth, the hum of activity, and a waft of odors that simply meant *home*.

Before Hodel was the marketplace, the synagogue, and the little schoolhouse. And there, Motel's tailor shop, the livery stable, Lazar Wolf's butcher shop, the fishmongers, and the messy roads that nestled up against endless fields like foals against a mare. The northern light that poured like honey upon the thatched roofs. The sound of Mordcha's clarinet singing from the flat above the Forbidden Piglet, his tumbledown inn. The hum and hush of home.

Yidishkeyt and *menshlikhkeyt*—Jewishness and humanness. These were the crucial values of the shtetl community, around which all their lives centered. These values were manifested in the synagogue as well as in the home, and all these actions led one toward the goal of living the life of a "good Jew." One's faith was present in the holiness of Sabbath, in the humdrum buzz of the market, in every corner of community and organization of the family.

"But why must there be such a rush about everything?" Hodel asked as Golde, dressed in black, darted back and forth across the house.

Motel's father was dead. Their family was doing all they could to help the Kamzoils in their hour of need. It was just that Golde's girls clearly did not understand what such a need entailed.

"We must bury the dead as quickly as possible," said Mama as she stirred a colossal pot of soup.

There were so many rules and customs, laws and traditions that Hodel did not truly understand; they were simply the reality of everything she had ever known.

"But Papa Kamzoil is no longer alive, Mama," Hodel said. "What difference does it make to him at all?"

She used to be afraid to ask questions, afraid God would be angry if she asked them. But through the act of living, her questions had become part of an intimate conversation with God, and traditions grew to be the manifestation of a faith she felt growing in earnest, deep within her heart.

"The body must reach its eternal rest as expeditiously as possible," Mama replied.

"But how, Mama? And why?" Hodel persisted.

Golde stopped. She placed her hands down in agitated fists upon the kitchen table and looked at Hodel with as kindly an expression as her nerves would allow. "In Jewish law, the human body belongs to its creator—it is on loan to us, and we become its guardian. So, when it is time for the body to be returned to the earth from which it was created, and the soul to the creator himself, we must make certain due respect is given. Respect for our deceased is the ultimate mitzvah—for the dead can neither help themselves nor help us."

"Because they are dead." Hodel nodded.

"Right." That much was clear.

"And so," Golde continued, "we recite *baruch dayan ha'emet*, cover the face, light candles, and place them next to the head. We ask forgiveness as we lower the body to the floor, then recite the proper psalms and arrange for the *taharah*. Then we must watch over the body so that the soul—which is transitioning from the world of the living to the World of Truth—can be at ease. Above all else, we show greatest dignity to the body and do not mar or harm it in any way. It must be returned in its entirety to the earth and to the creator, just as it was given, without any violence or interference. That is both the custom as well as Jewish law, and now I shall not say another word about it." With that, Golde took up her great black pot of soup and headed toward the door to go to Shaindel Kamzoil's house. "I will be back in a moment, and do not let me catch you picking at the chicken!"

Buried in the earth, thought Hodel. *How dreadful.* But tradition was tradition, law was law, and custom, custom. The fertile earth would claim the flesh, which would fuel the tender grasses, the soil for the trees, and thus the fruits that grew upon them. The body was the temple of the soul, the soul a vehicle to perform the good deeds called mitzvoth, and was thus imbued with sanctity. But that body would someday rot. For bodies must. The thought of it festered within her, made her hot and sick.

Still, she would continue the walk of faith. For now.

thirty-nine

H e is fine," The Gentleman said, soothing her. Hodel sat inert atop their bed. Without Perchik, the world beyond the taiga was incomprehensible; if only she could light a fire to illuminate the future.

"We merely have to ask him a few nagging, almost silly questions. . . ."

Hodel sat stiffly on her bed, like a fragile stack of cups about to topple.

"But fear not, my dear, for he will be out soon. It is all very standard procedure."

The Gentleman made a move to exit, but then stopped on his way across the floor of the Volosnikov house and hovered over her. As Hodel caught his eye, she saw him look at her strangely, as though he saw within her a kind of mirage.

His manner felt so incongruous with his ferocious vehemence the other evening in the moonlight. This was the tenderness of the other man she knew him to be: the man who had escorted her to Nerchinsk, had saved her from the nightmare of that prison. This was the man whose eyes she had seen look upon Irina with such devoted tenderness. The eyes that also flared with such tormented heartbreak.

But Hodel reminded herself that these eyes lay inside the sockets of a man who beat his daughter in his rage, who commanded the infliction of abuse upon his daughter's lover, and, of course, who was responsible for the disappearance of her own husband. . . .

But, still, she had never forgotten—and would never forget—his kindness. She admired his sedulousness. She was still grateful to him. . . .

"We must have a real talk sometime, mustn't we?" he said. "A nice conversation. Just get to know each other, I suppose."

He hovered over her still.

"I enjoy your company, Hodel."

She tried to speak, but today she was inarticulate with grief, her tongue limp and wordless.

"Ah, but I see you are quiet this evening. Perhaps another time."

The Gentleman turned on his heel and closed the door gently behind him. Hodel's mouth was salty, bleeding from the incomprehensible, infected with Nerchinsk's virus of disquiet.

How she would dazzle God with her patience.

Perchik attempted patience in his imprisonment. Within minutes of his capture he had been placed in the solitary torture device he had, until this point, only heard rumor of. How long he had remained within it he could not tell.

The call for torture always made itself apparent at some point, though the box was particularly severe—and mostly unheard of for political prisoners. Blindfolded and dragged in chains, Perchik was left in the guardhouse; he was chained to a chair before the overseers arrived. Before putting him in the box, they removed his chains, instructed him to strip, and verified a description of him drawn up at Kiev, then Moscow, then Omsk.

At the bottom of Perchik's certified sentence, the Chief Commander had instructed, *A special watch must be kept upon the unruly.* This extraordinary recommendation (penned in the Chief Commander's own hand) had made a deep impression on the main officer at Nerchinsk—a bulbous man they all knew to be The Gentleman. They had been watching Perchik forever.

The standing box was an upright coffin. The box was kept within an almost completely silent, windowless room; there was no light, save a single hanging bulb, and no sound at all from the camp beyond.

Had it been several hours? Half a day? A week? Time was passing; how swiftly or slowly, he could not determine.

He was alone; everything inside him was ablaze as he endeavored to grasp at his sanity. At one point, Perchik awoke to the warmth of his own urine spreading across his leg, and as he jolted at the sudden wetness, he knocked against the sharpened fragments along the inner walls. His back ached viciously, and his legs were quaking from fatigue. He was ravenous with hunger, mad with thirst. The box stank from the waste of his predecessors (the stench was torture enough). Every atom of the air within was filled with ammoniacal exhalations—the leftover smell of long-unwashed bodies reeking and rancid with neglect. Directly before him was a little window (no larger than for his eyes alone) carved into the door. Just as Perchik felt the chill of the air start to grip the sticky wet of his trouser legs, The Gentleman appeared directly before him. He was holding a small glass of milk.

The sight of the milk was its own torture. It made the juices of Perchik's stomach churn with desire. He ripped his eyes away from the glass and steadied himself, focusing instead on The Gentleman.

His orderly appearance filled Perchik with disgust. The Gentleman's sharpness and cleanliness, his upturned lips, the angle of his hands behind his back, the crispness of his uniform—all evidence of vanity and myopic self-interest.

"Well, here we are," The Gentleman said. "Since I have been made superintendent, nothing of this sort has ever occurred. Remarkable. You must be a very extreme case. This contraption is usually reserved for the irate prisoner. At times, the despondent one. Today, the political." The Gentleman made a little bow with his head. "Welcome."

At that he placed the glass of milk on the small table between them. "Beautiful, isn't it? Milk. So pure. So filling." Perchik's heart was racing; his mouth swarmed with saliva. The Gentleman stepped around the table and moved in close. "Would you like it?"

Perchik knew this had to be a trick, or some other form of cruelty set there to test his resolve, and thus he grunted, thrashing against both the walls of his captivity and his animal instinct.

"Come now—there is no need to fight natural urges," The Gentleman said, removing a key from the ring on his perfectly polished belt. "It will feel good to get out and stretch a bit."

Perchik felt his insides cry out for the milk with a starving infant's desperation.

The Gentleman inserted the key to the great padlock upon the door to the apparatus, and at the sound of it Perchik felt his guts churn with need. Could he restrain his need? He did not know.

At last the door flew open, and Perchik flung himself toward the table like a madman, grabbed the glass, and on his knees, in heaving gulps, partook of the rich cold milk within it.

"That's excellent," The Gentleman said. "Good for the belly. Just as I hear confession is quite good for the soul."

Perchik wailed. He slammed his hand against the edge of the table in a blinding anger, then all at once began to weep.

"There, now, this will all be over soon. Though how soon is entirely up to you." The Gentleman approached and helped Perchik to his feet. "Now back into the box with you, my boy. We can't have you running about." Perchik was too weak and too demoralized to fight him, so he allowed The Gentleman to return him to the contraption.

Through the window, The Gentleman smiled at Perchik, locked and quiet once more.

"You do understand, don't you?" The Gentleman continued softly. "You and I have had a slight deficit of trust. . . ."

Later that night, convulsions woke him. The pain in his cramping muscles and stomach was so great, he felt almost relieved by the cuts that raged along his skin, for they distracted him. Yet it was not the pain, nor the box's sharp walls, that made him yield to humility. It was what he knew of the human capacity to endure. Its ruthlessness. For endurance meant greater tortures to come.

The corporeal punishments of Nerchinsk were more or less death sentences: starvation, the slitting of nostrils, lashes with a birch rod administered with both hands. In addition, hundreds of convicts died from disease. There was a hospital of course, but convicts benefited little from it; smallpox wrought havoc three summers ago, and there had been a typhus epidemic or two. Scurvy was common, as was syphilis (thought to be spread by the homosexuals), and dehydration, of course. On some level of his conscious mind, Perchik already knew he was suffering from disease—such a thing was impossible to ignore—but he would not yield to it. Not for any reason.

That night, as he stood encased in the box and quite alone, he noted that his vision was patchy—his eyes were not sufficiently adapting to the dark room. He blinked hard, shook his head. He tried again, for he knew the dark held something new within it. Someone new, who stood just before his eyes but could not be seen.

"Hello?" a voice asked softly.

"Who's there?" Perchik uttered, desperate to see.

"Can you not see me, then?" whispered the visitor.

Perchik made no reply, his stomach boiling.

"Can you not recognize yer ol' friend, come to reprieve you?"

It could not be!

"Anatoly!" Perchik cried. "Anatoly, how the devil did you get in here? My dear friend, I am overjoyed!"

In a place where officers embezzled funds

and prisoners filched supplies, such a visitation should never have come as such a shock, but Anatoly was the last man Perchik expected to be visited by, and in such a state as this.

"Master yerself, man. Ye must be still. I have much to tell, but first open wide." Anatoly placed torn bits of bread through the face hole and directly into Perchik's mouth, then gave him water and a long drink of tea, the sublime warmth of which nearly caused his legs to buckle in ecstasy.

Anatoly continued in low voice. "You have supporters here, Reb Perchik—both here an' in sister camps an' cities. Followers who'd lay down their lives. But you must 'ave patience. Show full submission when't comes th' officers o' this prison. Please. Fer us and fer the cause, ye *must*."

Perchik could scarcely believe it. Anatoly Gromov of Vladivostok, a fellow comrade? *Things are never what they seem,* he thought as his friend related to Perchik the events that had transpired since his incarceration.

"All's prepared, friend. Our friends in Petersburg await ye. But fer now, master all displays o' temper. Soon you'll deafen them, comrade."

Anatoly quickly slipped him another drink of tea, then tapped the box's side and disappeared into the clouded darkness.

● ● ●

Many hours later Perchik awoke. He was no longer in the box but laid out on the floor of a prison cell. The cell was damp and fleshy and saturated with a peculiar odor unlike any other bad smell in the world—one so strong even Perchik, with his decaying senses, could detect it. *If Nerchinsk is indeed a dump for Russia's detritus,* thought Perchik, *it certainly reeks of it.*

"Is that you, Reb Perchik?" a voice in the darkness asked. Perchik immediately recognized it as the voice of Andrey Tenderov; it was sure but tired, the body of it broken but not the spirit. Perchik could almost feel Tenderov's heat through the stone.

"Tenderov!" Perchik said. "My, you have certainly been in here a long while."

"I have," Tenderov said. "You're out at last, then?"

"I am."

They both sighed as they sat along the cell walls—together but apart—having wisdom enough to share what was certainly only momentary relief.

"They despise you, you know," Tenderov continued. "You are so infuriatingly above reproach. However are they supposed to keep a watch upon you when you give them so little to watch?"

Perchik considered the silence for a long

moment before replying. "I suppose, Tenderov, you would know a great deal about keeping watch."

"I would," Tenderov said with his familiar, glowing laugh. "How long have you suspected?"

"Always," Perchik said, his voice just a whisper. "But it was the wine. The wine you stole and passed around that night Dmitri played Bach for us. The only alcohol in the storehouses is hard liquor. The wine is kept locked away in the officers' quarters. You would not have had it unless they had given it to you."

At that, Andrey smiled and laughed, a little sad.

"Though you are terribly good at what you do, Andrey—especially for one so young," added Perchik.

"I am not so very young. I only look it—part of the appeal, of course."

"Of course."

It seemed to Perchik that many things went into the making of a spy; but oh, poor Andrey—imprisoned beside the very man he was charged to keep a watch upon. Facing God knew what. Which made him wonder: "Have they locked you up in earnest, Tenderov?"

Andrey was silent for a long while. Perchik scarcely dared to breathe.

"They have never done so until now," Andrey replied at last. "I think they are going to kill me. Tell me it isn't true, my friend; tell me it is a lie."

But Perchik could promise no such thing. Thus, he remained silent and still.

"Well, never mind," Andrey continued. "There is no sense in living. Not without her. One would think that with all the loving I'd done, there was nothing left to be discovered. But oh, there was. She has a kiss as deep as Baikal." He choked on the thought of it. "I learned that kind of love from you, my friend," he added. "I learned that kind of love from you."

Perchik sat with Andrey Tenderov throughout the night. Still. Silent—both knowing what the morning would bring.

forty

In the absence of her husband, Hodel had little else to do besides rip open the letters given to her by Irina and pore over their words, every one of them from, of all people, Tzeitel. Each page was a kind of portal to a distant life—a home far away but not forgotten. Hodel held the pages between her fingers reverently, knowing that the thoughts had originated in Tzeitel's mind and flowed through her arm onto the very pages now in Hodel's hands. For a moment she thought she could almost smell Tzeitel, for her soul was ever present in the words upon the paper.

Hodel,

Where has the time gone? I cannot believe eight months has passed since our precious Jacob was placed into our arms (though I suppose I shall still be saying that in twenty years). Eight months of utter joy, of nurturing my child at my breast, of endless adventures.

A few weeks ago Jacob focused his eyes on me and smiled, his mouth just like Mama's and your own. Now he rolls over, sits up, and is just beginning to try to crawl. Soon, I suspect, he shall be all over the place! Motel and I are observing as he develops into the man he shall, God willing, become. How fascinating to be here to witness him grow every day. Nothing compares.

Nothing compares? Hodel thought. *What a classic remark from Tzeitel.* Hodel put the letter down and shook her head in indignation. In two little words, all of Hodel's life choices were suddenly obliterated by Tzeitel's sense of domestic superiority. Suddenly, Hodel was a child again, in all her petulant glory. *The Tzeitel in this letter does not know me—does not know all we have endured!*

All at once, Hodel felt a cold knife stab her with a terrible recognition: It was not that the Tzeitel in this letter did not know her; it was that Hodel did not truly know, or fully appreciate, the Tzeitel in this letter. The Tzeitel of the past. Time had doubtless altered Tzeitel as it had so altered them all. The Tzeitel that had, over time, also grown and changed, and enjoyed happiness, and doubtless suffered. The Tzeitel she might never see or ever know again.

Motel sends his love. You would scarcely believe, Hodelleh, what a man Motel has grown to become. His business is thriving (we finally received the sewing machine! It is almost as precious to Motel as Jacob!). The stitches are perfectly even and close, and it moves me to see him so enthralled with the progress of the world. But above all, I love watching Motel as a father. Jacob just adores him! Whenever Motel picks him up, Jacob cheers with delight. How wonderful that God chose to give us this baby boy.

Swiftly flying months of learning and growing toward becoming the mother I hope will honor our ancestors. Eight full, busy months. I'm so tired and so happy. But of course, eight months ago, you were still here, and Chava too, and things were not so very different and strained. So much has changed, dear Hodelleh, in your absence.

In moments of bliss, I always thank God. But it is in the moments of trial that I turn to Him the most—for in those hours we learn humility, we see how much we truly need His guidance. Daily, I ask for help to become the wife and mother my family needs. Daily, I ask Him for support.

Hodel clutched at her breast, for if she did not hold it in, her heart would surely lurch out in response to so much wrenching misery—and at the fondness for her now evermore remote youth in Anatevka. She read another:

Hodel,
It is important to tell you many things.
Weeks ago, Chava ran away in the middle of the night. We looked everywhere for her, and when we finally discovered her whereabouts we were shattered. She had married Fyedka in the Orthodox Church. Do you recall him? The young Russian we so often saw her speaking to in the bookshop?

Hodel remembered him very well indeed.

I knew, Hodel. I knew what they were doing, and I did not do enough. I have never seen our parents more heartbroken. I do not think they shall ever be the same. Our beloved Chaveleh. Our Bird. The betrayal. The loss too great for any of us to bear. I suspect this news does not come as an utter shock to you; you and Chava were always so very close.

Hodel pressed her hand against her mouth, keeping both sound and further feeling at bay.

But there is more. A few days ago, there came an order. The tsar has issued a decree that our entire village must be cleared in a few days' time. I do not know where any of us shall disperse to, but we must all manage as best we can. Surely the heart of the world is vast enough for us all. Motel and I are traveling to Warsaw (there are textiles there, and a vibrant community of our people), and Papa spoke this morning of leading the rest of our family to America.

I have, as of yet, had no word from Chava and Fyedka.

For now, I look to God, for I know He will respond to my questions. For I believe, in the deepest part of my heart, that He shall truly bring us into a frame of mind where we may hear His greatest responses . . . Perhaps not the final answers, but at the very least, the next response we need.

The world is changing, Hodelleh. As Moses spoke in the book of Exodus, "I have heard their cry on account of their taskmasters. Indeed, I know their sufferings, and I have come down to deliver them." I know how much you and Perchik wish to be a part of it—save the world, Hodelleh. But preserve it too: from the tyrants and the heartless.

God be with you, Hodelleh.

Tzeitel

Hodel was very still. Her hands limp, face slack.

The sisters were all strangers now. There was no home to return to. Everyone she knew, treasured, and loved on this earth was scattered, kept from her, kept from one another. And nothing—nothing she could ever do—would bring any of it back again.

She put down the letters.

There was a limit—a moment when knowledge, falling drop by painful drop, caused the spongelike heart to overflow. A moment when it could hold no more, too saturated was it, with suffering.

forty-one

Here it was: the cool of the morning. Andrey Tenderov waited. Three hundred blows with the rods had come at last.

"Siberian men are strong!" he cried, counting upon what he believed to be the toughness of his hide, as fearless as a man with nothing to lose. He cursed the tsar, his officers, and his fate, and in his soaring voice, he sang songs of love and war. "Russia is seventeen million kilometers long! I crossed the earth to find such love!" he cried, his spirit urging itself to madness, releasing him from fear.

"Now then, Tenderov, I hope you're ready to meet the devil—today's the day he'll finally snatch your soul!" one of the guards said.

"I shall live through the blows, I assure you, and we will share a glass of vodka together yet!" Tenderov slapped this emphasis upon them, and his voice at once resumed in song.

The Gentleman approached the scene, his body rigid and uniformed. He stopped. He looked at Tenderov and almost smiled.

"I shall not allow you to foul my family, Tenderov," he said. "I trusted you, and you have sinned. How you sinned, Andrey Tenderov, and with such clear eyes! Treachery within the walls of my own house." He drew a knife from his coat pocket and handed it to an adjacent guard. "Do not apologize! Betrayal should be impersonal, even when it is not."

The Gentleman licked and bit his lip at the thought. Then, with narrowed eyes, he ordered a guard: "Cut out his tongue."

Tenderov's friends stood beyond the barbed fences—Hodel listened to Irina's roars, which nearly drowned out the sounds of Andrey's own screeches as they ripped his songs out by the root. When it was done, the guards prepared him to receive the lashes of the birch rod.

After one of the three hundred blows, Tenderov fell senseless on the snow.

The Gentleman remained behind as they carted the body away to the hospital ward. Hodel looked on, scrutinizing his gaze. But all at once, the icy blue eyes were upon her, clutching at her for a frigid moment before The Gentleman moved away and out of sight. All that remained behind were boot prints, a tongue inert upon the ground, and the Nercha riverbank, now dark with blood. The songs of Andrey Tenderov had been drowned for good.

They stood there in a sudden access of horror; hope had somehow purged it from their consciousness, but now it flooded in—in swift, dark, bloody tendrils like the ones before them.

They felt it poignantly: Andrey Tenderov's fate was every bit their own.

"I hope that wasn't the pivot," Grigory muttered, turning away.

"The pivot?" Hodel murmured.

"The fulcrum. The turning point. In every story there is always a moment when the anchoring thread of the tapestry unravels. I don't know that I've ever been inside that story until now."

"But what do you mean by 'the pivot'? The pivot of what?" Hodel entreated him.

Grigory's expression was as pitch-black as his eyes. "Of disaster."

forty-two

D mitri scratched at his arms and neck until he bled. He had recently caught fleas from Yevgeny, who in turn had caught fleas from Mitya the dog, and all of them (except Yevgeny himself, of course) were in a volatile temperament. But Dmitri Petrov had also been riled by the incident with Tenderov, Perchik's unexplained disappearance, and the keeping of so many secrets. He was not cut out for internment, activism, or dogs.

The tides were turning. They had been assigned to the roof—a punishment for unruly behavior in the dining hall earlier that day (the men cajoled Yevgeny as he danced happily atop a dining table). Dmitri had hopes that Yevgeny's antics might afford him a few hours' respite. Instead, he was assigned to the roof as well, along with Grigory. Shame. The wooden roof was covered with natural debris in constant need of clearing; and though the air was fierce, the task imposed certainly was not. (After all, Anatoly had already been assigned to serve in the outhouse—by such comparisons, they considered themselves fortunate!)

"And anyway, Anatoly's been a brute recently," said Grigory below his breath. "All mighty and suddenly priggish about our stash. What a two-faced killjoy."

"Come, Grisha," cooed Yevgeny. "Is that any way to speak of your friend?"

"Oh, I make it a habit never to let friendship get in the way of a good insult," he said slyly. "Not that I have many friends."

The sky was dark, the hour late, and they were not allowed to leave until the job was complete. The overseer let them rest for ten minutes every two hours and never let them out of sight, so they worked tirelessly.

Yevgeny laughed with the whole of his body as he swept. His hair was wispy and hung down in his eyes when sweaty. Dmitri, for his part, was tortured less by the punishment and more by keeping the company of Yevgeny for an entire evening.

"You know," continued Yevgeny with a delightfully mischievous grin upon his face, "I will say: I prefer this duty to the furnace, I do. That I do."

Yevgeny had been carried to Siberia an already elderly man; his charm, manners, and the noble nature of his Jewish ancestors' misfortunes, as well as an almost childlike face of utter sweetness, all won him the good graces of the milder superior officers. Even The Gentleman, despite his better judgment, genuinely enjoyed Yevgeny's merriment and often kept him assigned to the head office on Sundays, even once admitting him to dine at the officers' table.

"I find The Gentleman to be of the old school. Far be it from me to understand his logic. All I know is punishment comes my way at least once a fortnight!" said Yevgeny.

His energy was lighthearted, his good humor infectious, his mind unworried—who could not care for such a man? But Yevgeny often forgot himself (especially if he had been drinking) and became recalcitrant—then The Gentleman would be forced to constrain him to the furnace for a week or so to tend the fire. Yevgeny would weep and feign infirmity, swear reformation, and remind the guards of the pettiness of his crimes. But soon he would find himself once more upon the roof, in the outhouses, or back beside the furnace.

"Please," said Dmitri, punctuating each new insult by kicking icy debris aside vigorously with his boots. "That man is deeply common; he's of both limited skill and education. His powers have been heedlessly awarded, and his behavior is as transparent as the air!" Dmitri removed his hat and wiped his brow in frustration.

"Now, now, Dmitri, steady there," muttered Grigory. "No need to get worked up again."

"But then of course, I have the fortune, or rather the misfortune, of always being in the very highest of spirits!" Yevgeny continued thoughtfully, settling down for their break in the labor. "So I believe The Gentleman punishes me very often to see if it will make a better man of me!" Grisha laughed with delight as Yevgeny continued, "I do not bow to him. That is what I believe makes him most enraged. He says I am . . . oh, what is the word? What is the word, Mitya? You are so clever! You are always so clever with words and things!"

"Impudent," Dmitri answered, eyes rolling to the back of his head from the irony of it.

"Impudent! Oh, Mitya! Bless you! I am so fortunate to have you looking after me!" Yevgeny ran and embraced him. "Promise me you shall never forget me!"

"Bah!" Dmitri spluttered and clawed Yevgeny off him. "I wish I could forget you!"

"But you shan't. For I have made such an impression upon you, haven't I? And I carved you that little cello out of dung so that you may be reminded of your music even when you cannot play! And to be reminded of Yevgeny long after we have parted! It is for you to have for always." Yevgeny poked his bunkmate on the shoulder and smiled as he shook the shock of unruly white hair from his eyes.

"Enough!" Dmitri could take no more. He threw his rake upon the ground and extended himself to his full height. His eyes were ablaze. "You have never done a thing in your life worth mentioning!" For all the insults he had flung at Yevgeny over the years, none, not a single word of it, did he mean in earnest. But his voice was different now. It frothed with bile, with every blackened hatred Nerchinsk and all her components had planted in his soul. And that hatred grew hot and thick within him—hatred that now stung with the deadly infection of angst. "You are a goddamn nuisance. A cretin. A good-for-nothing swine. Do you know that?"

Yevgeny's jaw trembled. Tears spilled from his eyes. But, dignity intact, he gave a laugh concealing all his agony. "I know that I make merry only because I could never make much of anything else."

Grigory spoke softly. "You do indeed, Yevgeny. You make us all quite merry."

Yevgeny smiled broadly at that, his face still soaking and taut. "Yet perhaps that is no bad thing," he said, shrugging as though none of it mattered very much at all. "How else would I get to see the world as I have, and meet such fine men as yourselves, without my inveterate naughtiness?"

Suddenly, the soft, wrinkled skin around his eyes appeared deeply shadowed, the rims red and wet and swollen. He clapped his fists against his heart, quivering from knee to belly, plagued by the weight no one had ever named until tonight. "I am not a wicked man. Just a useless one. A man who cannot—who could not ever—help himself." He fell upon the fragmented rooftop.

Dmitri caught Grigory's eye. Both turned cold. "That is not badness," said Yevgeny, weeping. "No, Mitya, you see. That is not badness."

forty-three

Weakened and woozy, Perchik reached for his throbbing head only to discover he was inhibited by chains. He gazed down at his hands in horror, as if seeing them clearly for the first time in many weeks. They were of a ghostly pallor, completely hairless, and so transparent that the blue of his veins stood out like routes on a train map, a nefarious etching of an atlas to oblivion. With spotted nails, his hands were covered in a metallic rash unlike anything he had ever seen before. Suddenly, an ache was in his guts, not merely at the sight of his skin, but from a sickness of thought, which rose within him like a gas. He twisted, then retched upon the floor beside his boots.

The room itself was constructed of stone and contained nothing more than the chair and table he was chained to and a large, imposing lamp hanging from the ceiling. The air was as thick and wet as the walls themselves—and stank of something like a cellar, with a more than slight suggestion of corpses. His innards buckled and he retched again.

When he rose from the violence within him, he wiped his mouth upon his shoulder and opened his eyes. Before him, upright—as though he had been there all along—and smiling with the faintest touch of contempt gracing his mouth was The Gentleman.

Perchik did not move. A bottomless silence broke open between them. Perchik eyed him coldly for a few moments before The Gentleman finally spoke.

"Do you like my cuff links?" The Gentleman polished their surfaces with the soft pads of his fingers. "They were a gift."

When Perchik made no answer, The Gentleman laced his fat fingers together in a fist, smiling broadly. The entire gesture was patronizing, as if to suggest he was both dominating and worshipping the prey he had finally caught. "My, it is wonderful to see you here. We have waited a terribly long time to get something on you!" The Gentleman laughed, his tone suggesting he was beginning to let his guard down. "Andrey Tenderov turned out to be rather a disappointing agent, wouldn't you agree? He came with the highest of recommendations from government intelligence. Shame. Beautiful singer, wasn't he? But as for his espionage, well . . . we all know he became *distracted*. But no matter! Pfft! All gone."

Perchik felt a serenity come over him—all these years of squalor had not made him skeptical; they had made him clear.

"A gang of hooligans up against the Russian

imperial government?" The Gentleman said. "Against a tsar who has been appointment by God? My, my. You idealists are such a headache. I think I despise idealists almost as much as I love ideals. But we knew you would misstep sooner or later. We have intercepted your coded communications and know with whom you have been communicating. Your grand schemes are void now—your affiliates have been similarly exiled, comrade."

The Gentleman adjusted his cuff links, which, now that Perchik looked closer, he could tell once belonged to Andrey Tenderov.

"I am happy to be the bearer of the news" he continued. "You are an enemy of Mother Russia. You wish to destroy her majesty in exchange for the creeping erosion of individual choice—until we are all faceless, choiceless drones, all digging one another out of human mess."

There must have been a lucidity in Perchik's eyes that The Gentleman could not decipher, for Perchik saw a shudder of agitation in his face—the feral look that precipitates panic. There was a subsurface barbarity that lay there; a raging violence almost always reined in, but kicking from deep within. They had all witnessed its full power but a few days before.

"Can't you feel it crumbling in your hands?" The Gentleman whispered as he reached toward him and slowly opened Perchik's palms to reveal the metallic rash within. Perchik did not flinch, did not unlock his eyes from The Gentleman's. He made no move at all.

"I was told to kill you, you know," The Gentleman said. Perchik had suspected as much. "But I could not do that. So the committee agreed we should slowly poison you instead."

Together they gazed down upon Perchik's hands, knowledge passing between them. The Gentleman smiled, and Perchik's intestines lurched. Poison. He had not accounted for that.

"I didn't—and I do not want to kill you!" The Gentleman cried in delight. "Kill you! Lord! What would I do without you?"

Here, in this room, The Gentleman could speak his truths without impediment.

"What would *she* do?"

forty-four

I f the truth of a man lies within him, then it stands to reason one might be able to simply open him up and grasp at that truth the way one carves into a carcass to extract the tenderest cuts of meat. But there are certain men whose inner truths are far too delicate, and whose constitutions are far too strong to penetrate. In such a case, one must simply wait for the truth within to creep out of its own accord, like a creature that may break apart if pressure is put upon it. Perhaps it was so with Dmitri.

How could the shackled heart, and the poetry that mocked within him; how could the stench of fear, and the cacophonous clamor of uncertainty, and the darkened depths of spirit; how could any of it ever be expressed?

It was the cello, in the end, that set him free. That gave him peace. Inside the chords, notes, and arches of melody, he found a space where all of what he longed to be could fit—that unnameable, unknowable self.

To look at him before Nerchinsk, one would think Dmitri Petrov had no reason for pain. His musicianship, his higher education, his rugged looks, and his lovely family—of course one would think he had no agonies. But there is pain and there is pain.

Once in Nerchinsk, no cold, no labor, no punishing treatment, no single thing could mar him more than the love that raged within his breast for her. The love he felt but could not utter; the love he knew—with every scrap of his being—did not belong to him, but to the only man he admired. The man he respected above all others. If only he could say what everyone already knew to be true. Everyone, that is, but her.

He felt that ancient barbed twine unravel itself and come between them. It lodged itself into Hodel without her knowledge, and once enmeshed it yanked and ripped at his already riled heart and made it throb in agony. One moment he would revel in her scent, the next he could weep with guilt.

The three of them were such a happy triangle. But Dmitri recognized he was the hypotenuse in a shape perfectly right without him—an excessive attachment, not at all unlike a third wheel on a cart—excessive, unnecessary for it to function. Countless times he nearly spoke, nearly moved to kiss her. *Tell her!* his mind urged. *Take her in the arms you know were designed to enfold her within them!* But every time, he thought of what would happen if he did. Crippled by loneliness, fear penetrated his love; the alchemical result was aloofness. Or often, viciousness.

He knew that he could never be alone with her without wanting desperately to touch her. Could not touch her without wanting to possess her, to make her his own. So he barely spoke to her at all. He would waste his life away beholding a painting upon the wall of a locked house he would never be allowed to enter.

There was nothing to be done. Nothing he could do but honor them. And play, of course. He could play his cello. Every strand of aching music, every forlorn concerto, for her.

He was tied to a chair. At least as far as he could gather. His eyes were blindfolded, his mouth gagged, head throbbing from what was certainly an injury to the side of his skull. Had he been captured in the night? They had brought him to a place where he could only faintly hear the cries of other men from what seemed like leagues away as though through water, or along the very darkest of nightmare-laden hallways.

Galvanized into action, Dmitri Petrov shook himself. He threw his head to try to free his eyes, bucked wildly against his restraints. The chair thudded hard upon the stone floor as every muscle in his long body burned to be unfettered. All at once, Dmitri heard a door open and then close. A presence had entered the room.

"Ah, Dmitri Petrov," the voice of a man spoke

at last, sliding in casually behind him. "The man who makes the music."

"Who's there?" Dmitri Petrov asked, for he did not recognize the voice, and in his consternation continued to flinch within his constraints. "Who are you?"

"That is not of import," the man replied. "Around here, they tend to simply call me 'the Voice.' I am quite taken with the title, truth be told."

"Come now," Dmitri scoffed. "This is unreasonable!"

The man suddenly went vivid in his coldness as he spoke again. "I don't do *reasonable,* Petrov. That is why they laud me."

The temperature inside the cell dropped with the remark.

"I shall scream, then!"

"But cries cannot go through the earth, can they? We are deep beneath the ground, my friend. And your cries, however musical, are not stone-piercing."

Dmitri's mind raged.

"Dmitri Petrov. *Mitya.* I assume you know why you are here? This is not the hour for loyal friendships or beautiful gestures. It is the age of *even exchanges*—a tit for a tat. I know this because I specialize in criminals—the only power any government has is the power over its criminals. Tit for tat: that's the system, Mitya.

That's the game. Once you understand it, things will be much easier."

Suddenly, Dmitri was overcome by the desperate need for music—for his hands to play his instrument, caress the wooden body, the wearing strings, and let it save him from this hell as the cello always had. His fingers twitched with it.

"Poor thing. Little Mitya, for whom no one cares. Little Mitya!"

Finally, Dmitri exploded. "Dmitri! That is my name. Dmitri Pavlovich Petrovsky. That is all. Nothing less. The name is Dmitri—everything else gnaws the man to dust."

"Well, all right, then, Dmitri," the Voice continued, unfaltering. "I simply need to know the plans you and Reb Perchik are embroiled in. Please. It is most urgent."

"Never."

"Come now—do not let your sentiment interfere with your politics. I thought more highly of you than that."

"I swore to him."

"Oh poo, you swore! Such a shame! Friendship is so sacred—no imperial rifles could ever shoot your promises to shreds!" The Voice bit hard into the air as he gripped Dmitri's hands, tied tight behind the chair he sat upon. Dmitri felt hot breath against his neck, heard the stinging clang of metal as a knife was opened wide, and churned with terror as the man wrenched the muscles of his tremendous, stifled arm and spread the fingers of his left hand against the cold sharp blade.

"Please!" Dmitri cried out. "No, please! Not my fingers!"

"Ah," The Voice cooed with pleasure. "But see, Dmitri, you are not in your world, and I am in mine." He shoved the blade into his thumb, and Dmitri felt the hot blood ooze out across his palms and flood onto the floor. "I see the concept has not been made fully clear to you yet."

Dmitri felt the man release him, and as his muscles sighed in relief, he heard a dragging chair, which the man placed directly in front of Dmitri. Dmitri heard the man sit down and could smell his odor, feel the heat of what must have been an enormous frame—if only he could see his face and appeal to his eyes.

"Even exchanges, Dmitri," the Voice continued, tapping him on the cheek almost playfully. "Something for something else. Easy. You see? You tell me what your friend is planning, and I will leave your fingers be. Or, I will not, say, reveal your darkest secret to the man you revere above all others."

Dmitri choked upon his shock. "I don't know what you mean," he muttered, quite sick with it.

"You do not know?" the Voice taunted. "How ever could you not?" He leaned in close to Dmitri's ear and whispered so quietly that it could have been the Voice of Dmitri's own conscience revealing all into the darkness. "Doesn't your blood beat hard when you see her coming? Doesn't her voice thrill in your ears, and the scent of her send you swelling throughout the night?"

It could not be.

"He makes her throb with his politics, his utopias," the Voice persisted. "He makes her tremble in her soul. Do you really feel you can compete with that, Dmitri? What do you give her? Remnants! Weakness! Standoffishness! When does your shyness and the enormity of your pathetic love become nothing more than arrogance? Why even here—in this gray frozen cunt of the world—why would a woman such as she even think to notice you?"

Dmitri flushed with despair.

"Now. Once again: What is your comrade planning?"

"I do not know, sir," Dmitri said sullenly. "He keeps so much from me. I do not know, and that is the truth."

The Voice was silent for a moment. But then he called out, "Guards!"

A gang of men entered the cell now. Dmitri heard their feet as they entered, thudding about and lugging in a heavy load. They surrounded him, and one removed his blindfold. His eyes stung—the light, however meager, had been kept from his eyes for far too long. His visual perception had been compromised, his mind unable to keep up. But there was no mistaking it. Standing before him, there it was, clear as morning.

His cello.

"Now, Dmitri," the Voice said from far behind him, reminding him that this vision before him was no dream but indeed a true and present and horrifying reality. "For the very last time, now: What do you know?"

Then, at once, Dmitri caved.

Without knowing himself, his voice expelled the plot. His afflicted mouth delivered confidences as easily as kittens.

Perhaps all men are enslaved in part by their little loves—obsessions that are not digestible, ideas that rub and irritate like sand in the belly of an oyster. They are defined by their servitude to such things.

As Dmitri watched the men destroy the instrument, he thought to himself that the cello, in such a place as this, was superfluous, and thus somehow squalid. It therefore had to be destroyed. He saw that now.

At least that was what entered his mind as he watched the men demolish it. Decimate it anyway, despite all pitiful divulgences. He could hear the music of it surge within his skull—the cello cried out from the corner, offered its forgiveness, told him he was clean and good, however helpless. The music turned to screeching, pleading, crying out for help; its timbre strangled, the tune harsh and dissonant. It all happened so abruptly, Dmitri Petrov did not know what to think. . . . As they thrashed its frame to splinters, fractured it to shredded shards and matchsticks, Dmitri thought, *My love*—the greater love, perhaps; for it was the only thing that ever loved him back.

"You are forbidden to see them again," the Voice whispered over the broken man, who wept soundlessly into his now unchained limbs. "Not that I suspect you shall ever want to. . . ."

Dmitri stared in disbelief as the guards smashed the cello—he had believed his confession would save the instrument. No: that pile of useless flinders might as well be him. He had smashed all promises to fire kindling and obliterated his friend and, worse, the woman they both adored.

forty-five

Waiting is a special kind of anguish. Perchik had been gone thirty-five days and seventeen hours, and in his absence, Hodel felt as though she were being buried, encased in dense, relentless clay; immovable, obdurate—the soil possessed with a consciousness intent on ending her. She knew her body had been taken from the earth and therefore must be returned to it.

God spoke it unto Adam: "For dust you are, and to dust you will return."

Yet man's soul came from above.

"He breathed into his nostrils the breath of life, and man became a living soul."

And when our earthly tasks have been accomplished, she thought, *that soul rises back to God, returns to its source.*

Was she returning now? Perhaps. She felt the walls of life close in, smelled the pungency of hot, wet earth as it continued to fall upon her—claim her for its own. But Hodel remembered Mama's words: *We show greatest dignity to the body and do not mar or harm it in any way. It must be returned in its entirety to the earth and to the creator, just as it was given, without any violence or interference.*

If that were true, how could she return to God

if she were interred within the earth without her heart? For Perchik possessed it utterly, and somewhere in this camp—in a location so near to her and yet so barred—he held dominion over her heart, and thus, prevented her from being taken. An ordinary woman might have shrunk from fear, but Hodel was no ordinary woman— she was afraid of nothing.

The Gentleman stood above her as she lay upon the bed, unable even to moan.

"He is weakened, my dear; I shall not lie to you," he said with eagerness in his tone, trying, possibly, to bolster her. "But he is being looked after. . . ." He trailed off, not knowing what to say next. "We are so very nearly done."

He moved a chair to her bedside and sat upon it, fiddling idly with his hat. He paused. He sighed. Hodel sensed he wanted something.

"Is there anything I may say or do to bring you comfort, Hodel?"

Nothing you can say will be worth saying, she thought but did not utter.

"Anything at all?"

No.

Well, there it was. In the wake of her misery, The Gentleman surrendered his own. Beneath the refined exterior, The Gentleman wanted, above all else, not to be revered or respected or even obeyed. He wanted to be loved. It could be that all his odd behaviors—all the sanctimonious child-rearing, the rigorous perfection of his personage—were attempts to attain it, while all his tortured rage was merely the petulance of the rejected urchin that lay below the surface of the starched collars and brightly polished boots. The urchin coveted such love, desired desperately to clinch it in his hands and caress it roughly, like an animal's pelt.

"Hodel, I do care so deeply for you. But we must learn to truly speak."

But Hodel could not speak. Her heart was missing.

The Gentleman stood, as if he knew the cause was lost. Then, pausing in the door frame as he moved to leave the house, he said, spite lacing his tone, "Your friend Dmitri Petrov betrayed your husband, you know. No matter. Betrayal is the way of the world."

forty-six

All traces of him were cleared before Dmitri returned from interrogation.

"What has become of Yevgeny, then?" he inquired of the overseer upon returning. "His bunk has been cleared." Dmitri sat down upon the empty mattress and looked around him. "Has he been reassigned to another barracks?"

The overseer casually rolled a cigarette in the corner. "What, the old man?" he said. "Dead. Cleaning the furnace. Cleared away this morning."

Yevgeny, it would seem, like any dullard worth his salt, died just as he had lived—with warmth.

It was in the furnace that they found him. Warm. With a smile on his face. Discovered on a Thursday after eight days of labor there, and two days or so of neglect.

The overseer reached into his jacket pocket and retrieved a box of matches. "And since the northern bunks are overcrowded, looks like you shall have a replacement in the morning."

Dmitri stared hard at him, eyes locked adamantly upon he who delivered so offhand a remark. He could not move at all. He felt his eyes might break apart and fall to pieces.

Dmitri turned on his heel, made swift haste of his exit.

Before long, he came to the middle of the seemingly infinite taiga field: arms held fiercely around his center, hatless, gloveless, without protection from the relentless winds that soon made him quite numb. He reveled in the harshness of the elements in this moment.

Grisha and Anatoly followed him, keeping a safe distance.

"They say he had a smile upon his face," said Grisha softly after a few moments.

"Aye, they did," Anatoly added, nodding.

Dmitri inhaled the biting air, the rime in his lungs oddly soothing.

At last he spoke. "Is it all gone, then?" He sobbed below his breath. "Did they—take the little sculpture of the cello?"

"No," Grisha murmured. "I have kept it safe."

Dmitri's jaw hardened. His eyes were steady. Yet his face was streaked with white, salty lines already turning to frost.

"Thank you." He spoke so quietly, perhaps only the wind could hear him. His friends stood there in the silence for so long a while, the dull dusk of evening turned to woeful darkness. "Do leave me," Dmitri uttered. They nodded and left him there, alone with his grief.

During the darkest days ahead, Dmitri would think back on his time in Nerchinsk—on the mines and his companions and, of course, Yevgeny. How he longed for a glimpse of all the moments he had so pushed and raged through.

But whenever he met someone he came to like, he always said, voice soft but full and genuine: "I so wish you could've known him."

forty-seven

H odel had promised her papa that she and Perchik would be married beneath a canopy. And so they were. The day after her arrival in Nerchinsk, a bed linen served for the task. The rest of the ceremony was ramshackle (and would have horrified her mother), but Hodel didn't mind. All she could do was give thanks fervently that she had arrived at this moment at all. She saw it as a sign from God: He arranged their love, and thus she would strive every day of her life to honor it. God in His grace would provide. So stated the bride's prayer: "God blessed them and said to them, 'Be fruitful and increase in number; fill the earth and subdue it.' "

The very first time with him was nothing like she had imagined. She was dissolving like a crystal into the source itself. She wept as she confessed to him that she had been defiled; but to her relief, he held her close, kissed her eyes, and insisted that in his heart he knew her body to be "as pure as the soul within it," and that was all that mattered to him.

She was still at first as they lay beside each other, but as he held her face and placed his mouth upon hers, she shifted beneath him. She realized she had never felt—for there had never been—bare skin upon her own.

An unknown feeling rushed up inside of her: a kind of hunger, a pining. *So this is desire,* she thought, and the absolute yearning of it was instinctive, ancient, and shared with every human who had ever wanted before them, and would ever want again—it filled her like a wineglass, then came to overflow above the edges.

Her breath was short; she caught it in quick gasps.

"I am frightened," she whispered, stopping him, for she was suddenly alive to her entire body quaking from so great a desperation.

"Hodel . . ." He shifted, bringing their bodies closer with a gesture of pure tenderness. "My wife," he entreated, enclosing her, "do not be afraid. . . ."

His diffidence delighted her, for it was comforting to see him as vulnerable as she. At last her mouth opened against his own, and she blossomed and unfolded into his infinity.

Something caught within; from the depths of her, the dull and lolling heat burst into a flame. In the freezing night, he beckoned to her essence— lifting her toward a summit she had never known before.

She grazed her mouth against his ear and summoned him away from this land of ice and labor, from the bustling intersections of his thoughts. Reaching for him, she found the knowledge of it present within her, the skill latent, waiting only to be released. She loved him.

Her insides heaved. She trembled with uncertainty, and all at once she realized he was trembling too. She felt his body, hot and clamoring, crying out in response to her own. She felt the sweat upon his face as he pressed it up against her, hearts pounding as they both seized, cried out.

Her eyes opened. They caught their breath. Incapable of speech. Wherever they had gone, they had traveled there together. . . .

"Perchik?" Hodel said in the compass of her husband's arms, in the earliest hushes of their first morning. "You have seen the world. What is the most important thing?"

His face grew grave. He placed the span of his great hand upon her heart and touched her chest with reverence. Locking eyes with her, he replied, unsmiling, *"This."*

Perchik could not tell if she was truth or figment, but as he stirred, he found himself clinging to her. He brought his fingers to his face and thought he might just smell her upon them— the hope of it alone still made him quicken. He was astonished by how inexperienced he felt in her presence, and laughed like a boy, in ecstasy that things could be as clear as this.

He loved her. He loved her because nature willed it. Because they were already united and of one body. The bare flesh on every part of her belonged to him. The scent emitting from her skin was his.

When he first laid eyes upon her, he had been terrified. There could never have been a creature like her before. An unsettling heat radiated from her eyes—an intelligence that seemed innate. It transfixed him. She had no knowledge of her beauty, not the full extent of it, and this made her all the more inescapable. As he looked at the length and ravishing curve of her form, and at the sagacity of the mind contained within it, he felt himself fill up, like a well surging from the deepest and most secret crevices of the earth.

Perchik had been no stranger to lust. He had surrendered to it countless times before, could write an atlas of the female form. But in his search for triumph (or, perhaps, for comfort), all he had ever acquired was worthlessness. Nothing more. All he had received was an utterly indifferent gratification. He was left only with his own debasement. A bitter emptiness.

Oh, Hodel, he thought as his mind rose from the reverie, *all women before you have turned to ash. . . .*

forty-eight

T he door clanged as they approached. Perchik felt the depth of cold within the stones along his body as he lay upon the ground facing the wall, and heard two sets of footsteps, only one of which entered his cell.

"We have released your comrade," The Gentleman said above his head. "Dmitri Petrov is to be returned to Petersburg. No longer useful. He told us everything, I'm afraid."

Perchik lay there, stunned. Stunned, of course, but not surprised. Steadfast he remained. *Oh, Dmitri,* he thought, *poor sod, too soft for such a world as this.* What must have been days ago, Perchik had stopped urinating, and his head screeched with pain as though his brain had shrunk and was clattering against his skull. He was starving. Swollen. Nearly blind.

"Don't you see, Perchik? You have nothing. You might have 'comrades' to execute your will here or in the cities, but I'm almost ashamed to admit that they are of little concern to me, personally. You are my concern. And I'm terribly sorry to tell you that we simply have no reason left to keep you here."

Perhaps there was a secret part of him that knew it would not work; a silent place within him

390

that knew it would end like this. Yet in his mind, Perchik could see a pillar high above the ground: a beacon of ignited truths that shone upon the earth below! Upon the unworked soil that churned to reach its potential. Upon the starving creatures scattered on it—the starving and the sick. Upon all humanity in this, its grayest and most desolate time of confusion. He felt he had been created to re-define the human capacity for fellowship; he had been appointed to prove man's greatness by a God he still fiercely believed in, despite it all. He believed. He passionately believed. Belief and passion were nearly all he had.

For he had her, of course: Hodel. And she was twice the strength of any antidote or nourishment, more formidable a force than even hope itself. In the battle against deathly cold and growing weakness, against poison and through despair, she was his bright torch, the pillar of fire calling forth to extinguish every darkness. The world he hoped to form was not for man; it was for her—and so he could not leave it. Not just yet.

"You heap such misery onto this world—it is time to bid farewell to it," The Gentleman said.

"You cannot rule me, sir."

"Nonsense. Your pain is our pleasure, Perchik. You see?"

"There is no way to rule another man. The only rule is brotherhood."

Suddenly, something occurred to Perchik: he

would never truly lead again. Never. He would be robbed of the chance before he had even truly begun. He began to laugh.

"Go on and laugh. Whom do you think you're fooling, comrade? That is the laughter of despair. And your despair is our satisfaction—don't you see? We have you in a corner like a rat, and you shall submit. You shall submit or else we shall destroy you."

"You cannot!" Perchik choked on his hysterics, his voice rising with determination.

At once The Gentleman attacked. Darting like a hawk, he lifted Perchik by the neck, slammed him against the wall, and breathed hard into his face, revealing his fat, buttery complexion flushed with sweat and fury. "How have we not broken you?" he said, his eyes boiling over to the edge of rage.

"It is her," Perchik said, his countenance serene. "It's her."

The Gentleman was riled. His eyes flickered with defeated dread. Perchik was revealing a superb endgame The Gentleman had never dared to conceive of as possible. Perchik saw the other creature living beneath his uniform; the buttons and seams on his shirt strained against the evil that was aching to escape. The Gentleman exhaled and, trembling, threw Perchik hard upon the floor as he all but ran away.

"Feed him, Irina," he called from down the

corridor. "We must keep him alive. That is, until we kill him."

Irina knelt beside Perchik and gently spooned soup into his mouth, which stung his insides as it went down. Between each taste, he gasped great drinks of air to adjust. Irina's face was drawn—hollow-cheeked and barren-eyed.

"How have you survived this place, Irina?" Perchik whispered. "How have you survived *him?*"

Irina looked deep into his eyes, and Perchik felt his heart frost over at the edges with the intensity of her expression. She placed the bowl upon the floor and buried her hands within the folds of her skirts. She was quiet for a long while, as if in prayer for the shame she was about to reveal.

"My mother was from Hulunbuir, a small town in China ruled unofficially by the Russian government. Mother was from a tea-making family that exported brick tea to this region along the railway. Father fell in love with her at first sight when he and other young soldiers went across to patrol the railway, so he captured her and brought her to this place against her will, along with a cartload of other forced female settlers. The camp was not as large as it is now; it was more of a village, and there were very few women—one for every ten men.

"Mother constantly attempted escape, but her

plans were always thwarted. Father dragged her back and beat her, only to turn about with soothing words and loving little gifts. Were it not for my birth, she most likely would have killed herself. She lived to protect me from the swinging temperament of my father. She taught me languages and poetry, femininity, and, most of all, about the ancient art of tea." Irina drifted off in thought for a moment. "The art of tea my mother gave me, which father used to poison you."

It locked into place at last: Perchik had been poisoned by the tea that Hodel brought back from The Gentleman's office—the tea he knew she never drank.

"I loved her," Irina said. She described all this so simply, as if none of it—not a single nauseating detail—mattered anymore.

"When I was just thirteen, just on the eve of my womanhood, mother died of smallpox. The village was riddled with it. And straightaway, father was altered. Not by grief, exactly, but by something almost . . ." Perchik watched her as her mind grappled for the right words. "Something far more wicked than that. It was as though something very deep inside of him very quietly snapped, like a lock on a door no one heard turn. My mother's death opened up all the truly mad things within him. Things that had perhaps always been there, but lay dormant."

They sat still in the airless room. No breath, no pulse, no clamor of anything could be heard.

"Father kept saying I was 'too much like her.' That I was going to be thought of 'any day now as a free girl,' one that the men of this camp would quickly tarnish. He could not stand that. And so, before long, I came to take my mother's place."

Perchik could not breathe. He barely found the breath to whisper. "Irina. Whatever do you mean?"

Irina could not meet his gaze. Those eyes— so icy and identical to The Gentleman's own— turned milky with the truth of it. Her face lost color as the monstrous revelation left her lips. "You see . . . I am also his *girl.* . . ."

His eyes grew wide, his blood halted as his heart stopped beating, and his stomach fell with the news of a horror far worse than Perchik ever could have feared.

"And he felt that Andrey sullied me, you see— beyond what any ordinary father could abide. But what occurred will reoccur. It shall become some kind of odious pattern."

forty-nine

I n prison, a home life seemed impossible. But Hodel scraped together a sense of home in this little room at the Volosnikovs', and in her growing solitude, the plague of restlessness envenomed her. If she tried, she could imagine Tzeitel's voice echoing from within her memory: *We must transform a simple house or dwelling into a home.* In Hodel's prior life, such concepts seemed a nuisance. The recollection ate at her; how duplicitous are memories—sweet one moment, torturous the next, seen through many filters as time advanced ever onward.

Hodel took refuge in filling the place with welcome and warmth. That little room stood in unrelenting silence, existing in a ceaseless allegiance to the evils of Nerchinsk.

It was in such a state that Dmitri Petrov found her when he stole away in the moonless shadows of the camp on the eve of his departure from it.

"Tea?" she inquired over her shoulder. She yearned for the energy to greet him with kindness, but her resolve was weak, her nerves frayed, and every scrap of energy went to preserving her own sanity in her husband's absence.

"Please," Dmitri replied uneasily—they had

not seen each other since any of the horrific incidents.

She moved to heat the pot. Dmitri Petrov shifted his weight from one foot to the other. He was suddenly aware that he had never been alone with her. His guilt filleted him—exposed his inner flesh, which flinched and shrank away with every passing moment in her presence. The wind shook and howled about the house. He owed her many things.

"Hodel," he began, staring feebly at the floor as if the words could be discovered there, picked up from within the wooden planks. "Hodel, I—I want to say . . . I feel I owe you . . ." He was terrible at this. "Well, I owe both of you, really, without a doubt, the most sincere—"

"Dmitri, don't." She cut him off, putting him out of his evident misery. "Don't." Her face displayed not even the subtlest hint of emotion. "No need. It is done." She grabbed the tin pot by its long wooden handle and placed it on the stove above a spasming flame that gasped for life, convulsing desperately in short, bright bursts. "*Ver derharget!*" Hodel cursed in Yiddish as the fire went out. "Now we shall never start another—never, never!" She threw her hands up in fury, all hope extinguished with the flame. She turned her back toward Dmitri and slammed the pot of frigid tea down upon the counter. Posture wilted, one hand covering her face, and with fingers clenched about her eyes, she exhaled heavily—she had needed that fire.

Dmitri edged toward her, removing a flask from his jacket.

"Perhaps this will serve . . ."

"Whatever do you mean?" Hodel said, still riled.

Without meeting her eyes, he nestled in beside her like a tamer might approach an angered animal in the wild. "Here. . . ."

Dmitri poured the liquor from his flask, covering the bottom of a small tin mug. He then placed a finger to his lips—*Quiet,* the gesture spoke—as he reached across her body for the box of kitchen matches and struck one hard against the wall.

How it blazed! Dmitri Petrov's fingers held the tiny light, the smell of it intoxicating: all possibility and heat. The struggle between them vanished as their faces were illuminated by the little orange inferno. Dmitri took care of her in this moment. He was Dmitri Petrov: knowledgeable, capable. How grateful she was. How greatly she needed him. But Dmitri's magic was not yet done—he dropped the tiny match just above the rim of the cup. The alcohol burst into a sudden flame. She gasped.

"This is how we melt the snow down in the mines when we are desperate."

"Incredible."

"Isn't it?"

Her eyes filled with the incandescent blue of the flame. Rimmed with sleeplessness and tears, the darkness of her eyes reflected the depth of the fire's power. And then she found herself clutching at Dmitri's limbs, embracing him, weeping.

Dmitri Petrov did not know what to do. So confusing and surprising was this contact, so crippling and loaded. Her body felt like the body of his cello—as familiar and as right. Yet he merely stood there. He allowed Hodel's embrace for so long, he could not determine if the stabbing pangs he felt were of pleasure or of shame. In impassioned, swirling gusts, his love for her heaved. At last he raised up the great span of his arms and wrapped himself around her trembling body.

Dmitri Petrov ceased existing in that moment— he was suspended in fantasy as he held her. The wind outside ceased to howl; the pulse of blood ceased to pound within him. This was much more than any moment that had come before—or, he was quite certain, would ever come again. But in a heartbeat, the moment had crested. Time stirred once more, contracted back from suspension, and crept cruelly on. Then, all at once, there came a knock upon the door.

"Who's there?"

"It is I, Hodel," The Gentleman replied beyond the door.

Dmitri Petrov desperately searched the room for a means of escape, but it was of no use. Hodel grabbed him by the coat and threw him beneath the kitchen table, then covered him with the cloth that lay upon it.

"Not a word," she whispered. He nodded. "Not a breath." Hodel gathered herself, straightened her headscarf, cleared the tears from her face, and opened the door.

"Good evening, Hodel," said The Gentleman.

"Good evening, sir."

Without invitation, The Gentleman moved past her into the body of the room. He stood, taking the place in. He seemed caught in the net of his thoughts.

"Hodel," he began in a somber tone, "I'm afraid I bear some rather awful news." He pulled a chair toward the kitchen table and settled himself just inches from Dmitri Petrov. Her stomach turned. She saw something terrible in The Gentleman's countenance—the veins in his neck stood out, his face was quite red, and his expression was one of both self-satisfaction and quiet hysteria. His latent nature had been exposed the night he stood by the destruction of Andrey Tenderov and had only continued to creep out from the darkest corners within him. If she thought about it—truth be told—she had seen it always.

"I am so sorry, Hodel," he said, "but Perchik is dead."

At once, the world around his face went dark.

"The elements quite ravaged him, my dear."

His voice echoed, reverberating through her as slowly, and darkness gathered around the image of his face. She lost her grasp of the world entirely. Every sound and sight smudged out around her until nothing glowed at all except the ice within those eyes—those eyes that stared so intently, they caught her by the larynx and gripped upon her reason. Eyes that blazed with cold—the last sight that she caught before she fell and darkness took her altogether.

When she came around many minutes later, she found herself inert upon the bed. She turned and started—The Gentleman was too close beside her, his eyes bearing down.

"There, there, my dear," he said with gentleness as she moved to protest. "No need to speak a word. I quite understand." He raised his hand and moved his fingers along the length of her hair. "Do you remember, Hodel, what we discussed the night that we first spoke?"

She did not. She stared at him unflinchingly.

"Do you?" he bit, voice harder than before.

She shook her head.

"Your eyes are beautiful, Hodel. So beautiful. But they are also tired and full of lies. I know that you remember. For how could you forget so magical a meeting?"

There was a part of her that thought, *This*

cannot be—but the rest of her knew it had been so all along.

"I looked at you and said, 'I would like to request that you accompany me to Nerchinsk. Would you consider this proposal?' Then you said, 'I would, sir.' And then I promised that I would personally see to it that no harm would come to you, and I have kept my word. Have I not done so faithfully, my dear?"

She could not take her eyes from him as he unraveled.

"And then I said, 'Do we understand each other?' And you nodded. You *nodded*, Hodel, and that was when I knew you understood me, and I rejoiced in the knowledge that this day would one day come!"

She knew so well how solitude could twist and inexplicably warp the soul of a perfectly ordinary man, drive him to covetousness, to cruelty. The Gentleman had deformed in his deprivation. The realm beyond hunger is starvation, and the realm beyond starvation is a world of empty, miserable lightness. It is only in that realm where such leaps to the unthinkable—to evil itself—are no longer leaps. They are but steps. Footprints in the frozen mud, spotless boot by spotless boot.

"I knew he would eventually break," The Gentleman said, rising from the chair. "Eventually, they all do, in one way or another." He

402

smiled down at her and took one step too close. "You see, you are a free girl now, my dear."

Her jaw was set, face gleaming with tears despite the fire in her eyes—the tears a fuel, an accelerant that thrust her up and toward him with all her fury. She wailed, biting as he thrust himself upon her. His breath was hot and rank; she could feel it on her face and smell its fetidness. He panted hard before her, his sex riled. "Everyone breaks, my dear." He picked her up and slammed her against the wall, his mouth opened wide upon hers as if to suck the very life from her.

Her pent-up rage exploded upon him—her strength quadrupled in the presence of his gloating phallus as he wrenched it out and up beneath her skirts. But, in an instant, he gave way.

The Gentleman clutched his throat as Dmitri Petrov attacked him from behind, wrestling with a ferocity he had never known as he wrung a scarf tightly around The Gentleman's neck. The Gentleman fought to escape Dmitri's grip, his erection wet and heaving toward the woman they coveted.

Free from his clutches, Hodel lunged, kicked his quivering prick, and watched him collapse with a howl before gathering all the acidic hatred in her heart and spitting it upon him.

"You should die for this!" she railed, watching him writhe as saliva trickled from his mouth and encircled his bulging head. In the cacophony of everyone's panting breath, Dmitri moved toward her.

"My friend—" he gasped, quite full of feeling.

"Don't touch me!" Hodel wailed.

Dmitri stalled in horror. "Please, Hodel, I only wish to help you, I—"

"A lot of help you did me, Petrov—a great deal of good you've done us all!"

He knew it to be true. He was wholly worthless. Not that it mattered anymore. Dmitri turned from her, contorted by his shame—he had murdered his friend, betraying all he ever cared for.

"Dmitri—no!" Hodel cried, for The Gentleman had struggled to his feet again. He swiftly bashed Dmitri across the head with a cauldron from the kitchen and watched him crumble to the floor. The Gentleman turned toward Hodel once again.

"You think you are so great, with your smug expression!"

He pinned her down onto the floor beneath the enormous heft of his body, now dripping with sweat from anger and exertion. He moved his gluttonous hands up her skirts and squeezed hard at the back of her legs. "No one makes a fool of me, you filthy little Jew." He ripped the meeting of her underthings. "You little witch! You have beguiled me so, and nothing is ever denied to me!"

She felt his weight give, his panting cease. The Gentleman's head lolled, collapsing upon her chest, and he was out cold on top of her. The room was deathly quiet.

Gazing upward she could see, with the cauldron clutched in his hand, a wheezing, determined Anatoly.

"Seems we got here just *after* the nick of time," said a stunned Grigory Boleslav.

Footsteps rumbled outside—people wondering what the commotion was about. Grigory threw Anatoly a look. They knelt to move The Gentleman's body off Hodel.

"Roll him over, Anatoly; we must get him across the floor somehow."

Freed from beneath The Gentleman's enormous body, Hodel found herself in Grisha's arms. "Deep breaths, my darling," he soothed. "It is all right."

Grisha gestured at Dmitri and nodded to Anatoly to tend to him.

"Come along, Mitya!" said Anatoly, picking him up by the collar and shaking him vigorously. Dmitri was motionless.

"Dmitri Petrov, come along—for the love of God!" Grisha bellowed. Anatoly removed Dmitri's spectacles, then smacked him hard across the face. At last, Dmitri stirred, and

Anatoly took him into his arms as they heard the footsteps of guards approaching up the lane.

"Quickly!"

Then they ran across the fields. Pursued by guards, they ran as though from fate itself. Toward what location or which fate, Hodel did not know.

fifty

They diverged with Anatoly along the road as he carted Dmitri back to the barracks.

"We shall see you at the meeting point!" Grisha called as they ran.

Grigory took Hodel by the hand. They darted through the shadows and approached The Gentleman's office. He smashed the front window with the edge of a pocketknife and opened the door from within, then moved to the back room with greatest speed. He lifted a floorboard beneath the shelving.

"What is going on?" Hodel cried.

He made no answer, but from the floor he produced a handgun and shoved it into his jacket. Then he handed Hodel papers. A map. Money. A long scrap of fabric. A box of sulfur matches. A key.

"Grisha, tell me what is happening!"

Grigory stood. He gripped her hands. "Hodel, listen to me." His black eyes fixed upon her. "Perchik is alive."

Alive! Her mind swirled. Even amid the horror of this place, he was alive, and that was all that mattered.

"Anatoly and the others have gone to break him out of lockup. The rest of us are ready to keep the officers at bay so that you and Perchik may escape. Do you hear me, Hodel? Perchik's escape is of vital import to many, many people."

She nodded fiercely. "Tell me what I must do."

"Take these things," he said, shoving all into a satchel and placing it around her neck. "The identity papers are false, the map and money for beyond the barriers, and the key is to the hut."

"The hut?"

"Yes. Our meeting point. From this office, you run east. Far—to the very edge of the camp. There lies a small storage hut; food, medicine, weapons, and alcohol, all used by the officers. It is locked, but it will open with this key."

"Where on earth did you get it?"

"Courtesy of Yevgeny—turns out he actually was a very good thief." They shared a momentary smile.

Hodel was suddenly seized with fear. Had she received this second chance by error? Might it be taken from her if she missed a single step?

"When you arrive safely at the hut," Grisha continued, "signal to me by igniting the long scrap of fabric with one of the sulfur matches. And then from there you run. You run like hell. The hut is mere meters from the fence. Anatoly and I will then enact the final part of the plan."

"And what is that?"

"Hodel, no, there isn't time."

She gripped him hard. "What is that?" she cried again.

"We are running into the mines," he said almost reverentially. "Led by Irina. There is a secret escape burrow prisoners have been working on for years. Dozens of us can escape through it in minutes, perhaps a hundred within an hour. With Irina inside, the officers will follow, and we shall blow it up as they do, trapping them within—like your Moses trapping Pharoah as he crossed the Red Sea!"

"No!"

"Hodel, please, there is no time to argue!" His voice shook her, telling her there was no more to say. "We must move."

As they approached the door to the office, Hodel could already hear the prisoners swarming like bees and gathering in droves beyond the hill.

"The train passes only one and a half kilometers from the fence," Grigory said as he removed the gun from his jacket and held it at his side. "It should arrive before morning. Board that train while it is moving and take it toward Ekaterinburg. Perchik will tell you the rest."

Grigory and Hodel bolted through the door, down the steps, and out into the night. In the face of almost certain defeat, there was a glorious validation in their solidarity—as though they took upon themselves the leadership that she supposed her Lord God might have.

"But, Grisha, what of you? And Dmitri Petrov, what will become of him?"

He looked at her hard, shook his head, and smiled.

"What is to become of us all, Hodel?"

The noise was growing from beyond. Hodel turned toward it, trying to comprehend that this was, indeed, happening.

"Grisha!" she cried out, looking back toward him with uncertainty. But he was gone.

There was nothing left to do but run.

fifty-one

A nd so she ran. She pelted hard through the woods, hid behind barracks and outhouses, darted past the officers' headquarters, crawled behind the women's lodgings. Her lungs blazed within her, her mind faster than her feet. But before long, she could see the hut in the far distance.

She stalled and turned about as she heard shouts, pounding feet, gunshots. She stood in the middle of the field, halfway between the chaos in the mines and her future freedom. Men ran from every direction toward the mouths of the mines, as if it were swallowing them up. Atop the hill stood Irina, glowing in the resplendence of her purpose; Hodel thought she saw, for a flicker of a moment, Irina's gaze meet her own, before she too was consumed into its blackness.

At then, at last, emerging through the mist from the edges of the camp: she saw him. His body was weakened, but not his majesty. She saw him as she had seen him at first sight across the hills of Anatevka, as miraculously as she had the first day they ran toward each other in this wretched place.

Perchik. Her only one.

"Stop, criminal!" the voices called. Hodel

looked about her. The guards pursued from far behind.

She pelted down a hill, and as she ran, the guards were tackled by the prisoners, leaving her free to race toward the hut—toward him and all he stood for. Time slowed itself, playing out as through a sheet of water. She wept, her heart exultant—this purest of moments, this most absolute wholeness of life.

"Hodel!" Perchik cried, grasping at her hand. "Hodel, follow me!"

They sprinted together on the frozen ground, the hut mere feet away. When they reached it, she clamored in the satchel for the key and placed it roughly in the great iron lock upon the door—escape too near to be believed! And then: a call.

"Hello," someone said.

But this was not just any voice; it was the calm and steady iciness of the Voice himself—calling out from just behind them. He had been waiting in the shadows.

"Reb Perchik!" the Voice called out, smug, calm, and uncannily certain.

Perchik turned.

Hodel saw his face ignite with the expression of recognition. He smiled and opened his arms in greeting.

And then: a gunshot. It occurred in an eternity, pierced the silence of the air.

Perchik clutched his shoulder and fell upon the ground.

The moment filled Hodel, like the inaudible memory of an explosion. She could not hear her own screaming. For an instant, she was wild with derangement before flying down upon him. The sight of blood surging through his shoulder: pure and bitter on her corroded eyelids. She knelt there dumb, soaked in and reeking of despair.

"Hello, Hodel . . ." the Voice said, emerging at last from the shadows.

She turned to see him. He removed his hat to reveal the face. . . .

Perhaps within every man there lies a seed that can rot the fruit if we're not careful. Perhaps such a seed makes us stronger—better, somehow, for overcoming it. But perhaps in some, the seed incubates too long; it shoots up, polluting the vestiges of all our goodness, so much so that wickedness becomes a need.

Hodel could not, in any way, believe her eyes: it was none other than Anatoly.

He stood there, above them and beyond, gun smoking in his hand. A thousand words could never leave so deep an impression as the vacant chill within his eyes. At last he spoke.

"Well, how touching," he said. "Sometimes, you have to wait things out and take care of them yourself."

The words emitted from him in the perfectly

clear voice of an aristocrat—no trace of common accent in any corner of his speech. He moved toward her. "It really is disgusting how you let that conceited insurrectionist order you about, Hodel—haven't you any pride at all?" His question was thick with held grudges. "My grandfather was murdered by Decembrists; I shall never let our motherland be blemished by mutiny again."

He lifted his arm and clicked the gun into position, intent on shooting her too.

"Anatoly," she pleaded, searching his face for the man she swore she knew. "No. . . ." Her mind went numb. She braced herself. Her body stiffened as vibrations pounded through the frigid air.

The shot rang out.

But to her shock, her body was unmarred. She felt no pain or infirmity. Her eyes lifted.

A hole within his head leaked only the slightest hint of blood; it oozed like a tear down his brow and around his eye. His eyes went blank as the great hulk slumped to the ground, and behind him, gun still smoking, stood Grisha.

Grigory Boleslav locked his blackened eyes with Hodel's, and it was clear that he knew. He knew more than any words could ever say.

He ran at her and buried his hands in the satchel, removed the sulfur matches and then the scrap of fabric and ignited it to signal the mines.

Shoving the matches back in her bag, he pushed Hodel, who was motionless with shock.

"Go!" he whispered before disappearing back up the hill into the brawl.

Below her, Perchik groaned. And so Hodel faced the door, turned the key in the lock, and kicked the door wide open, then lifted Perchik's body and dragged it into the cabin.

fifty-two

Dearest Hodel,

I hope these letters reach you somehow.

We have a daughter now; her name is Luba, and I love to watch her grow. It all goes so fast. The time we have together is so precious. Times are turbulent; we are torn apart from loved ones long before we think it may be time to ask forgiveness. To say goodbye. That makes every day a gift.

Each day I tell the children about our family. I so wish you could know them. And they you. The other night as I prepared her for bed, Luba asked if she would ever meet you, and I realized, Hodel, that I did not know the answer.

The children pulled their sheets down, Jacob helped little Luba lift her tiny self into the bed, then Jacob said he did not understand: If he had never met you, if he had never touched you or seen the place where you lived, how could he know that you loved him, and how could you feel his love in return?

Every day, I am blessed. My own children showed me that, in our separation, our love is just like God's. I cannot point to His house upon a map, just as I cannot point to yours. But still, I feel your love from far across the Urals, as I trust you feel mine in return. So it is with God. So it is, I hope, when we leave this earthly realm and return to our ultimate home.

"But is this not home, Mama?" Luba asked. And I relayed, Hodel, that one day we shall all go home.

Home, Hodelleh. That place beyond the place where we rest our heads every night. Where our centerpieces, our sewing, our carefully prepared meals, simply do not matter. Where our petty little differences and competitions with one another do not matter anymore.

And I thought of you.

It is odd, Hodelleh. Because I do not know if you shall ever read this, I feel compelled to tell you more than ever. Home —where love shall reign supreme. The kind of home you always held within your heart, my dear sister, the kind no meaningless skill of mine could ever fully capture. How I love you, Hodel. It aches within me that I failed to show you in so many ways. That I provided you with every comfort but the comfort of my heart.

Yet I know that we shall both, as we always did, return to each other. For the love beneath our struggle is so strong. Perhaps in time, the Lord shall reveal to us why it is so difficult.

As the prophet Isaiah spoke, "Fear not, I have redeemed you; I have called you by name and you are mine. When you pass through the waters, I will be with you. And through the rivers, they shall not overwhelm you. When you walk through fire, you shall not be burned, and the flame shall not consume you."

I am convinced that what joins all humanity together is our capacity to endure. Endurance is the condition under which we may feel both the glory of our distinctiveness and the depths of our sameness. Endurance, which is distinct from suffering. I have not seen the world as you have, dear sister, but I can see that endurance unites us. Endurance that is, thus, holy.

I trust that, somewhere, we shall be together again. Until that day, I send my love out to you and shall continue to do so, Hodelleh. Until, one day, we can finally go home.

Tzeitel

fifty-three

H odel secured them both inside the cabin. She bolted the door, locked it fast, then pushed heavy shelves in front of the doorway. She laid Perchik out upon the floor and ripped apart his shirt to reveal the wound in his shoulder. The shot was clean, through and through. But his body had been ravaged. He lay there, white and wheezing as he convulsed with shock. Hodel surrounded him in blankets, her mind roaring. Life had been an endless test of transforming misfortune into faith. Surely this was no different.

Perchik reached for her hands and smiled.

"Hodel," he said, struggling hard against the torment within. "This is for you now." From within his mouth, Perchik pulled a tiny key. He wiped it off and placed it tight within her hand. "You must take it. In your satchel, there is an address—in Kiev. It is a bank. This key opens the safe that contains all of Gershom's fortune."

"No." Hodel shook her head. She pushed the key back toward him as if refusing to take it might prevent him from leaving her.

"Hodel." Perchik's voice was firm. "Please, listen to me. From there you must go straight to

Petersburg and find a man known as 'the Pen.' He is a high-ranking member of the movement and my comrade. The map—the map Grigory gave you? Contained within it is a coded speech, my darling. You must give that and half the fortune to the people you meet there. It is the summation of my life's work. Promise me."

"I cannot."

"My darling, please." Perchik's eyes were pleading as he lifted a trembling hand to the softness of her cheek. "Please, promise me."

Her heart lurched, her brain flooding with agony, for she knew the moment that she gave her word, she would begin to lose him.

"I promise," she vowed, and placed her hand upon his own.

Perchik nodded in gratitude, then smiled wearily as he sighed, drinking in long, lasting looks of his wife. "Somehow . . . somehow, I always knew the journey here held no return." His lips were cracked, his speech labored. His body quaked.

"No!" she wailed. "No, my love. You cannot leave me. Not like this. Please, my beloved, you cannot!"

"I must," Perchik whispered. His hand was cold. "It is time." He shook as he pulled her closer to him. "Oh, my love, believe me— this is easier for me. It is so much harder," he said, fighting for breath, "to be left behind."

The home they would never have. The children that would never be.

"Do you recall what I told you when we first parted at the train so long ago?"

The entire life she would live without him.

"Oh, Hodel." He smiled. "We cannot be stopped."

"Your revolution?"

"No," he answered, his voice a shadow now. "You and I."

Hodel could not reconcile with such realities as these. Not here, in the frigidity of all that surrounded them.

"Take part . . . take part in the world, my love. Do not shirk from it."

The once achingly soft skin around his eyes cracked as he smiled; the cavernous depths of the lines that had formed across his face were appalling and unfamiliar—slits into the abyss draining the very life force from the eyes they surrounded.

"But there will be such an emptiness where you once were."

"The world will not take note, my dear."

"I do not mean for the world. The emptiness will be beside me." She could not bear it.

"Oh, my beloved," he said, choking. "But you are alive, and I shall live within you."

He gasped for breath, clutching her hand with

unwavering strength—as if this steady grip upon her were his last hold on the earth.

"Hodel, my wife, my dearest love. Do not withdraw from the world; take part in it. Do away with misery, with fear, and, above all, with regret. Demand more. Of yourself. Of man. Of this finite, beautiful time. It is too brief and too special to be squandered on despair."

She nodded bravely, desperate to keep both of them together just a moment longer, to burn his presence into her eternal memory.

Her face was soaked in sorrow. Perchik: her husband, her only one. He was a tiny flame now, feebly clutching at the wick. How grave the darkness when so bright a light begins to dim.

"I love you, Perchik," she uttered. "I love you. I cannot say goodbye. I cannot—"

"Hodel, we have never left anything unsaid, therefore we needn't say goodbye." Perchik gripped her hand tighter and tried to stroke away her tears. "We have the clearest union I have ever known—and who knows what is possible?" He winced, kissing her hand with dry lips. "Anything, I think. Anything is possible, with a love like ours. And that love continues, Hodel. We shall find it together; we shall throw a bridge over that mysterious divide, and we shall find it, one of us on each side."

From far beyond the hut there came a rumble, and the explosion of the mines filled the sky with thunder. Perchik winced again, trembling; his eyes locked into hers.

"Oh . . . my love . . ." he whispered. Then, like a candle whispering to smoke, his eyes went out, and he was gone.

fifty-four

They were coming! Hodel heard the cries of soldiers from just beyond the hill. She sprang from the floor to look about, grabbed Grisha's satchel, flung the key inside it, and threw it around her shoulder. She returned to Perchik's side and took the clothing from his body—shirt first, then trousers, jacket, blood-soaked undershirt, scarf, and heavy boots. She ran to a supply closet and stuffed the boots with surgical scissors and medical bandages as the guards came pounding hard upon the heaving seams of the cabin. Finally, as if without thought, she grabbed two bottles of rubbing alcohol and reached into the satchel for the box of sulfur matches.

The tumult intensified outside. She removed his hat, arranged his matted hair, and kissed his broken lips, stealing a few fleeting moments.

Yidishkeyt and *menshlikhkeyt* . . . Jewishness and humanness . . .

The voices of her faith were calling to her. Suddenly, she was gripped with conflict: What was she to do with Perchik's body?

It is the sanction of Torah law to bury the dead as quickly as possible. . . .

If she left his body behind, no one would ever bury him properly.

The human body belongs to its creator—it is on loan to us, and we become its guardian. . . .

The guards would doubtless have their way with it.

We must make certain due respect is given and shown. . . .

They would desecrate it far worse than any abandonment, than anything she could choose to do in this moment. *Respect for our deceased is the ultimate mitzvah—for the dead can neither help themselves nor help us. . . .*

As she gazed once more at his now empty face, she thought, *Perchik's soul no longer resides there.* There was no sanctity left but her love of him and all he stood for—the sacrifice of Perchik. No further evil would ever come. No one would ever harm him, touch him, or torture him again.

Kneeling next to his body, she closed her eyes to ask forgiveness. Then, in both love and horror, through tears, she opened the bottles and doused his body in the alcohol.

The sounds from the door grew louder. Shots rang out. Male voices were raised in rage. It was time. She gathered the pile of his clothes and climbed atop the sturdy shelves to the very highest window. She turned back, gazing at her husband as she struck a sulfur match and threw it upon the body. It instantly ignited—a white, angelic flame, his salt-encrusted skin cracking and hissing in the uproar—and for a moment he looked well again. She pushed the window open, threw the clothing to the ground below, and hoisted her body through, jumping out just as the guards burst into the room.

"The window!" they cried, and they climbed the shelves to follow her.

Her chest began to split as she ran wildly to the border fence; she could hear only the muffled shrieks of the guards' growing desperation as they grew ever closer, wretched and sharp behind her. Then, in a surge not at all unlike the one within her breast, the hut itself detonated, erupting into a soaring tower of flames.

She reached the fence and searched desperately for a way to scale it. All at once she saw it: Yevgeny's dog, Mitya. He stared at her from just beyond the fence with the same keen expression he had always displayed. He had dug a deep indentation of earth below the fence; it seemed as if he'd made it just for her and for this moment. Her savior was the handiwork of Yevgeny's blessed dog! It was narrow, but she knelt down and began to dig. When at last she had made space enough for herself, she threw the satchel and all of Perchik's clothing over the fence.

She looked behind her. No one was following

her! They all must have been blinded by the sight she'd left behind. Astonished, she gazed at the inferno for a fraction of a second before turning back around and lifting the bottom of the metal fence with all her strength, until it shifted just enough for her move underneath it. Mitya barked. Tearing away her cumbersome skirts, she wriggled her long body below; her stocking catching feebly on a barb was Nerchinsk's last peevish attempt to keep her trapped within its confines. As she emerged, the dog panted joyously, jumping and licking at her hands to celebrate their reunion. God knew how she had done it; all that was certain was that she had. It had almost been too easy.

There is a kind of transaction that occurs between a person and a place: you give the place something, and it gives you something in return. In years to come, Hodel would know for certain not only what Nerchinsk had taken but what it had given her as well. She gathered up the bits of scattered clothing, then stood and turned back. All that remained was the sight beyond the fence.

A rush of biting Siberian wind threw itself around her; it pushed hard against her flesh and threw her mane of hair about her face as she fully beheld the summation of her days. The life. The love—and, looming high above it all, the overwhelming greatness of the sight she left behind her . . .

The pillar of fire . . .

And in a flash, she ran again, concealed at once by the veil of the forest.

Nerchinsk would be warm at last.

Acknowledgments

The *Pirke Avot* (written around the year 200 CE) is among the most recognized texts in Jewish thought. In Chapter 4, Verse 1, it offers the following: "Who is rich? Those who rejoice in their own portion." Today, I rejoice. There is no need to wonder how I would feel "if I were a rich man," for the riches are here. Thank you all for making *After Anatevka* a reality.

A person should consider herself extraordinarily lucky if she has even a *single* spectacular, life-altering teacher in her lifetime. I have been blessed with many. In the world of books, literature, and writing, I have to thank Joanne Devine (who literally taught me to read), Jean Gaede, Howard Hintze, and Judy Chu, who all taught me to read and write with meaning.

To the great Sheldon Harnick: What can I say to such a "Dear Friend" that would ever suffice? You and Margie have been personal cheerleaders, supports, and the grandparents I wished I had had. But, above all, you are the ultimate tribal elder; you are the voice of our community, giving language to countless characters that will live eternally and continue to move and teach us for centuries to come. You are one of our great creators, and it is an honor to call you a colleague, and, above all, a friend.

Thank you to every member of my *Fiddler on the Roof* families—from Sheffield to London to Broadway—for all your support and inspiration, especially Natasha Broomfield, Lindsay Posner, Damian Humbley, Henry Goodman, Danny Burstein, Jessica Hecht, Samantha Massell, Melanie Moore, Jenny Rose Baker, Ben Rappaport, Adam Kantor, and Bartlett Sher. And, above all, my beloved Beverley Klein, Julie Legrand, Tomm Coles, and Frances Thorburn. As Samantha Massel says, "In the theater, one does not make friends—one finds family." Thank you for making me a part of yours and for allowing me to share the glimmers of your creations in the pages of this story. You are forever embedded in these pages, my memories, and my heart.

Thank you to Ken and Fran Steinman, David Montee and Robin Ellis, Suzi Dietz, and Lenny Beer for your lifelong support; to Santino Fontana, and Bobby Steggert; to Vadim Roshin for the memories in Moscow; to Arielle Doneson Corrigan, my chosen sister and real-life Tzeitel. Thank you to Lance Horne, Rachel Beider, Katie Indyk, Sarah Radtke Welsh, Alyssa Weytjens, and, of course, to (the real-life) Rabbi Syme. Thank you to Nick Bantock, my artistic idol who became a dear friend. And my deepest gratitude to "comrade" Kit Baker: the scope of our

Siberian sojourn could never be put into words, but, suffice it to say, our journey, in many ways, made this book possible.

Thank you to my first readers, whom I feel honored to call friends: Jason Alexander, Danny Burstein, Ted Chapin, Jeff Gilden, Jessica Hecht, Ken Ludwig, Terrence McNally, and Richard Schiff.

Professionally, there are those who always believed in this project, saw its potential, championed its reality: Matt Geller, Rick Joyce, and Jeff Berger (who always says "let's give it a try," and without whom none of what I am or create would be possible).

To my literary agent, Joelle Delbourgo: Thank you for taking a leap on an unknown writer. Your honesty and indefatigable faith mean everything to me.

And to my editor, Iris Blasi, a fellow warrior of the soul, thank you for this opportunity to share this story with the world—and for everything.

To my parents, Michael and Catherine Silber, who inspired the nature, devotion, and intensity of Hodel and Perchik's love: thank you for your constant support and championing of my efforts to be my best self—from places I can point to on the map, Mama, and to those I cannot, Papa. Everything I create, achieve, and have become is because of—and for—you.

The greatest degree of gratitude goes to Louise

Lamont, without whom this project would never have existed and without whom I would not be a writer in any capacity. You were my first reader, my first literary champion, and friend, and my gratitude to and for you could fill a novel of its own.

Center Point Large Print
600 Brooks Road / PO Box 1
Thorndike, ME 04986-0001 USA

(207) 568-3717

US & Canada:
1 800 929-9108
www.centerpointlargeprint.com